G000134402

THE
SHADOWS
of
WREN

THE SHADOWS OF WREN

JEN BLITON

First published by Jennifer Bliton 2023

Copyright © 2023 by Jen Bliton All rights reserved.

No part of this publication may be reproduced, stored or transmitted in any form or by any means, electronic, mechanical, photocopying, recording, scanning, or otherwise without written permission from the publisher. It is illegal to copy this book, post it to a website, or distribute it by any other means without permission.

This novel is entirely a work of fiction. The names, characters and incidents portrayed in it are the work of the author's imagination. Any resemblance to actual persons, living or dead, events or localities is entirely coincidental.

First edition ISBN: 979-8-9883247-1-3

Cover art and interior design by Rena Violet
Editing by Erin Young
Map created with Wonderdraft by Jen Bliton
Audiobook Narration by Meg Price

DEDICATION

To those who find their strength in the face of what
could defeat you.
For Jackson and Archer. I love you.

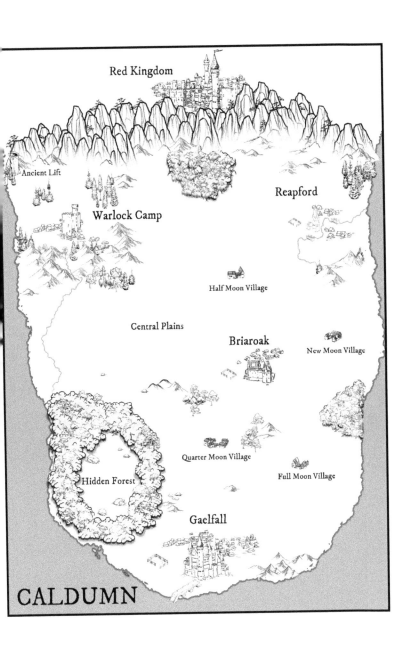

Red Kingdom

Ancient Lift

Reapford

Warlock Camp

Half Moon Village

Central Plains

Briaroak

New Moon Village

Quarter Moon Village

Full Moon Village

Hidden Forest

Gaelfall

CALDUMN

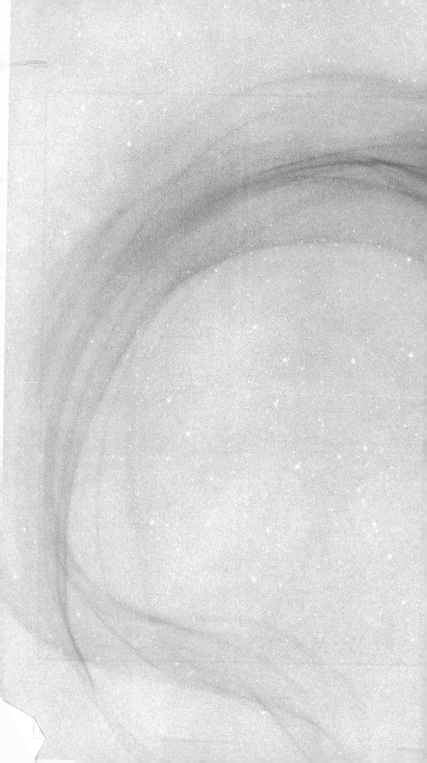

CHAPTER 1

Tendrils of cool misted shadow moved over my arms and down my hands, twisting around my fingers. I sucked in a sharp breath, trying to hold their magic in place, concentrating enough to get them to envelop my bare skin.

"Focus, Wren." Bergen said, standing at my back.

"I'm… trying…" I forced out, as my concentration faltered and the bands of shadow thinned.

I gritted my teeth and pushed harder at the ancient magic I held. The shadows responded eagerly. Too eagerly, in fact, and before I could pull back on my efforts, the shadows fully consumed me in a burst of magic. I let out a gasp before hearing a shout from Bergen.

"I'm alright." Bergen said, as I turned to face him.

The staff he held protected him in a shield of air that kept back the magic that emanated from my misstep. The raw white crystal on its top glowed faintly and dimmed back into nothing as Bergen corrected his stance and stood straight again.

"I'm sorry." I said, in a whispered panic.

I stared at the ground, looking at the familiar stone floors and dimly lit space of the basement we trained my shadow magic abilities in. It was a forgotten space under the library, old boxes of damaged books, and different furniture that no longer had use were stored along the walls. A threadbare rug sat in the middle of the floor where I was.

My attention was drawn back up when the door creaked as it opened.

"Aye, is everything alright in here?" Viggo asked in his all too familiar lilt, concern showed in his eye.

I pulled my auburn braid over my shoulder and picked at the ends to hide my embarrassment.

"We are fine. Wren pushed a little too hard in that attempt." Bergen tugged at his long silver-gray beard, deep lines were etched into his face as he smiled at me, "It's a balance, this sort of ancient magic can fully consume you, and if you can't control it, you might not be able to break its power from showing at times where it'll bring you more harm than good."

Viggo nodded and looked back at me. He pressed his lips into a thin smile of support. His strawberry blond beard was full and manicured well. I don't think I'd ever seen it looking out of place. A scar on his left eye from a battle long ago left it closed. He was a fierce warrior, fighter, and head of our Sentinels, but he was also my father.

"I'm alright, Dad. Give me another few attempts. I'll finish up work here at the library and see you tonight." I said, trying to shake out the residual feelings of unease.

"Try to put as much effort into your combat training as that shadow magic next time we spar, alright?" Viggo teased.

"I haven't trained with you in months, if at all this year." I scoffed.

"Aye, happens when you get your tail beat by the best."

I rolled my eyes, but felt the heat in my cheeks cool at his jokes. My shadow magic always freaked him out a little. It was once feared and hunted down, being seen as something that would bring doom to the one they worshiped. The majority of those views now remained within the Red Kingdom to the north, but I could see the fear in him at times when he watched my training sessions with Bergen.

I sighed as Viggo shut the door behind him, heading back to his duties within Gaelfall. The Sentinels protected our town from threats of monsters, criminals and anything that would want to breach the walls on its outskirts. While that wasn't common, most often they kept peace within the hustle and bustle.

At the center of Gaelfall, and with most towns to the south of the Red Kingdom, was the library. Ours was stunning. White quartz walls stretched to the sky with two tall towers on either side. The roof was crafted of slate that had a deep blue hue to it. Silver trimmed edging adorned the windows and rooftops.

Bergen cleared his throat, "Let's try this one more time, I want you to focus not necessarily on what you want your shadows to do, but feel the power as it moves within you. Feel how it responds to the Aura. Become familiar with that before we work on cloaking or shielding."

I nodded and got to work.

The cathedral arched ceilings with skylights allowed for natural light to illuminate the white quartz interior of the library. Rows of ebony wood bookcases lined either side of the great room, giving a stark contrast to the light, which made the books on display seem to jump out at you. Each town had its own library, and each one was uniquely beautiful. The library acted as a place for education, but also for our history and record keeping. Nearly every library in Caldumn had a Wizard assigned to it, and I worked closely with ours.

My shoes made a light tap against the checkered floor of gray-blue and white marble. The smell of wood, old books, and a hint of vanilla lingered in the air permanently. Near the end of the rows of bookcases sat a large wrap-around white quartz desk with Oona perched in the center. She looked tiny compared to the tall counter height desk.

"Compliments of your second home," I said in a posh tone to Oona as she looked up above her glasses. I pulled a linen wrapped loaf of sourdough bread from my satchel that still smelled divine and handed it to her.

"Ooo! I love Endora so much!" She squealed as she took the bread, and set it to the side of the wide desktop. Her dark, almond eyes were shining as she tucked her chin length, jet-black hair behind her ears. Oona was our night watch and Wizard in training.

"What are you studying?" I asked as she moved her hand across the open book, finding her place once again.

"I'm trying to expand my shielding," she sighed, "but it's proving to be... difficult."

I clicked my tongue in response. "Wish I could help, friend, but I'm afraid you're a bit farther along with that than I am."

She gave me a smile and looked back towards her reading before replying, "Tell Endora thanks again for the bread. It will be some excellent fuel to get me through this exercise today."

I gave a gentle squeeze of her hand and walked to the back of the room. I never thought about focusing on my magic after I discovered I could use it. Not like how Oona seemed to delve into trying to understand it. Bergen has worked with me on controlling it in line with my emotional outbursts so I would avoid burning down the house or injuring someone.

While my Mage abilities are prominent, we discovered I have a deeper magic within me. Shadows had slipped around me as I slept one night at the orphanage, and Endora wasn't sure what to make of it, asking for help from Bergen. Since that event, I had been on his list of being particularly noteworthy.

I was three when Endora found me hiding in the alleyway that my parents tucked me in while running away. When she brought me back to the orphanage, there was an initial attempt to find my parents. We learned they had been killed that night. The magic my father held had been of the hunted kind .

Endora was from Briaroak Village, the town of Witches, located to the north of our town. She came to work here in Gaelfall long ago, when a need for an orphanage matron came up. Her ability to use potions and elixirs to aid in healing or sickness was welcomed. The Witch's magic, focusing on nature and life, made her a herbalist and a healer.

I lived with her at the orphanage until I was nine, and a particular event that set things into motion as to how I was adopted.

I remember the first time feeling the conjured fireball as it flew from my hand. My emotions burst through me in wild, unrestrained anger. The fire shot through the room, barely missing the children who had been relentless in their taunting and bullying.

"Sweet child, what were you thinking?" Endora chided gently.

I looked at the scene before us after the fire was quickly put out by Endora. Charred walls framed a hole the size of a kickball that let in the light from outside. How embarrassing.

"I'm sorry," I said quietly, tugging at the loose strands of my hair, trying to mask my emotions once again.

Endora looked at the children who stayed huddled together at my outburst. She gave them a stern look while placing her hands on her hips.

"Well, I don't suppose we're going to get an explanation? Who did what to Wren this time?"

The biggest of their group spoke, feigning innocence. "We were just playing. Wren always takes things so literally."

I looked down, not wanting to show the tears welling in my eyes. They were always awful. I endured the hitting and kicking, name calling and hair pulling, but they destroyed the only things I had considered my own. I looked over at the tattered pieces of my stuffed rabbit and the pillow I had since being here.

Endora followed my gaze and pressed her lips together tightly.

"Come child, gather your things and we'll try to fix them."

She gave another silent stare to the children as they hung their heads in a sorrow that was only in the moment. I knew it would never be genuine.

Viggo appeared not long after inquiring about the commotion, taking notice of me after hearing the story. It was directly after that incident that Viggo decided it would be better to have me come home with him. To adopt me and give me a chance at a better life. Endora became a caretaker for both Viggo and me, beyond her matron duties at the orphanage, making meals and taking care of our small cottage during the times Viggo was with the Sentinels. I finally felt like I had a home and a family in Viggo and Endora.

Beyond that showing of magic, I hadn't tried to use it more until I made my way to the library one day to inquire about working there. The thought of an endless supply of books to read outweighed the need for a weekly salary greatly. My job at the library was to be Bergen's assistant and library keeper, but mostly it turned into a way to work on my magic, honing my skills and helping me understand my Mage abilities as well as the shadow magic I held.

On either side of the great hall, there were additional hallways. The hall to the right had rooms for quiet studying as well as places to hold meetings and public hearings when needed. The hallway to the left was off-limits to the public. It was where the more important books, manuscripts, and ancient texts were kept, along with private offices. I made a left and walked a few doors down until I came to Bergen's office.

A messenger cat was making its way out as I approached. The slender white calico looked up at me with glowing green eyes as it slinked through the opening. Seeing that its harness was empty told me that a message had been delivered. It wasn't uncommon to get messages this way. Many messenger cats in town were large and well-fed, receiving treats as payment for delivery. It made it easy to tell apart the ones that came from neighboring towns, as they were thinner with longer distances to travel.

Bergen was bent over an old tome on his desk, pulling at his beard as he read. I wondered if he realized how often he did that when he was deep in thought or processing information. His blue eyes looked up at me briefly, nearly hidden by his bushy brows, before looking back down to finish the last bit of text.

"Hello again, Wren," he said.

"Hello again, Bergen." I copied him as I set my satchel down on the small mahogany secretary's desk that was tucked into the corner.

"I've got a couple things to go over with you today. Give me one moment, and we'll begin."

I nodded and set the book I borrowed in a box of tomes to shelve later today, and looked through some of the work that had made its way to my desk. The number of old books piled up told me the choice of the white tunic and tan leggings I wore was a poor decision. I'd be scrubbing the dust marks out of them this evening.

Bergen's office was a mess. He called it 'chaotic organization', but it really was simply messy. I looked over to what lay on his desk and decided on yet another attempt at helping him straighten things.

"Let me organize these stacks of papers for you," I offered, grabbing at one of the many piles on his desk.

Bergen hurried toward them, laying his hand on top of the pile to keep it from leaving the desk. "Thank you for the offer, but I know where everything is that I need in there."

"Are you sure? It could be quicker if things were organized for you into genre? Alphabetical? Anything?" I tried appealing.

His bushy brows furrowed to a pained expression as he shook his head.

"It's an organization of mine that allows me to find what I need. It's kind of you, but I know where things are as it is."

I knew my attempt to re-shelve the piled books or, at the very least, offering to stack them neater would be met with another polite decline.

Beyond the mess, Bergen's office was different from the stark white and ebony of the great room. Rich mahogany wood panels decorated the walls. Ornate wood carvings of ivy and other flora crept through the crown molding along the ceiling. Intricate rugs were layered on the floor in varied colors of reds, greens, and purple to give some warmth and sound dampening to the space. Built-in floor-to-ceiling bookshelves filled with even more books and scrolls of every kind sat against the wall. The age of the texts varied from recent to ancient.

Bergen closed the large green leather-bound book. A puff of dust came from the pages, and he waved his hand to clear the air as his dusky blue robes with white trim swished. In the low light, I caught a glint of the robe's silver embroidery forming small woodland creatures around the edges in an active game of fox and rabbit. He pulled his eyeglasses from the oversized cuff of his sleeve and looked at me, "We've got a problem."

CHAPTER 2

Bergen had a way of keeping his expression cool and collected even when something was wearing on him. You could almost judge how bad something was by how still he'd make himself over it, and at this discussion, he stilled himself with one breath, appearing almost frozen with those dusky blue robes and silver thread creating a winter chill about him.

He began. "I've just received word from Agatha that their library has been attacked."

I gaped for a moment then collected myself. "What sort of attack? Are they alright?"

Agatha was the Wizard who kept records at Briaroak Village. I hadn't met her, but I knew she and Bergen regularly kept in touch more than any of the other Wizards within the other towns. The messenger cat came to my mind again. How those green eyes stared at me as it walked past. I wondered for a moment if it knew what message it carried.

"It appears there was a group of bandits who bypassed their wards and quickly sought after a few of the ancient books stored there before…" he paused, swallowing once and met my eyes, "before they set fire to the building."

Each Wizard warded the library to alert them of any sort of entrance that wasn't welcomed. A series of spells would fall into place to shield or hide anything within the library that needed to be protected. To bypass something like that was unheard of. I only knew of an occurrence like that happening once, and even then, it was a vague recollection.

"We had something like that happen here, correct? Before my time?" I asked.

"Yes, once. A radical group from the Red Kingdom wanted to destroy any history of ancient magic. The same group that led to many deaths throughout Caldumn. If you remember back to the studies I put you through when first training with me, you'd recall that many of the ancient books we keep are written in a way to hide the history itself." Bergen spoke with a hint of reproach.

"You'd also remember that those ancient texts were written in that way, only able to be translated by those who know what they are seeking. The play of words, the hidden meanings, all help those who are looking to find what they need from them."

I nodded, now remembering how utterly boring I had thought it was going through all the stacks of reading he wanted me to do when I first started training with him. A pang of regret hit me. The Red Kingdom looms as our ruling hierarchy. The south worked tirelessly to earn the trust of the King to be able to govern our towns without their soldiers and rule heavily placed on us, but their reign still weighs heavily on many of our towns.

"The wards held then, hiding the texts from them, and they left empty-handed. What needs to be remembered is that history needs to be preserved and cared for at all costs."

"So, this time was different," I concluded, looking down.

Bergen stood from his chair and brushed at the invisible specs of dirt on the front of his robes. The solid mahogany desk he used was much more substantial than mine and matched the same wood stain of his walls and shelving. He made his way around the wide desk and stopped at the head of the table, clasping his hands together in front of him.

I grew as still as Bergen continued. "One of their overnight bookkeepers on watch was killed in the fire. The texts they lost are irreplaceable. We will need to find out how they knew where to find the books they were after."

Heat rose to my cheeks, burning at my face as my eyes stung with tears. I placed a hand on the small desk next to me to steady myself, and could hardly feel the cool hardwood as I thought about Endora. I wondered if she would have heard about this by the time I made it home. I hoped she didn't know the bookkeeper who lost their life. I thought about all the lost history stored in that library about the Witches, and all the important books we had shared amongst each other for generations, but that now no longer existed. I looked out the window behind Bergen, which had a direct view into our Sentinel camp. It's where the soldiers who protect our town trained, gathered, and lived. Much like our Sentinels, the witches have a Battalion that keeps watch in their town. There would have been a group of them stationed at the library.

"What happened to the Battalion on duty?" I asked Bergen. "Did they see anything?"

"Agatha only said the two stationed near the doors were found dead outside of the town gates. Whether they were lured out there or dragged after being killed, we don't know yet. I'll be planning a visit to see what assistance we can offer in rebuilding their historical texts. I know Agatha had safeguards in place for some of the more important texts to the Witches' history, and I'm hoping we can do something to restore them."

A ball of emotion worked its way into my throat, making it hard to swallow. My vision wavered for a moment, and I sunk into the soft leather chair next to my desk. My hands ran across the wood of the arms, which were worn down to smooth grooves. I focused on some breathing techniques I learned when I was bullied in the orphanage.

Breathe in, count to four... Hold... Breathe out, count to four... Hold... Repeat.

I took one more long breath and asked, "Do we have anything here they would want? The ones that burned their library?"

"I believe we do," Bergen said, "Which is why I gathered these texts. These are some of the most important pieces of history and records we have here, and they will certainly be after them." He turned back to his desk piled with a few metal-clad scroll cases, two small books, and the green leather-bound book he'd been reading. "We've been the keepers of the history books of Aura, the uses of light and dark magic, and the history of those who could harness both. The scrolls are maps of the Ancient War and locations of concentrated Aura that we need to keep a track of." Bergen turned back to me after finishing.

I was once again open-mouthed at the depth of what was contained in those books and scrolls. My hands were sweaty and stuck slightly to the wooden arms of the chair.

"As you know, with Aura being the lifeblood of magic sustained in our world, being one with our environment, as much as air, plants, animals, and people…" Bergen began speaking as if he was about to give a beginners lesson in magic.

"Right, it is consumed, used, and then expended and restored to the environment. The endless cycle of life." I interjected.

"Indeed, the upcoming celestial events could be the reason for the attacks and robberies of our texts." Bergen said. I had loved learning about the celestial events, especially because one of them falls on my birthday in late fall, the Aurarius Lights. Golden starlight rains down from the sky, and beyond it is a beautiful event to watch, the surrounding Aura becomes denser and more powerful. When I was younger, I'd wonder if being born that night had made me different. Special. As if the shadows that appeared when I was younger were part of the Aura.

Not everyone is gifted in magic casting, but it's said that our lives are extended by the use of magic. Many of those who are gifted with it live hundreds of years, while others might have a full life at just over one hundred. The magic works with those that allow it through them.

"The people in the southern lands of Caldum have followed the balance of Aura due to the teachings of the Originals who walked among us. Those who were of the same shadow magic you hold." Bergen said, continuing his lecture that I knew I'd heard a few times now. Especially the shadows part.

I casually tried to change the subject. "And what about the map scrolls?"

I had tucked them away some time ago on a high shelf in his office and recognized them.

"Ah yes, the battlefield maps of the War of the Originals." Bergen couldn't help himself as he went in on another history refresher. "We are aware of the three Originals, those who were of pure shadow magic. From what we have gathered in the ancient texts, there was a disagreement between them. One that could have caused great harm to our people and our world if Marion and Jareth hadn't stopped Ismael." He adjusted his glasses as he peered at the open field encircled by trees on the map. "It's said the battle between them left a concentration of Aura within that field that can be felt by even those who have the smallest showing of magic."

"What happened to them?" I asked, thinking about what it would be like to see them still in our lands. A chill went up my spine thinking how old, gaunt and withered they would be at living a thousand years.

"We believe Ismael was destroyed. Marion and Jareth then left the world, and your family line has carried one of the shadow lineages since. However, the Red Kingdom seems to believe Ismael will return one day to regain his power. Fanatical religious sorts, but it's a theory, nonetheless."

"Has anyone tried to make it over the Great Northern Sierras to see what the Red Kingdom is like?" I asked, pivoting from the shadows once again, but I knew he wouldn't mind a teaching opportunity.

"If anyone did, it would certainly be something for history records, however, in an official capacity, we haven't had reason to."

I knew there were risks to the journey. Unpredictable and sudden weather changes, monsters, and the sheer face of the cliffs to climb. The ancient lifts that used to allow travelers between the lands had long since been destroyed.

The scroll map we looked at was old, and I took care as I lightly touched from the Red Kingdom, back down to the battlefield's location to the west of Gaelfall, in the center of the Hidden Forest.

"Traveling to the Ancient Battlefield is dangerous enough."

"Hmm, very true. Many do get lost or end up food for the monsters and creatures," Bergen said.

I paused and looked at him. The tone in the way he responded made me wonder if he was aware of the dry humor he held in his words at times.

"The stories about the battlefield are enough to keep me out of there." I said, focusing back on the scrolls.

Children loved to tell each other spooky stories about the battlefield, incorporating things like wailing ghosts who haunt its plains, wraiths who ate your soul, even down to Necromancers and Warlocks going there to use their dark magic for rituals or other demonic activities.

I can't say I hadn't had a nightmare or two from hearing some of the tales.

I thought about everything Bergen said, trying to think if the texts contained the answers as to what the bandits were after. If they had always been hiding in the open, sitting on the shelves of our library open to the public. As I got closer to the books Bergen had set aside, I could feel a shift in the surrounding air. Not the familiar shielding spell or a ward placed on them, but the hum of deeper magic emanated from them.

"I can feel these books without touching them," I said.

"Mmm, yes. They do like to sing their own tunes." Bergen quipped. "I'm going to shield these and that should quiet them enough, but most importantly it will hide them away, warded and protected, and I need to show you where I put them. If I'm not here before anything happens, I need you to retrieve them and get them out above all else."

I nodded and watched as he gathered them up. He turned to the bookcase nearest his desk and pulled on a vase that sat atop the shelf. The shelved books below the vase slid to the side, and a small alcove appeared behind the bookcase itself, carved into the quartz wall. There was just enough room to set them in and have it close smoothly.

"I'll need to get your imprint for the vase, so you can open it as well. No one else besides you and I will access this alcove," he said.

I nodded again and held out my hand to him. Bergen gently placed his hand on mine and I felt a light tracing of magic along my palms and fingers. Within a few seconds, it was done.

"There, try to pull the vase."

I walked over and touched the smokey glass that sat ever so inconspicuously. A light pull at the top and the shelf below slid open with ease just as I saw with Bergen. The texts all sat peacefully in their new home, quietly humming.

"Good. It's done. I'll work on shielding these and getting the wards put around. Go ahead about your day, Wren." Bergen said in a manner that was right back to his everyday work tone.

My gaze fell to the layered rugs again as I went back to my desk, following the patterns and designs while thinking about the responsibility I had just been handed. I grabbed the box of books to take with me for shelving. It felt light compared to the heaviness of the whole conversation we just had.

"Oh, one more thing, Wren," Bergen said, as I walked toward the door, "I think it would be a good idea for you to get more involved with your father's combat training. If we have bandits on the loose and you should ever come across one, I'd like to think you could fight as well as you use your magic abilities."

I thought it was another one of his dry jokes, but he sat at his desk and started writing something down.

"What about Oona?" I asked, still not wanting to accept the newly prescribed training orders.

"I need her here. You'll do well there with the Sentinels as you already know so many of them."

"Thanks." I said flatly, after staring at him another moment in silent affront, and made my way out of the room.

While the thought of a looming threat hung over me, I still couldn't shake my distaste in combat training. I barely felt like I could spar correctly with magic use, and now I was going to have to actually learn how to hit and kick and fight with weapons? I wasn't frail or out of shape by any means, I regularly ran and tried to keep a good regime of activity. Viggo and I had trained here and there, but it was nothing compared to what I'd seen him put his Sentinels through. I couldn't help making a pained face while I rounded the corner into the great hall of the library.

Oona caught my expression as I set the box of books down with a thud on the back side of the desk. I pushed open the small swinging door that was fastened to its side and sat at the seat across the inner open space, keeping my back to her.

Oona wore a simple white summer dress with small, embroidered eyelets in the shapes of flowers. Light blue ribbon laced around the arm sleeves and neckline. She always dressed so well compared to my blouses, tunics, and pants or leggings, but I honestly didn't envy it. I had a limited supply of dresses and always hated wearing them when it couldn't be avoided.

"Looks like you were assigned something you aren't too particular about." Oona said as she swiveled around the stool she perched on to stare at my back.

"Oh? What makes you think that?" I replied, trying to hide the weight of the news that had just been hurled at me. I tried to smile as I turned to face her as well.

"Tell me you have to work on your shielding with me. I can't seem to get beyond the bookends at the far wall there." She said, pointing to the small stand of featured books we set out for the public to view. Quite a considerable reach for how recently she had been working on shielding.

I looked back to Oona as she tucked both sides of her hair behind her ears again. She did this often when focusing on a task.

"I wish that was it." I said, "but guess who gets to start combat training tomorrow?" I pointed both thumbs to myself and gave another fake smile. Oona looked at me in silence for a moment before erupting in laughter.

"Good one, Wren. I can see you out there with the best of them now. Your Dad will be so proud." She continued laughing.

That fake smile faded, and I could feel sadness grow in my eyes as everything I had just heard sunk in that she didn't know. I continued to stare at her.

She paused, "Wait, really? No way." She still couldn't believe what I was saying.

"Yeah, I guess I'm checking in with Viggo tomorrow morning, and we'll see what sort of skills I'll learn. He really will be so excited over this." I groaned and turned back to the box of books and started taking them out to organize them to the sections they were to go back to.

I kept myself busy to not overwhelm myself with the emotions that churned within. Endora always said I was highly empathetic, but pile that on with my childhood trauma and the depressive thoughts of worthlessness, anxiety and panic that I battled continually, I knew I had to remain focused on my work.

"What exactly did you two talk about in there?" She finally said in the silence between us. Oona tucked her hair behind her ears again. She also did this when nervous.

"You'll want to talk to Bergen. I'm sure he's probably going to call you to his office any time now to go over what we just did... It's not good." I couldn't look back at her knowing I'd break down and start crying, the tears were nearly toppling over my eyelashes. The idea of this happening in our lands, and the possibility of it happening here had me feeling overwhelmed.

I balanced one stack of books in my arms for re-shelving at the farthest end of the hall. I could see out of the corner of my eye Oona's gaze follow me as I walked away. By the time I came back to collect the second batch of books, she was heading down the left hall towards Bergen's office.

CHAPTER 3

WORK IN THE library seemed to fly by that afternoon while in the haze of thoughts of the attacks. I didn't see Oona much after she spoke to Bergen. Her face was ashen when she came back to her desk and immediately pulled her book open to start more research on shielding abilities. As I went to gather my things and leave for the day, she still sat in the same place buried deep in the book. I gave her a light touch on her shoulder before heading back to Bergen's office.

It was always quiet in the library, but my footsteps seemed to echo louder today, making my presence known to anyone in the building. As I walked into Bergen's office, I welcomed the silence of the rugs.

My satchel was still perched on the small desk in the corner, and I couldn't help but be drawn to the last bookcase against the wall where the hidden alcove was. The twilight filtered in from the window on the vase, its gray glass looking smokier in the dim light. I shuddered to think of having to open it again under different circumstances. I couldn't allow the panic to rise, though, and tightly closed my eyes to scrub the memory from my mind.

Bergen had already left for the day, which wasn't uncommon, and was easy to recognize when the staff he kept with him wasn't propped up against the corner wall behind his desk. I wondered if he actually went straight home or if he was exploring more ways to help protect this building. If anything, he most likely ended up down the road to the Sentinels, figuring out what could be done to bolster our watch.

I bit my lower lip while I headed back out to the hall, listening to the reverberating sound of someone's shoes echoing down the hall before seeing Oona down a row of bookcases, slowly walking as if she was taking inventory, or looking for another book to further her studies. I wanted to reach out and help her, to be able to shield things in the way she could and studied, but I knew she'd want to do this on her own, and shielding in the capacity of Wizardry was something I wouldn't be able to achieve.

Like me, Oona had a hard time managing anxiety. I masked mine and looked normal on the surface all while on the inside I writhed with something so awful. Oona would show outward symptoms and then act to alleviate the problem, much like tucking in her hair, and then digging into a book for answers. It was something I needed to work on myself. Finding answers and not just sitting with the emotion, letting it eat me up.

Oona had only once opened up about her past. She'd suffered abuse from a family member that had visited.

It broke my heart to think someone as wonderful as her had gone through something like that. I think it added a level to our friendship that would be hard to break. She knew about my parents, and the way I was treated in the orphanage.

We worked together trying to find records or history of who killed my parents when we first started working together. We looked for anything that could give us a hint about why they'd been running that night, but couldn't find a single thing. Oona said she wouldn't give up the search, and I believe she still looks to this day whenever she's reviewing something from the time they were alive. While I now know the reason for their deaths, it was still a secret I've kept from her. My shadow magic was something only Viggo and Bergen knew about.

Stepping out into the fading light of the day, I took a deep breath of the coastal fresh air. A slight crispness signaled the turning of summer to autumn. It would soon be our rainy season. It never got too cold where we were in the south of Caldumn. Something about how the coastal waters help regulate our temperatures came to mind for a moment. A wool jacket in winter was sufficient, as it was a rare occurrence to get snow, and if that happened, it was only a dusting that disappeared with the warmth of the day.

The streets were still alive, as I passed many of the townsfolk who were packing up their day trades and others who were setting up for the Gaelfall Night Market. It was a nighttime festive event that happened one night each month, put on by those with small businesses and guarded by Sentinels for peace of mind so that the long evenings could be enjoyed without worry. The lovely smells of cooking meats and spices wafted in the air and I felt my stomach rumble in protest for supper. It was a lot of fun seeing the town alive at night. Music played, and colorful lanterns were hung over the street. You could eat and drink till the sun came up with friends and neighbors, but this particular night was not one for celebration.

I upped my pace off the main road to our quiet street and headed straight for our home in the distance. The lights were brightly illuminated through the leaded glass windows, which let me know Endora had made it home. I slowed my pace the last few steps to mentally brace myself for the conversation that was about to happen.

The white oak door creaked open as I crossed into the warmth and smelled the lovely aroma of potato and cheese soup, our go-to meal on hard days. Even under these horrible circumstances, the homey feeling comforted me somewhat. I hung my satchel up on the hook adjacent to the door and walked into the small open space.

"Hi Endora, I'm home. Need help with anything?" I offered, making my way to the sink to wash my hands. She was sitting in the worn purple upholstered chair next to a warm fire, Her brown eyes were glassy, reflecting the flames, and a forced smile that would normally illuminate her smooth, umber skin didn't quite reach the usual glow. The tight curls of her dark hair were pulled up on top of her head with a colorful scarf. .

"Hello dear, how was your day?" she replied. My heart twisted in pain, hearing the sadness in her voice.

"I… heard about what happened in Briaroak. I'm so sorry."

Endora always told me how vividly emerald my eyes turned when I was emotional, and I knew they must have been vibrant in this moment.

She turned back to watching the fire in silence for a moment, then said, "What is Bergen doing to protect you and Oona?"

I took a breath. "We're hiding away some of the more important texts. I'll be working on combat training with Dad now, and Oona's shielding is nearly perfect." I dried my hands on a towel and tried to sound convincing that we had things covered. "The Sentinels are strong, and they'll be adding more support to keep watch over the library."

She stood from her chair, meeting me in the kitchen, to check the boiling soup. "Your father should be home soon. I'm sure he'll be pleased about you spending training sessions with him again."

"Yeah, I'm sure he's really going to love telling me what to do without my protests." I laughed, trying to lighten the mood. "I might need you to mix up some healing elixirs to save me from the sore muscles I'm about to have."

She only chuffed at my feeble attempt at a joke while she kept her focus on the soup, but a small bit of light returned to her eyes.

Viggo came home not long after, more silent than normal, but that was to be expected. I knew Viggo had spent time in Briaroak, and after coming here to head the Sentinels, he was the one who told Endora about the position for an orphanage matron. They had been friends since childhood.

"Hey Dad. I don't know if you've heard the news yet, but guess who's training with you tomorrow?" I said with a small smile.

He gave a grunt of a chuckle as he put his things away and came into the kitchen for dinner. "Potato and cheese soup. It'll be much needed tonight."

I pursed my lips as I served up the bowls of soup and placed them on our small kitchen table.

We ate mostly in silence. Viggo held Endora's hand and they had an unspoken moment between them where I could see the sorrow they both felt. There was history for them at Briaroak, and an attack like that was completely unexpected in our peaceful lands.

We said our goodbyes as Endora headed back to the orphanage for the night after we cleaned up, and Viggo and I sat together by the fire. I stretched out on the shabby velvet green couch while Viggo sat in the chair. His persistent silence told me that he was pondering something more than usual.

"This attack is pretty bad, isn't it?" I asked, pressing him to open up.

"It is. We'll do what we need to protect Gaelfall, but it will give me a peace of mind knowing I'm getting you ready for anything that could happen." He continued staring at the fire.

I could see there was more behind his stare. His piercing blue eye nearly glowed against the reflection of the flames.

"I know it must be hard on Endora to hear, and you spent time there too, right?" I asked. I didn't know a lot about Viggo's past. Only what he told me if I had reason to ask.

"I don't think I've told you why I adopted you, have I?" Viggo said after some time.

I remembered asking when I was little from time to time, but the answer was always that I was special, or some joke that he could see I was a fighter after the fireball incident. I shook my head.

"When I saw you there, after everything that happened. I saw myself, and what I experienced as an orphan."

I sat up quickly and stared at him. "I didn't know you were an orphan. Why hadn't you mentioned that before?"

"It didn't need to be said at the time," he looked back to the fire, "I was adopted by a kind Witch and brought to Briaroak at a young age. It's where I met Endora, and have remained friends. As soon as I was old enough to enlist into the Battalion, I trained to fight, and was then sent off as we established these lands further, working with the different soldiers and fighters of the different towns. My abilities as a warrior grew and I saw how I aligned with the Sentinels. I ended up coming to Gaelfall, being brought on to head a few of their ranks, and as time went on, I became their leader."

"I guess I wouldn't have thought this all to be super interesting when younger, but thank you for sharing now." I teased.

"Let me finish," he smiled in return, "I adopted you because of what that kind Witch showed me. That I could be nurtured and loved, helping me to become the person

I am today. I saw myself in you, I saw what you could become, and I wanted to help you become that."

"So I'm the next great warrior?" I asked, not as much teasing now.

Viggo's laugh echoed in the room. "Not that I expect you to be pushing me out of heading up the Sentinels, but I do believe you have something great in you. You have those shadow things that creep out from you," he wiggled his fingers around, making me laugh along with him, "But you are special, Wren. The moment when I saw you, something told me you were different. I acted on that feeling and it has been the best thing I've ever done."

"Thanks, Dad." I said, feeling warmth not just from the fire.

"Whatever is coming, I'll make sure you're ready for, and Bergen better keep on his toes before you knock him on his backside with your magic again." He winked.

I shook my head. "I've got to go to bed, training first thing in the morning and all."

"Aye. Be ready, girl. I don't expect you'll be feeling great these first couple weeks."

I headed up to my room to pick out what to wear for training tomorrow. After changing into a comfortable pajama shirt, I pulled some black leggings out and a tight tank top undershirt that would work well during the exercise. I'd wear a billowy white blouse over it for any work in the library after. I set out a pair of black boots that tied up to my ankles. I used them more for hiking but thought they would offer some stability during the training.

Before crawling into bed, I stared at the moon which dimly lit the smoke rising from the chimneys of the neighboring townhomes. I cupped my hands around my eyes to block my interior light, trying to see if there were any ships with their large sails in the harbor, but it was too dark to see. I wondered if the night market would keep the bandits away from the library tonight. Enough people would bustle about until the early hours, that I'd like to think we were safe. I yawned and realized just how tired I was from the day.

I wrapped an arm around a favorite pillow and moved my feet into the cool room air from the side of the cloud-like blanket. I forced my eyes shut, sinking into the black. We were safe tonight; I kept telling myself. We are safe. Safe.

Breathe... Inhale, count to four... Hold... Release. Count to four...

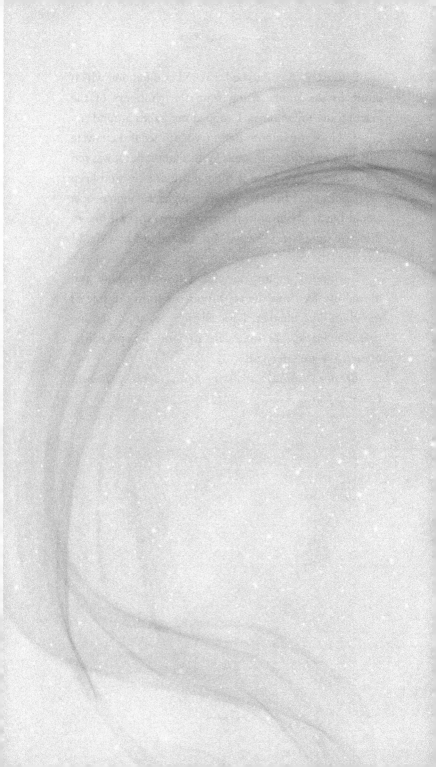

CHAPTER 4

WAKING UP THAT morning was easier than expected for the restless sleep I had. I kept dreaming about the last night I had with my parents. Parts of that night came to me clearly, and yet others were nothing more than the fog of being so young. My father was again holding me in his arms, running away from whatever was chasing us. I kept lifting my head over his shoulder to see what we were running from. I dreamt of multiple versions of that same moment. One time I saw horrible wolf beasts chasing us with glowing red eyes. Another was wraiths and skeletons hunting us down.

The most disturbing one was of us being chased by me, or at least it looked like me, but it wasn't me. I was full of shadow and smoke; I watched my mouth open and a piercing scream rang from it.

I awoke startled in a cold sweat from that one. I saw bands of shadow dissipating around me, disappearing quick enough that I wondered if it was just remnants of the dream, but I was left trying to settle my racing heart at the thought of not knowing I had allowed my shadows to show.

The memory of my mother crying while running next to us as my father carried me was stuck in my mind forever. I remembered her fear as she looked back at what was chasing us.

A burst of fire shot from her hands toward whatever chased us, but I never could clearly see just what they were. Blurs of voices and shouting, my parents' heavy breathing, my silent fear, as we tried to escape the nearing enemy.

I steadied my heart again, pushing out the thoughts of that day.

I stretched my arms up high above my head, arching my back to get the blood moving within my muscles. I tried to calm my nerves by thinking I'd be a trained fighter soon enough and I'd know how to defend myself against any of those monsters from my nightmare.

The bare floors gave the familiar shock of cold from the night as I placed my feet down and let them warm the wood underneath. A quick trip to the bathroom to freshen up and I was back in my room to change into my training clothes. I stood looking in the mirror for a moment examining how I looked in all black, appearing a lot more confident than I truly felt. I tied my hair up in a topknot to keep it out of the way of whatever we were planning to do for the first day of training. The billowy and soft fabric of the large white blouse felt like just enough of a barrier to my cool room, and I wondered if I'd need another layer for the chill of the morning.

I entered the kitchen and noticed Viggo was already gone for the day, heading to the barracks to begin barking his orders to the soldiers. I could smell eggs set on a candle warmer for me. I opened the top lid covering the pan and was happily surprised with a delicious omelet. It wasn't a regular thing to have breakfast made as he left so early, along with the fact that I was almost twenty and should make my morning meals, but it was a sign that Viggo was thinking about my training this morning, and a good breakfast would be important. I took in the smell and sighed happily as I pulled the plate from the warmer and dug into the food.

I walked to the familiar path to the library at a quicker pace than usual. It was hard to think about anything but the dream. These were the roads where my parents had been killed. Although I took these roads nearly every day without a second thought, today I could feel anxiety and nervousness creeping deeper with every stride.

There were still some late-night townsfolk along the way; some who were sleeping off their partying in places not otherwise meant for sleeping, and others slowly making their way back home in a drunken stupor. The Sentinels still stood watch on the street corners where the festivities had been. They were always fixed in certain areas of our town and the harbor. Easy to forget, blending into the background of our town, but there when you need them. Someone you could ask for directions or assistance, and protection.

I turned the corner to the main road of the library when I saw there were now four soldiers instead of the two who normally stood guard at the library entrance. Other Sentinels were paired up and patrolling the grounds surrounding the library as well. Bergen was quick to bolster security, visiting Viggo at the Sentinel base when he left the library last night. I walked past the library entrance and around to the back side where a small path led to the training grounds.

A rail fence that encircled a giant dirt arena appeared first when walking down the road. I had spent some time here when I was younger, running through the fields on days when Viggo had taken me with him to issue a few rounds of work to the Sentinels. As I got older, and took more of an interest in the soldiers than playing in the fields, Viggo had Endora keep me busy at home with her. Beyond that were more fenced-off areas with different wooden dummies and weapons racks. To the far end beyond those fenced spaces stood three stone buildings. The armory bunker, the barracks, and the Central War Building where their day-to-day operations took place.

The sky was clear and made the heat from the sun more noticeable as I continued to feel the nerves circle around in my body. I wasn't sure why exactly I was more nervous to meet with him this time, but figured that once we got in the swing of things, I'd calm down. I walked further into the courtyard of the Central War Building, noticing more of the Sentinels going about their daily tasks.

Becoming a Sentinel required intensive training. You had to live in the barracks where you would eat, sleep and breathe their training. Some possessed magical qualities, and both men and women joined, it didn't matter, but the focus was on combat training ranging from hand-to-hand, to weaponry skills. There were skilled fighters and then special operations, like spies, sword masters, berserkers, and bowmen. The most prestigious was the Watch, who reported directly to Viggo, and assumed control of operations as needed.

I looked at one of the heavy broadswords in a rack as I passed and wondered if I could even pick it up. The effort it would take to swing a sword like that and not fall from the resulting force would be an exercise itself.

Viggo appeared in the doorway of the central building as I walked into its courtyard. His shaved head glistened with beads of sweat that the heat of the sun would soon bring more of. He pulled on his full beard with both hands to straighten it. I always thought he appeared young due to his round cheeks that peaked above the facial hair, but his eyes showed years of battle and training.

He wore a white tunic hidden by a leather breastplate with fighting trousers and boots. I looked like a true novice next to him.

"Wow, we're going full on fight mode already?" I said, noticing his armor.

He only smiled, "You're lucky I won't expect you to stay in the bunkers, but you'll be training with me first thing in the mornings until lunch. Then you're free to check in with Bergen." He continued with a bit of a laugh, "I'll be holding you to the same standard as my Sentinels."

I nodded quickly, giving a feigned salute of a fist over my chest. "May the Valiant Prevail."

"That will earn you extra laps around the ring." He sharply warned, raising a brow.

"Sorry. It's the nerves." I blushed.

Viggo gave a nod and motioned for me to follow him as we walked out of the courtyard and into a small fenced in ring that had soft grass growing within.

"We haven't had to use this one in a while, might as well start and get some of this grass worn down." Viggo joked, "I'm already going easy on you by giving you a soft landing for the first day."

I smiled as I looped my shoulder bag around a fence post and removed my oversized blouse before returning to the center of the ring.

"First thing we are going to do is see how your balance is, your breathing techniques, and flexibility. We'll be doing a lot of stretching techniques today." I sighed in relief before he continued, "But don't think that you won't be feeling sore by the end."

With that, we moved into the first stretching positions. Viggo spoke and worked alongside my movements, explaining what they stretched and how it would affect mobility. It was different from how I trained before. The way he spoke, and the time he took explaining things made me see he truly wanted me to understand the technique and movements. He had a way of being matter-of-fact and it helped me look at him as more of an actual teacher than my father.

We worked on leg strength, creating smooth movements while keeping our breathing in line. I don't think I've ever held a lunge as long as I had today. Circling our arms high above our heads, then out to the side, while keeping our breath in line was key. By the end of the training session, I moved into different 'Warrior' poses, as he called them, seamlessly.

"Aye, good work, girl. We'll pick up tomorrow with some core work. You've got some good balance. I thank myself for that." he joked as I nearly collapsed into the grass on my back.

"Sounds great." I said, keeping my breath even, but feeling like I was nothing more than jelly.

"Have you heard anything more about the attacks on Briaroak Village?" I'd been wondering if there had been more news halfway into our workout, and finally had the time to ask.

"We received some information from the Battalion General. Seems like the bandits are a troublesome group, but we've bolstered our patrols and units. No identification on them yet."

"Do you think the reinforcement of more soldiers around town will be enough to keep them from here?" My nerves showed near the surface as I asked.

Viggo smirked, I wasn't sure if it came from reassurance, or the eagerness of something to battle.

"Keep to your training and focus on what lies ahead, leave the planning to my Watch."

I nodded, hoping to have something more to calm me, but the truth of it was, we truly didn't know.

Viggo gave me a pat on my shoulder as he strode back to the main building.

"I've got to check in with the coastal soldiers securing our taxes to the Red Kingdom. Tell Bergen I send my regards," he said, and I let my face scrunch in pain, knowing I still had an afternoon of library work ahead of me. "I'll see you tonight."

I wanted to lay there all day in that cool grass. Little white flowers danced around in the high spots while the deep blue sky remained open and welcoming to spend as much time as needed staring at it. I laid there thinking of nothing before slowly getting up and made my way to the library.

The walk wasn't far, but it felt like five miles when I made it to the back steps of the library. I opened the side door and slowly trudged through the right-wing hall towards the center. I threw my large blouse over my head, and almost had both arms pulled through the sleeves when I came into view of Oona. She was perched on her stool in her usual spot behind the desk, wearing dark trousers and a thin fitted sweater. Her eyebrows raised and eyes went wide as she saw my huffing.

"Training… went well?" Is all she could say. I pulled my hair from my ponytail and wiped at the strands that stuck to my neck from the sweat.

"You could say that, sure," I said and dropped my things at the back desk, then honestly replied with a groan, "I'm going to be so useless this week."

Oona shook her head with a silent laugh.

"You're a star, Wren. Keep going."

I rolled my eyes but gave her thanks as I slowly moved my heavy legs to Bergen's office to check in for the day.

Bergen was deep into a stack of papers when I entered. He only nodded to me while I gingerly sat down in my seat and looked over what I had laid out on my desk to do for the day. Luckily no books to shelve. I flipped through the stack of indexing cards to get done and started organizing and filling out the paperwork needed.

"I'll need you to check on a few lists of duplicate books we have to donate to the Witches once their rebuilding is finished," Bergen said.

I looked up from my papers and nodded. It would be a task to check through the inventory sheets, but worth it to help them. It still hurt to think of not only the loss of life they experienced, but the loss of the literature, too. So often we take for granted the ability to read a story, and now with some gone forever for them, it would only be the right thing to help where we could.

"I take it practice went well today?" Bergen asked as I grimaced while trying to cross my legs.

"There was a lot of balance and movement today," I said. "I'm not sure what holding poses does for my fighting skills, but I'll keep going to see where this leads to."

Bergen let out a grunt in response.

"Have you heard of these 'Warrior' poses? Do they actually fight holding a lunge? No. They don't. I'm very confused at that, and all this arm and hand movement." I blurted out, still thinking about why I was making those movements. I waved my arms in the arc over my head that I had to do repeatedly to show him what I meant.

Bergen then smiled and leaned back in his seat. His hand moved up to the side of his gray beard as he pulled on it, "You'll enjoy yoga. It's a wonderful practice that is known from other lands."

I gave a shrug and shook my head not fully believing his words.

After indexing, I went out to work with Oona at the main desk, and chowed down on the mixed nuts, bread, and cheese I had with me. I quickly realized that I'd need to pack a more substantial meal next time if I wanted to feed my body for this… yoga. Before I finished lunch, Bergen let me know he was heading back to his home for more research, and that we would work on additional spell casting exercises after my training with Viggo tomorrow. I smiled at the small reprieve.

The day passed quickly while Oona and I finished work in the library. She was committed to expanding her shield work, and we made it a point to not bring up the worries we shared. We masked the anxieties with gossip and talked about a few guys in town that we may have had a thing for. Oona had a type, and found Sentinel soldiers particularly attractive.

"Who'd you train with today? Anyone I know?" Oona asked.

"No, just my Dad today. Most of them steer clear of him, so I don't think I'll be mingling with them as much as I'd like. The less attention on my training the better." I laughed.

"I can set you up with someone. Have them take you out to dinner, maybe a nice massage for those sore muscles?" She wiggled her eyebrows.

I jokingly hesitated, giving it thought before declining the sweet offer.

Walking home in the evening was painful, but I managed to make it back without looking too worse for wear, or so I hoped. As I opened the front door the welcoming smell of dinner wafted to my senses. A couple small glass vials sat atop the table, and I gasped.

"Endora, you are amazing, have I told you that?" I said, and nearly dropped my bag to the floor before making my way to the vials.

"Drink one now, and another in the morning before you head out for the day. It'll help ease the pain," she said as she turned from the stovetop.

"You have no idea how much Dad is loving the torture he's putting me through." I said with a laugh.

She smiled and came to the small table to place a mixture of vegetables, seared tofu, and pasta down. I could smell the aromatic garlic sauce and my mouth watered. I sat down and waited for Endora to take her seat as well before diving in.

"You'll want to take a warm bath tonight and use the herbs I've put in the washroom. It'll relax your muscles this evening and prevent any cramping,"

"Thank you again. I don't think I'd be able to walk up the stairs later tonight if it weren't for these." I said, and tipped the vial back to drink.

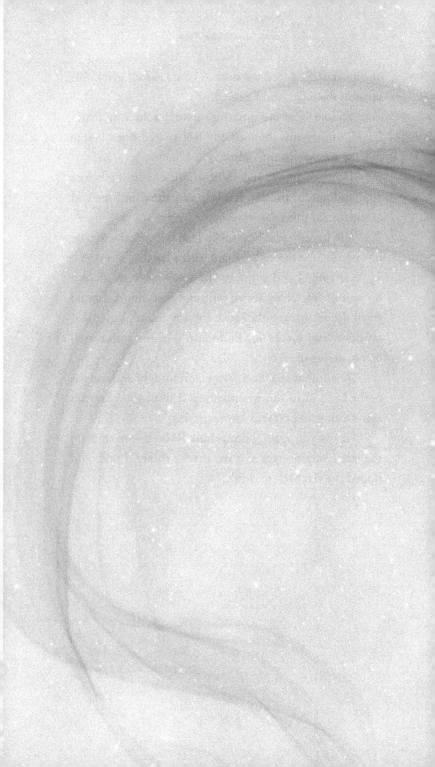

CHAPTER 5

THE DAYS MELTED into weeks, and I continued to focus on my training, hoping that with enough physical effort it would give me dreamless nights, but my nightmares continued. The combat came with gradual ease and power with the strengthening of my muscles, and I started to build not only confidence in fighting, but in my appearance as well. My posture was straighter. My arms toned up, my core became tight, and my thighs had new definition that I noticed in the mirror when changing one morning. It would be near torture without the help from Endora's elixirs, but the need for them lessened until I no longer needed them at all, and I learned to greet any twinge of soreness with my excitement of the new muscle and strength forming.

Magic training quickly turned into one of the harder parts of the day. I worked on understanding Aura, allowing the magic to flow through my body and willing it into what I wanted it to be. I could endure longer sessions of casting and I tried to expand the size and power of what I could cast, but self-doubt would grab hold of me and I'd lose that continual flow and connection to Aura, eventually hitting a wall. The haunting of my shadows within would beg me to let them out beyond the control I put on them, and it was even more work to understand how to properly balance them.

Bergen watched and helped correct my focus when he saw me wavering. I tried to work past the self-doubt and the anxiety that seemed to spread deep roots throughout my mind. It felt like pulling at a root to remove it only allowed for another to spread elsewhere.

Some nights I would be so exhausted from the day that I would sit alone in my bed, feeling despair and self-loathing. It was what Viggo and Bergen had said to me; I was worth the time spent, that I was meant to be here, that kept me going. Even if I didn't see the path that they did, I knew it would be the only way to fight my insecurities.

More attacks started to happen, and not only to towns with libraries. The bandits were ruthless. Burning homes, torturing people, and leaving nothing but death and fear in their wake. We pored over any information we received from those that came across their path of destruction, the bodies, or narrow escapes, learning that they continued to attack under the cover of night as a cloak that kept their victims from confidently identifying them. Anyone who survived and caught the smallest of glimpses couldn't give more information than what we learned from their blurred recollections. Human, but something was off. Masked by hoods, voices unnatural. Viggo spent countless hours with his closest Watch going over their attacks, trying to find patterns or areas that would lead us to getting ahead of them, but nothing made sense.

I rolled over to my side for a moment to allow the burning in my core to subside from our training. We were almost done with the day's torture, and I was looking forward to the moment of stillness we would do after I completed the last set. I rolled onto my back again and looked up at the blue sky. White fluffy clouds slowly danced through my field of vision and I steadied my breath.

These attacks lingered in my mind. The insecure part of me made me feel so insignificant to what was going on, however, a deeper part of me felt like I would somehow be responsible to our lands and our people. I would be the one to help them.

"These books that we are protecting contain information about Aura, light and dark, and the magic that can be done. What sort of dark magic can they learn from them?"

Viggo responded, looking up at the sky across from me. "Magic isn't my specialty, you'd be better off asking Bergen what they could do with them."

I propped my elbows up and looked toward him. "Have you ever seen dark magic? When you've fought in battles, have you seen it?"

Viggo looked at me and then back up to the clouds, more of them moving into our vision.

"Yes, and you don't want to go looking for it. Dark magic is wielded by the Necromancers and Warlocks. You don't want to mess with their likes," he paused, "And beyond them, there are much worse creatures out there that can use it to do unspeakable things."

I knew the Necromancer and Warlocks resided along the border to the north, and mainly kept to themselves. The Warlocks were nearly a myth, but I had heard of Necromancers who occasionally passed through the small villages between our main towns. Something about the way he mentioned there being much worse made me wonder if it was shadow magic he was referencing. What I held.

"I wouldn't put it past the Necromancers to be behind these attacks," he said before I could ask if it was my shadow magic.

"Got it, stay away from the Warlocks and Necromancers." I said, and he turned to look straight at me.

"I'm not kidding. If you ever cross paths with one of them, get away. Fast."

I didn't say more at the finality of his tone.

We only took a couple more moments of stillness before Viggo got up and warned me of tomorrow's workout to build upper body strength. I wondered if my core would allow me to lift my arms over my head after today. We bid our goodbyes, and I made my way to the library for a quick change and a bite to eat before remembering that I'd be heading to the clearing near Bergen's home to continue my magic training.

The magic fields were an open grassy spot away from town that allowed for any stray spell that went awry to land into the trees or ground, avoiding any buildings, or people, for that matter. It was the spot we went to when we focused on my Mage abilities, leaving the shadow spell work to be done in the library's basement. I ate an apple from one of the nearby trees in town as I walked, making my way toward Bergen's home.

He had a narrow, tall home. It had multiple floors made of wood and stone, and a flat roof top area where a chair and telescope sat as a fixture of the exterior of the home. Bergen would frequently be up there studying the stars and celestial events in our world. I had only seen the main floor interior of the home, which consisted of a small front room and kitchen with stairs against the wall. Stacks of papers and books littered the space, keeping true to his office and the 'chaotic organization' he liked to say he kept.

The magic field was to the right of his home. The grass was a light green, which soon would go to yellow and eventually dormant for the winter. Pops of small late summer flowers poked up through the tall blades, giving hints of pink and white.

Bergen stood out in the middle of the field, holding his staff in one hand as it rose nearly as high as he did. The impressive raw white crystal set into the carved top glowed in the rays of light that dappled the field. He was dressed in a simple brown linen robe, a stark difference to the more ornate and richly colored ones he wore in the library. When I asked him about why Wizards didn't wear the same robes when out, he told me that wearing plain robes outside of the library was meant to show equality to the people of the town that they served, while the color and intricately designed robes showed reverence to education, and enlightenment when it came to the library.

I was just glad I didn't have a dress code to adhere to at that level. It was well known I didn't prefer dresses and robes. Wearing them only made me feel more out of place. Endora always told me I'd find a reason to enjoy wearing dresses one day, and I wasn't sure if that would ever actually happen.

It's not that I hated how I looked, I loved my green eyes, and the slight point of my chin, the straight line of my nose, and the dusting of freckles over my cheeks, but dresses just didn't seem to fit with my features. At least to me. Tunics, sweaters, and leggings is where I felt myself most.

Bergen and I had a quick greeting before we began with some standard casting abilities. I felt my fingertips warm to the fireball I held in my hand and then released it to dance through the field in a large circle around us. I moved it back towards where it began and extinguished it. A fire then erupted from the ground to the far left of the field. I kept it contained to the small singed area we had dedicated for this, to not further burn the flora. I thought about this spell as the same one my mother cast as we ran that night. I let the flames die out quickly as the memory of the most recent nightmare flashed in my mind.

Moving on, I created shards of ice that formed in an arc over my head. I shot them out, and they slammed into a large trunk of a tree, splintering the bark and sending it flying. A giant wind of blizzard chill circled out from my palm, twisting the grass and leaving frost on its tips. I then encased a boulder in ice that was a few inches thick, twisting my hand, and causing it to crack in two.

I could feel my mental energy wavering as I ran through the spells, but couldn't shake the dream and the chill that slipped through my body. My weakness was in maintaining the spells I could cast. Learning the spell and casting it with ease wasn't hard, but my ability to expand on it and make it stronger was lacking.

Bergen noticed my dip in energy and held up his hand for me to stop my cycle of spells.

"I need just a moment. I'm a little distracted from training earlier today, is all." I tried to apologize, but Bergen smiled and put a hand on my shoulder, as we both stood side by side.

"Viggo is impressed with your effort. I can imagine it's impacting you some," he said, "But we have to increase your endurance. We're going to spend additional time with your spell work during library work hours."

I stood silently as my mind sorted through the past few days. I wondered if I was the right person for them to be putting this effort of training on. What if I wasn't enough?

A flood of emotion and anxiety slowly moved into my subconscious as we started back up with the spell work. I moved again into the fire spells, creating different orbs, blasts, and sparks around us. I could feel the anxiety grow more as I got lost in my mind again. A different magic swirled deep within that I couldn't quite pinpoint where it was coming from.

Uncertainty and despair continued. I was weak. I couldn't do anything to save my parents. I wasn't worth all the work going into me. Why did I think I could be someone to save our people from these evil bandits?

Shadows of darkness swirled around my vision as I lost view of the fields before me. I could hear a thrumming of magic in my ears as a faint scream rose within me.

"WREN!"

Bergen's commanding tone rang out, snapping me out of my haze. Dark swirls of shadow dissipated in small, glittering stars, twinkling and dimming away.

I went to choke something out in surprise that I had let my shadow magic slip, but Bergen cut in. "I think we're done for today."

I wanted to apologize, but I couldn't get the words out. The emotions of fear that someone had seen, along with the embarrassment for lacking control mixed into something unsettling. The icy burn of the shadows tingled so familiar as it lived deep within me. I could feel the hot streaks of tears on my cheeks before I realized they had fallen.

I looked around in a panic, hoping to not see anyone in the distance be a witness to what happened. Bergen grabbed both my shoulders and looked directly at me. His blue eyes were dark.

"You are alright, Wren. I need you to know first of all that no one saw." He moved back to holding his staff, "I'm asking something of you that no one should have to go through, but you wouldn't be here if you weren't supposed to be."

"I don't know if I should be the one to waste this time on." I finally whispered as tears fell. I was only adding another layer to a danger already present.

He pulled at the corner of his beard, lost in thought for a moment before speaking, "I would like you to visit Agatha in Briaroak. I have some things to deliver to her, and I think it would be better if you did. Think of it as a lesson."

I wanted to protest, but after everything I just nodded.

"We'll get the details worked out this next week."

The next day Viggo came bursting into the library.

"We found a trace of their magic. My Watch just sent word. They are on the fringe of the Hidden Forest. I'm preparing a small band of Sentinels now." His words rushed out and I almost couldn't catch it all. "Aye, girl, suit up. You're coming along."

I looked at Bergen in shock, not quite asking for approval, but he nodded, and I ran with Viggo to the training grounds.

Viggo barked orders to the half dozen Sentinels that were now ready to leave. I had my boots and gauntlets on, but couldn't quite get my breastplate fully strapped before we set out to the fringe of the forest. I always avoided venturing too close to those woods. The fear of the monsters and beasts that roamed in there kept me away, but I didn't feel the stress of that thought as I was amid a group of armed soldiers.

Four men and two women were armed to the teeth. Swords glinted on their backs as they marched with smooth speed. I hadn't trained for the pace they kept and jogged here and there to keep up. It quickly reminded me I needed to get back into running, even if my days were full of other methods of training. The forest's edge took just under an hour to get to, and Viggo met with one of his Watch who came out of the clearing.

"The tracks are still fresh. It looks like they were chased here from the north. Warlocks, maybe. They made a loop nearby, circling back. It's when we sensed them and the others have been getting closer to them as we speak. We'll have to hurry to catch up to them." The Watch's voice had a hint of excitement to it.

We entered the forest too quickly for me to fear the shadows that lingered within the trees. It was well known that Viggo had appointed three Watch soldiers whom he trusted to do a lot of the spying and intel for our town. Most of the time they were used to track criminals within the city walls, or maybe hunt down a monster that was being a nuisance and too close to regular foot traffic, but I could see the excitement emanate from them, being able to use their abilities in this way. Like they longed for what they once fought against in the old battles for peace within Caldumn.

The people of Caldumn battled each other for lands until the towns were formed. After a particularly brutal battle, a treaty was formed within the southern lands. Our towns were to each remain as their own separate entities to govern as they wished, but any of the surrounding villages would be neutral territory, being assisted by the nearby main towns as needed. We still sent our taxations and exports to the Red Kingdom via ships at port, but I didn't venture to the harbor of Gaelfall often to see the large ships as they came and left with supplies.

The band of soldiers formed a straight line, and each person took a wide span from each other to prowl through the forest. It was an excellent method to make sure we could still hear each other, but with the advantage of a large range of vision.

We marched deeper into the forest and the sound of birdsong within the birch and oak trees faded away, giving way to our voices, footsteps, and breathing. Soon the brush became thick, and it was harder to see and hear one another. I stopped for a moment, listening intently to catch a familiar voice to make sure I hadn't fallen too far away from them. Viggo's voice called out as he met with another of his spies while we trudged through the brush. He called for us to push forward quickly. We must have been close.

The group started moving faster, and I heard Viggo call out movement up ahead, "In the trees! Weapons ready, move forward team!"

I tried to keep up, my steps crashing in the brush, as anxiety rose through me at the quiet that grew. I stopped, only hearing the faint shouting of orders. I fell too far behind to know what direction to go, and my body froze with fear being lost within the Hidden Forest.

Suddenly, something deep within me tugged. From my magic, it responded, calling me to follow the lure of whatever was trying to lead me. I strayed more to the interior of the forest, feeling the pull. The thought that it could maybe be a tracking potion that one of the Sentinels used to help us stay together came to mind, but it wasn't familiar. I slowly moved as I went deeper into the forest, lowering the sound of my steps. I continued to walk in the direction that was calling me. *Magic?* I thought as I could feel it swirling within me. Something familiar, yet novel? It was leading me somewhere, and it was when I moved around a small outcropping of boulders when I saw what pulled at me.

Not what, but who.

The scene in front of me had me trying to process information quicker than I had time before being noticed. The woods opened into a small, grassy clearing. On the other side of the boulders were more trees and thick bushes. In the center, a deer had been gravely injured, gutted, and laid bleeding out. A man had its head in his lap, stroking its cheek, and whispered something. Jagged final breaths escaped from the deer and it went still.

His expression was soft as he looked up from the deer to meet my gaze. His hazel eyes had flecks of green light that slowly dimmed away as he rose to his feet away from the deer. His silver hair hung down past his shoulders, tied half up. My vision traced to his strong jawline and masculine face as I noticed how handsome he was. He looked powerful, broad shoulders met with large biceps where his white tunic clung tightly. His sleeves were rolled up, showing his impressive forearms. Slight amusement crossed his face as I glanced at his black trousers and boots that flattered his strong legs before looking back up to him to notice his smile. My cheeks probably went a shade of red.

I scowled at him and asked, "Who are you?"

I could feel that mysterious magic swirling in me, making my stomach flip, but I couldn't trust it, or him, just yet.

"Hello. I think you got separated from your group. You shouldn't be out here alone with the beasts you'll find in the forest," he replied.

I couldn't tell if his tone was one of warning or genuine surprise.

"Who are you?" I demanded again, standing my ground across the clearing, keeping a good distance between us.

"My name is Tyran," he said. The small, amused look remained. His eyes sparkled in the dappled sunlight, but not in the same way as the green light I saw before.

"What did you do to that deer?" I asked, my eyes darting to it for a moment then back to him. He looked so casual about our meeting, and I knew I had to keep my guard up if it was a tactic he was using against me.

"I should ask who you are first," he said, curiosity appearing in his expression as if he was feeling something within him, too.

I stayed silent. I knew not to answer. If he was one of the bandits, I had to be prepared to fight, and be able to yell for backup, but this pull towards him made me pause.

He waited for a moment for my response then let out a soft chuckle, and answered my question, "I found her attacked and lying here in pain. I helped her pass on without being alone." His eyes went soft again as he looked back at the body of the animal.

I kept my eyes on him, and the memory of who uses that sort of magic flooded my mind. I tried to keep the shock from being visible, but he saw that small flicker of recognition in my eyes and spoke before I could.

"I am a Necromancer."

The words hit into my stomach and everything I was told about them being dangerous, their use of dark magic, and all that Viggo warned me about them, flooded my memory. They couldn't be trusted. Viggo was so sure they were the ones behind these attacks.

"You are the ones that did this," I accused him through gritted teeth. "You've destroyed towns."

His brows furrowed at the accusation. "I don't think I'm the one you should be worried about. As I said, there are far more dangerous things out here in this forest. I am the least of your concerns."

I put my hand on the hilt of my dagger that hung on my hip and got into a defensive stance. "You're the ones responsible for the Briaroak library burning." Anger slipped through me. "Why are you stealing ancient texts? What are you doing?" My voice grew louder, and in the distance I could hear Viggo calling my name.

I shouted, "Return them. Now!"

Tyran's expression changed to something serious, but tinged with hurt. "You think I did that? No, I'm out here looking for the same criminals you are."

His eyes went cold, and I could feel another swirl of that magic within me. Something continued to beckon me toward him, making me hesitate, wondering if he felt it, too. Viggo called my name again, this time closer, and

I responded to him, letting him know where I was, while continuing to stare Tyran down.

"Well, the meeting was wonderful. I hope to see you again soon." He smiled.

Wren.

I was startled at hearing my name, but his mouth hadn't moved. His voice was as clear as what our previous conversation had been, but in my mind.

He turned his back to me and cast a rune on the ground, glowing in a green and purple dance of color.

"Be careful." He said with a smile before stepping into it and disappearing.

Viggo came crashing into the clearing with the Sentinels behind him.

"Wren! Are you alright?" He had a hint of panic to his voice as he looked around to find any sign of an enemy.

"He, he just disappeared." The rune that once shone brightly, dimmed to nothing.

My body was frozen, processing the last moments of our interaction. The dead deer lay beside the now-empty space, and a soldier walked over to inspect it.

"Who was it?" Viggo asked, coming to my side.

"A Necromancer." I finally spoke. My vision was blurring from my stare.

The Sentinel came back and confirmed that the gutted deer had the same magic enchantment of the bandits we were tracking. Viggo spat at the ground in disgust.

"He said he wasn't responsible for the burnings and thefts," I said, finally shaking out of my trance-like state. "He said he was hunting them like we were."

Viggo scoffed at my words. "Liars." It was all he could manage. I could see the anger writhe in him. It wasn't just towards a Necromancer either, I saw what looked like lingering frustration toward me.

As the sun set, we headed out of the forest. I chose not to say much and instead listened to the conversations of our group, finding out that they hadn't been able to catch the bandits, either. They would see glimpses of trees moving, or brush trembling as the forms of cloaked figures would rush through, but no one could get confirmation of what they were chasing.

I wondered if it could have been one of the many beasts or monsters that lived here playing games with us. The pull of the magic I felt earlier with Tyran was nothing more than a faint tugging now, and I tried to pass it off as one of the many tricks of Necromancers. There was a part of me that knew this was something that went deeper than some blind trickery, though. That magic I felt was a part of me, and my shadows. But why had it pulled me to him?

It was dark by the time we made it back to town, moving slower than we did heading out. I was exhausted from everything. From the unanswered questions, from the threats, and from the mixed feelings of who Tyran was. It was a frustrating curiosity more than anything, and I told myself that it was probably the only time I'd ever cross paths with him. Yet, that pull of magic told me differently.

CHAPTER 6

THE YELLING WAS faint at first as it drew me to a drowsy state of alertness. I fell asleep quickly and didn't have energy to keep my mind going after my eyes were closed. I rolled over, and the commotion grew louder. My eyes opened slowly, expecting the morning light to be filtering through my windows, but it was still night. Blinking a few times, I focused my hearing on the noise.

Shouting.

"Fire!"

Adrenaline soared through my body as I shot out of bed, throwing my comforter to the other end of the room, and ran to my window. I could see a faint glow of orange over the rooftops toward the center of town.

No. Not yet.

It's all I could think as I ripped open the drawers of my dresser and pulled on the first pair of pants, leaving my nightgown top on. I shoved my feet into slippers and raced downstairs, out the front door, slamming it behind me, and took off running towards the library. If Viggo hadn't woken yet to meet with his Sentinels, he certainly would now.

My breath was quick as I sprinted down the road. The homes I rushed by were mostly dark save for seeing a window or two illuminated from those waking to the noise I could begin hearing much clearer now.

"Fire! Fire! Get the pumps! The buckets!" The voice of a man yelled out.

Quickly turning a corner, the library came into view.

I nearly stopped breathing as I saw the horrid sight before me.

The glistening white of the quartz was bathed in orange. Dark, thick smoke billowed from the rooftop, blacking out any light from the moon that would have been hanging above it. Flames licked at the windows and the smell of burning books, wood, and building material hit my nostrils. Silhouettes of those helping left long shadows on the road ahead as I continued to make my way through the beginnings of the crowds coming out of the taverns and homes.

Oona.

Her round face flashed in my mind. Her straight black hair tucked behind her ears, and her glasses perched on the bridge of her nose. I thought of her smile that always seemed to greet me. She was our library's Nightwatch and lived in the upper quarters of the building. I looked up to the higher floor's windows, seeing the orange flame glow, threatening to break through the windows. I had to help her.

I ran to the foot of the entrance steps. Heat blasted me, and the giant wood doors were wide open while flames licked along them. Black forms were slumped at the doors, and I tried to make out what they were as the smoke plumed out and obscured them. A small break in the billowing shadows revealed the full extent of the horrors to me..

I turned to the side and started to retch. The nausea was instant as I realized what those forms were. Burned bodies of the Sentinels hung on the doors. Four figures, blackened and charred, and I could only hope they had met quick deaths before the fire took them. I turned back and looked once more, hoping I wouldn't see a fifth–her small frame would be barely visible.

I tried to send a chill of air out in front of me, to douse the flames with ice, but only white steam erupted amongst the unquenchable flames. The fire was too great, and even the best of Mages wouldn't have the ability to extinguish it by magic alone. My breath hitched, and I could feel the anxiety rise in me. Tears formed from the feeling of helplessness. I was about to fall to my knees when a small arm wrapped around me and pulled me toward them.

It was Oona. I let that wave of relief flow, sobbing out her name as I grabbed her and hugged her tightly. I pulled back to look at her, wanting to check to make sure she wasn't hurt. Soot covered her face and down her bare arms. She was in pajamas as well and coughed for a moment before speaking.

"I tried to save what I could. My shields were holding when I barely made it out. I couldn't save them all," she said with a croak to her voice.

Her dark almond eyes showed the sadness of failure.

"Oh, Oona. You're safe. That's all that matters. I'm so sorry I wasn't there," I said and held her close again.

"The bandits," she continued, as I pulled back to look at her again. "They moved so fast. I heard the screams of the Sentinels and saw them nailed to the door before I came downstairs." She coughed again, trying to clear the smoke from her lungs. "I heard them down the left hall. I only had a moment to focus my shield before having to hide again. They were in Bergen's office and I could hear crashing and breaking wood. They called out when they found the books and made their way out while lighting everything on fire. Wren, the little I could see of them, they were human, but also... monsters." Her eyes widened as she remembered the moment.

"I'm so glad you hid. I'm so sorry you had to see that, Oona," is all I could reply before we felt the cool mist of water from the carriages that held large barrels of water. The pressure from the pumps sent the water spraying from the connected hoses, while many of the Sentinels worked with the townspeople to spray the hottest flames.

We stood for a moment and watched the water dance on the flames while the smoke increased, changing from dark black to gray and white clouds. The white of the quartz returned as the glow of orange became dampened to the flow of water. Oona shivered in my arms, and I noticed her look away from the burned doors.

The bodies were near skeletal as they came into clear view. I guided her away from the front of the building and made our way to the side. While passing by a group of Sentinel soldiers, I overheard one mentioning that the Sentinels who were on patrol around the perimeter had also been killed. My blood ran cold. Their throats were cut, and the bodies were dragged to the base of the building in hopes of them burning along with everything else inside.

"We need to get you water," I said to Oona and walked across the road to an open window of a tavern serving those who were agog with the scene. She didn't speak, but came with me to the open window while I requested tea and water. I sat her down on the ground against the wall and she sipped the water, then gulped it down in relief.

"I'll get you another one," I said as I stood to ask for a larger container of water. I noticed Viggo appearing from around the back of the Library. A wave of relief ran through me, knowing he was already here and alive. I grabbed the large stein that held water and quickly thanked the bartender.

"I need to speak to my Dad, we'll be just there to the side of the Library, stay here until I get back?" I said as I handed her the water. She nodded and tipped back the large container, nearly the size of her head. I turned to catch sight of Viggo still near the building and made my way to him.

He was already dressed in battle leathers that matched the Sentinels. His forearms were clad in leather bracers that covered his knuckles, adorned with iron spikes around them. He had a bandolier strapped across his chest that held daggers and a sword sheathed on his back. I marveled at the stark shift of power that radiated from the changes to his appearance. He slowly stroked his beard as he tipped his head toward one Sentinel flanking him, receiving information before he looked up and saw me approaching, "Don't worry about notifying the Red Kingdom, we'll get this under control."

The Sentinel nodded once, and left to check in with their fellow soldiers.

"I'd hope you wouldn't have heard the noise," he greeted, looking at me briefly, then the scene of chaos behind us. I folded my arms across my chest finally realizing that my nightgown was a stark difference to most soldiers around me. My senses began taking over after all the adrenaline from the night.

"I found Oona. She's safe. I saw the guards at the door. I…" I couldn't finish as nausea roiled in my stomach again.

"Aye," he said in his familiar lilt, with sorrow to it. "They gave their lives trying to protect our town. I can't think of a higher honor. May the Valiant Prevail." He spoke in reverence, "Oona shielded a good amount of our history. She's a hero for that."

I nodded, and my voice was raspy from the bile that had crept up. "She caught a glimpse of the bandits, or monsters. She said they were human, but not quite."

He listened to me, bowing his head to watch the small streams of water from the pump carriages slither their way across the cobbled road we stood on. I could see him processing what I said before finally looking up.

"We'll need to have a chat with her. I know she's probably in shock, but the sooner we can get this information while it's fresh, the better opportunity we have to identify what she saw."

I agreed and pointed in the direction where I had left Oona. She still sat against the wall of the tavern, now sipping on the tea I left beside her.

Viggo was gentle and kind to Oona when he spoke to her. We moved into a quiet booth inside the tavern. No music played and most of the patrons were outside still watching the ongoing crisis management.

"Now Wren mentioned that you may have caught a glimpse of these bandits?" Viggo spoke softly.

"They were unnatural looking. I haven't seen them before, but they mentioned who they were stealing the texts for. Someone named Rhonin," she coughed once, still clearing her lungs, "Do we know anyone by that name?"

Viggo's expression had already hardened at the mention of his name, "I just might." Followed with cursing the Necromancers under his breath.

My heart raced, thinking back to my meeting with Tyran. How I really was in danger. But if he was partly responsible for the attacks, why did he let me go?

Oona nodded, and I refocused on her, seeing the sadness in her expression.

It was a feeling I knew all too well. That feeling of not doing enough, of not being enough. Viggo had motioned to one of his officers, asking to bring a blanket for Oona. She allowed for a smile of thanks when it was brought to her and wrapped it around her small frame.

Bergen hadn't even crossed my mind once through all the events of the night, and I realized he probably wasn't yet aware of what had happened. He left last evening from our training to Briaroak, to work with Agatha on repairing some of the texts they lost. Viggo saw the sudden change of my expression when I remembered and waited for me to speak.

"Bergen. He's not here. He went to meet with Agatha," I said.

"Aye. I already sent a messenger cat with word of what happened earlier tonight. I expect he'll be returning in the morning."

I pursed my lips and tried to fight the images of him seeing our beautiful building in the state it was now in, swirling my emotions. I was supposed to get those books out. I was the one he trusted to protect those texts, and I wasn't there to do my job. I felt the pain of inadequacy sink deeper. I should have stayed with Oona, knowing that Bergen would be out of town. All the regrets that I couldn't change pierced me.

The conversation slowed as Viggo was called off to continue investigating the attacks. I invited Oona home with me to get a few hours' rest before we'd have to meet with Bergen and go over the events of the night again. Oona didn't protest as we made our way back to the cottage, and kept the blanket wrapped tightly around her. Endora had come to the cottage and had the lights on, waiting for us at the kitchen table.

The relief on her face when she saw I brought Oona helped relax some of the anxiety I had. She already had a fire going, tea, and gathered calming herbs of eucalyptus and lavender for Oona to use in a warm bath to wash away the soot and charred wood smell.

We headed up to my room after Endora felt like Oona was cared for enough and headed back to the orphanage to check in with the children. I held my friend as she slipped into an exhausted sleep. I wasn't able to rest so easily, Tyran and the Necromancers were still on my mind. I watched as the dark night disappeared into the growing morning light.

CHAPTER 7

*T*ENDRILS OF SMOKE *weaved around me as I channeled that unknown magic, much like I did with Aura during training. I willed it to move and creep around my arms and legs, feeling the cool mist against my skin.*

"Where are you?" I whispered into my shadows and sent it out from my body, watching it slowly move into darkness.

Visions of Tyran in the clearing came to me. His face held that smile of amusement at his first sight of me. The image faded away, leaving nothingness around me, when something came my way. The tendrils of mist that appeared were not of my own. They slowly moved towards my feet and curiously licked at my own shadows. The sensation caused tingles down my spine as it wrapped around me, exploring. The shadows I sent out met with a form of another. Someone like me; I recognized, as the sensation grew. A meeting of one and the same.

The sunlight that filtered into my room was brighter than I normally woke to. I slept longer than I had in a long while. Oona must have already got up and left for the day. My comforter was twisted around me tightly, showing evidence of my fitful dreaming. I untangled myself and stood to stretch tall before changing and heading downstairs. I hoped Viggo wouldn't be too upset at me being late after yesterday.

A soft scratch at the door had me opening it to a messenger cat, brushing himself against the door frame. His familiar blue-gray tuxedo fur and full body told me already who it was from, and I bent down to pick up the letter that was harnessed to his back.

"Good morning, Newt." I smiled down at him.

He purred expectantly in the open doorway at the clay pot we kept near the entrance. I sprinkled a few cat treats out for him as payment for the delivery. His very audible purrs erupted between the crunches of the treats before he prowled off.

I grabbed some granola and fruit as I sat to read the contents of the message, knowing it would be from Viggo. Newt was the Sentinels cat, a stray that made its home there, then trained to deliver local messages from their location. The letter Viggo sent told me to take the morning off, and we'd pick up tomorrow. He added I'd need to check in with Bergen and go over the events of yesterday with him.

I sighed as I put the letter down and took a bite into a nectarine. I wasn't sure what to make of everything yesterday. My dream was something completely different from anything I had experienced before. There was so much that felt familiar with the magic and shadows, and I couldn't help but wonder if I'd ever be able to shake meeting that Necromancer.

What I did know was I wouldn't miss a day of training, even if told not to come. Viggo probably thought I would have jumped for joy straight back into bed, and normally I would have. But after last night, I knew I had to be prepared more than ever against Rhonin and what attacked us.

There was a weird mix of apprehension and anticipation about what the library would look like as I made my way towards the center of the town. My bare arms were warmed by the sunlight that kept the morning chill tucked into the shade that receded from its full size. My ponytail swung and tickled the back of my shoulders. Even without sleeping last night, and the visible purple around my eyes, I could feel a renewed level of energy running through me. I wasn't sure if it was going to be short-lived once I started training, but I wasn't about to let it go to waste.

The morning air smelled like the fall blossoms of marigolds, then twisted with a salty damp coastal campfire aroma. The last of the smoldering bits of the previous night still lingered. The street was still wet from the use of water to extinguish the flames.

When the library came into view, my heart tinged with sadness. The white quartz was mottled in soot and black marks. The exterior of the stone still stood, but the right tower's roof was badly damaged and partly collapsed. I noticed the center roof had also collapsed in on itself.

Windows were broken out, and the silver trim around them was melted from the extreme heat.

I didn't see any sign of Bergen within the building, and decided it would be best to continue on my way to check if Viggo was in the middle of training others. I didn't think I could stomach going through the damage alone as it was, and to do it twice when I later met up with Bergen wouldn't serve a purpose.

After training, I found Bergen standing at the entrance of the library's side door that went straight into the hallway to his office. The fire hadn't burned much at this end, but I knew the smoke and water used to extinguish the flames could cause just as much damage.

"You trained this morning?" Bergen asked, almost surprised.

"I'm regretting it already." I said, as he held open the door.

The tap of our steps were met with muddled splashes, as the water still collected in areas of the floor. The air was cold inside, and I felt my arm hair prickle in response. The smell of damp burning was thick, and it took a moment to not feel like I was choking on invisible smoke. We made our way into his office, and the scene was shocking.

His office had remained untouched by flames. My desk was still in the corner, completely untouched. The mahogany panels had only a slight hue of soot, but that was all that remained of familiarity. Bergen's desk had to weigh a considerable amount for the size and solid hardwood, but it was turned at a 45-degree angle, bunching the rug it sat on. The window behind his desk had been broken out and glass littered the ground. The built-in bookcases were torn clean off from the walls. Only the holes remained on the quartz walls where they had been bolted in. I finally looked at the alcove, now bare and completely open to the room. The pain twisted, starting in my stomach, then my lungs, and finally in my heart as I saw that empty nook. Bergen stepped over the mess of books and wood strewn about, moving closer to examine where the ancient texts once hid.

I didn't dare move. Heat flashed in my face and for a moment as the magic stirred within me. I could sense my vision clouding in mist before I hurried and placed a mental block on the shut door that held those shadows, focusing on the broken window while steadying my breathing. Bergen turned to me and noticed that infinitesimal moment where I pushed back what almost showed.

"They were attuned to find these books. Even with the shielding and wards we placed on them, there's nothing you could have done to stop them. They broke them with a power I haven't seen in some time. I can feel it lingering." He looked at his desk, sitting askew, and sighed. "It's better you weren't here, and I will need to thank Oona again for her bravery. She could have perished with the Sentinels." He glanced around the room, and could only say, "It would have been even more devastating."

I stepped over the mess and looked at the alcove for any sign of the magic he mentioned, but couldn't see or feel anything. I knew it would be something I would probably need to train for in future magic practice.

We left his office and made our way to the great hall. Oona did indeed save a great portion of the library, the first third of the library near the entrance burned and the roof collapsed and broken, but beyond that and where we walked, the books stood untouched. Bergen and I went in different directions, taking in all that was saved. I noticed a row of books that normally were placed closer to the entrance were moved to the safe zone, and found a few more rows similarly done. It dawned on me the day I left the library after we heard of the attacks that Oona was walking through the aisles taking inventory of what to move within her shield's reach. She saved so much for our town and people. I admired her even more.

We walked together and assessed what we could fix. Bergen kept a hand pulling at his beard near the corner of his mouth as a smile slowly formed. "All is not lost. We will be able to repair what is damaged. It'll take time, but Oona, not only saved our history, but the library as well."

I smiled, looking around at the wreckage, imagining it being restored once again.

"Now, while I would have liked to use the basement for training your shadow magic today, I have a feeling it too will need to be drained and taken care of." Bergen had gone straight back into his work mode way of speaking, "I mentioned how we would be sending you to Briaroak, and it's the best time to do so. With the bandits having hit both our towns, there will be minimal risk of you running into them, and I now have pressing matters of texts I need to get to Agatha."

I nodded, and we walked together down the hallway to his office. "Who am I going with?"

"Just you." Bergen said.

I stopped. "What? Why not a Sentinel escort or, Oona, or someone to go with me?"

"I'm offering this as a time for you to work on your mental clarity. I want you to look at your self-confidence, what you can do, and how you do it as a strength to your ability to wield Aura. You are strong and capable of many things, and sometimes I think that you don't always get to rely on yourself to believe those things when there are others around. Now you get to put it to use," he said, entering his office and grabbing a few old books he had in his desk drawer. They had luckily escaped any damage.

There was a part of me that felt uneasy knowing the bandits were still on the loose. Knowing I technically could run into them going somewhere outside our town, but I felt a renewed sense of purpose within my body stir, and the magic that it contained moved with it.

I have become powerful without magic, and with. My belief in myself is what mattered. Now I needed to keep those thoughts at the top, to drown out the negativity that I so easily sank to.

"You'll be leaving tomorrow. I've already cleared it with Viggo. Check in with me in the morning and I'll have the items ready to send with you."

I didn't know what to expect as I packed my satchel for the couple night's stay in the village between here and Briaroak Village. It felt like so long ago when Bergen asked after training in the magic fields if I would deliver some scrolls and books to Agatha at their temporary library. I tried to make the best of it and thought it could be an opportunity to pick up supplies and herbs for Endora. I packed the last of the clothing and books, and slung my bag over my shoulder as I headed out to the library before venturing to Briaroak.

The crisp air continued its drag into autumn, and I took in the musty smells of damp, decaying plants as I walked the quiet roads. My evening was spent thinking of who Rhonin was and what Necromancers wanted with our texts. There was also something that wore on me about my interaction with Tyran in the Hidden Forest. I knew Bergen would have at least some knowledge about them, and thought to ask before leaving.

"I was wondering if you could tell me about… Necromancy?"

Bergen only showed a hint of surprise at my direct question, foregoing a greeting as I entered.

"I met a Necromancer in the forest the other day, when we were chasing the bandits. Viggo told me how dangerous they could be, and yet, something was telling me differently. Tyr—," I paused, "This Necromancer was helping a deer that had been attacked. There wasn't a hint of malice or dark magic that I could detect from him."

I almost had said Tyran's name, but chose not to. I don't know why I was hiding his name from them, but I hadn't told Viggo it either when he came to me in the forest. Why I was protecting him, I wasn't sure, but it felt right to do so in the moment. "He told me he was hunting the same bandits we were."

Bergen listened as he sat in his office, now cleared of the mess. The walls were still bare without the bookcases. He propped his elbows on the arms of his chair, fingers lightly interlocked, and spoke. "It sounds like you ran into a typical Necromancer. Moreso, a kind one who went out of his way to help a dying deer. I wasn't aware if they all knew about the bandits, but it's reassuring to know there are more on the lookout for them."

It wasn't exactly the answer I was looking for, the complete neutrality of it, so I pressed on. "Why does Viggo seem to have such a disdain for them, and why is the narrative of them so bad in the stories we hear growing up?"

Bergen let out a soft chuckle and adjusted in his seat. "Children's tales are just that. Made of wild imagination and creation. I'm sure Necromancer children have their own tales of Witches and Mages being just as scary." I gave a sarcastic half smile, and he went on, "Sometimes people fear what they don't understand. Whether that's by choice or not." He pulled his glasses from the large sleeve of his robes, "As for Viggo, you'd have to talk to him about it. There was a period during the territory battles that he experienced enough to validate his feelings towards them."

It was easy to forget that Viggo was older than he looked, and that he fought in those battles for territory within the lands of Caldumn.

I didn't press further on Viggo's feelings towards the Necromancers, but asked one more question. "Can they lure you in? Make you feel drawn to them?"

Bergen tipped his head to the side slightly in a quizzical expression. "Not that I know of. Is that something you experienced?"

I wasn't sure. I searched along the patterned lines of the rugs on the floor for a moment before speaking. "It felt like it was coming from within me, but yet it pulled me in his direction. Familiar, but new."

Bergen kept his head tipped, and I saw he made note of my experience from his thoughtful gaze. "To finish answering your first question, Necromancy has a stigma of evil due to the fact that they walk closely to the edge of light and dark magic. The balance of life and death. They have the ability and choice to wield dark magic, but it comes at a cost. It's a knowing decision to go into dark magic, and it'll tear your mind into something else. A decision most Necromancers wouldn't dream of making."

CHAPTER 8

BERGEN PULLED OUT the final manuscript and gave me the items. Two books and a scroll container that was absolutely packed, and definitely the heaviest of the materials to take with me. I was relieved to see it had a substantial leather loop and I could strap it to my back. I tucked the other books into my full satchel and slung the case around my body. I assumed I looked like I was some merchant off for an adventure.

"Take the road that leads to the north, then the one that goes off to the west, and stay at the Quarter Moon Village. I know it's a short distance out of the way, but it'll be quieter, and less of a chance to be run in by the bandits." He instructed me as I nodded, taking mental notes. "Oh, and when you get to Briaroak, let them know I sent you on a request from Agatha. The Battalion shouldn't be too confrontational. They are really lovely."

Viggo seemed to be still upset over the events of the library attack, but I couldn't help but feel a lingering resentment at what happened in the Hidden Forest. Training was canceled due to my upcoming travels, and while I had every intention of heading out toward the villages right away, I found myself marching down the dirt trail of the Sentinel training grounds.

I continued to play back the events of the Hidden Forest. I had worked so hard to not feel like I was weak. I assessed the situation, and I needed to know more. Whether he would hear me out or believe me, I'd just have to wait and see.

The Sentinels standing at the opening of the central building didn't stop me as I walked through the entrance, and I followed the sound of Viggo's voice where he stood at a table in the middle of a war room. His Watch gathered around him, assessing the map of Caldumn. Marks within the Hidden Forest showed where we had been, and before I could turn around to avoid interruption, Viggo looked up and stopped speaking.

"Wren. No training today. Safe travels." He dismissed me, and I felt the heat of that anger simmer more under my skin.

"I need to talk to you," I said sternly, not knowing how fully out of line I was being when it came to military standards. Viggo stared me down in silence, and I could see his subtle changing expression in his eye, going from the immediate rage of what would have unleashed at any one of his other soldiers, to a reined in smolder.

"Outside. I'll be there soon."

I turned and walked out, cursing my boldness. The anxiety over what I was going to ask rose inside me. I was interrupting his meetings to ask him about something that could have and should wait. Did I even have the right to ask him this? What was I doing? My hands were sweaty, and I started pacing back and forth, remembering my breathing techniques.

The Sentinels involved in the meeting streamed out of the building, and I watched Viggo follow the last of them out. He beckoned for me to follow as we walked around the training grounds.

"I'm sorry," I started. "I shouldn't have interrupted. I should have waited to speak to you until you were finished."

He pushed his lips together tightly, his beard and mustache met and it looked like he didn't have a mouth for a moment.

"I'm glad you came. We needed to talk about a few things. I shouldn't have asked you to come out so soon when we were tracking the bandits. You're good, Wren, but I haven't been able to fully train you as the soldiers we had out there, and that was a weakness." I furrowed my brow in question and he went on. "You weren't there with the group when we were close to the bandits, and I had to make a decision. Find you and let them go, or continue and hope you weren't being attacked by something else in the forest."

I knew the decision he made, and my body went hot. Embarrassment. What an embarrassment. We were walking faster now.

"You're lucky that Necromancer was so passive. He's lucky we weren't there either, or we would have torn him apart." I felt the frustrating curiosity replace the embarrassment, and I stopped dead in my tracks and turned to him.

"Why when you didn't see him? He said he was chasing what we were too, and he took time to help a suffering animal—" I stopped as I saw pure anger form on Viggo's face. "What did they do to you?" The anger in his face paused as he recognized the depth of my question.

"They are monsters," he sneered and turned away to keep walking.

I almost tripped as I started to jog up to his pace again.

"Please, I need to know," I said, as we kept a quick stride for a minute. The rails of the fences continued on past us.

I needed to know. I needed to know why I felt what I did in the clearing. Why I was drawn to Tyran. If it was something to be curious about or wary of. Viggo finally let out a deep breath and slowed his pace.

"It was the last battle we had for territory, nearly 100 years ago now. The Necromancers wanted to expand their land into the Central Plains, and it would have been interfering with our travel paths and trade routes, so we went to battle for it. My partner..." he choked up for a moment then went on, "My partner, Mikhail, and I had fought side by side through many battles. There wasn't anyone I cared for more than him. With his grace, and power, we felt unstoppable defending our lands." I could see the pain in his expression. "The Necromancer General was unhinged. He wasn't following standard rules of engaging in battle. Reanimation, mind controlling monsters, you name it, he was raising it and sending them our way. My partner and I, along with our fellow soldiers made work of them, severing heads from bodies and burning the corpses so they would stop coming back to life. One night we were ambushed. Beasts descended on our camp and started tearing our army apart. Mikhail and I rushed from our tent and started fighting off the monsters. They were viscous, unrelenting, and as I battled I lost sight of him, of Mikhail."

Viggo was getting more emotional as he went on. I was, too. He never had spoken about the battles he endured much, and while I had only heard once about him having lost a love, this was something beyond what I could have imagined.

"I heard him call my name as they were pulling him away. I saw their General and the wicked smile that grew around his face as I rushed after them. I was tackled by two soldiers that came with the General, and they held me down as I watched him torture *my love*. They sliced him into pieces and then let the monsters feed on him. I will never forget the fear in Mikhail's eyes as he looked at me one last time."

Tears were streaming down his face, and I lost my control, allowing the stinging tears of my own to fall. Mikhail wasn't just a partner in battle, he was his partner in life. His *love*.

"I snapped. I lost it, and I broke free of the soldiers. I killed them by ripping out their throats with my bare hands. All I could hear was my screaming as I ran towards the beasts, consuming the last pieces of Mikhail. I picked up his blade left nearby, and I sliced their stomachs open. I ran after the General, but he had cast a rune and was gone."

I thought of that rune I saw Tyran use, and the relation of it in Viggo's memory shook my core. I had to push the thought of Tyran aside.

"I was covered in blood and still screaming as I turned and saw the beasts fleeing. The next morning, we assembled our forces and pushed the Necromancers back. They ended up retreating. We went after them with war crimes, and the Necromancers said they would have a trial for the crimes committed. We never heard of the outcome, and it wasn't long before all the towns came together to form the treaty and the neutrality of the outlying lands."

It was hard to swallow, and I wiped at the tears that had fallen down my cheeks. I took a deep breath to settle that feeling, and then hugged Viggo, to try to quell the sorrow I resurfaced for him. There hadn't been a solution to his suffering. He never learned of the outcome of the mad General, and I couldn't help but feel his pain.

"I'm so sorry, Dad." I said.

The wind danced along the fields that stretched outside of town. A sweet, dusty smell of dried grasses and wildflowers moved around me as I walked along the cleared trail from Gaelfall to the small villages that were scattered across the neutral lands. The storm clouds had slowed to a crawl and while the incoming rain would be a welcome, I really wanted to try to get to my next stop before getting caught in a downpour. I could feel the chill in the air that normally would have made me want to add an extra layer of clothing if it weren't for the load I was carrying. I could feel the cool sweat under the heavy scroll case against my back, and the leather belt that sheathed the daggers Viggo had me take in case of any problems that should arise on my travels.

There was something particularly freeing about walking alone outside of familiarity today. It wasn't the first time I'd traveled out of our town, but I was always accompanied by Endora, and this road was one we didn't take. We usually went on the eastern roads to the Full Moon Village. It was an easy way to obtain herbs and supplies from Briaroak Village without having to make the full journey.

When I told Endora about my upcoming visit, she almost jumped in excitement to join me, but the orphanage had recently taken in a new child that she was helping feel comfortable with their new surroundings. I knew she would love to see her hometown again, and meet with family and familiar places she loved when growing up. I hoped one day we could come back and she could take me to all of her favorite spots and share the fond memories they held with her.

The song of the wind moved around me as I walked. It shifted every so often as cool and warm air mixed. I thought about practicing my spells and lit a fireball, allowing it to hover in my palm. I held it out and shifted the form and size. Round, oval, long, smaller, larger. The flames danced around until I extinguished it as quickly as I had set it alight.

I shifted the air around me into small bursts, having an imaginary fight with the winds that came towards me.

I'd try to meet them across the field and watch the rippling it caused through the grass that became caught in the soft tussle of winds.

I lightly grazed my fingers over the tall fronds of wildflowers with the last dying blooms and watched the frost grow on them at my touch. I could feel the Aura playing happily inside me. No stress of training, just pure entertainment for myself.

A small swirling of that magic appeared. The shadows licked at the mental wall. Alluring. I looked around me at the empty path I walked along. I was away from people, away from causing harm. The Aura work I'd done was already so pleasing, and in the moment of confidence with my spells, I allowed my shadows out.

For a split second, I thought it would burst out at me, that I would be fully consumed and wished I hadn't, but it didn't. The magic slowly swirled and circled around as it moved into every part of me where I channeled the Aura.

I opened my hand and held my palm out watching as I formed swirls of shadow and darkness. I let it weave between my fingers. The smoke soon obscured my hand into translucent wisps, making it nearly invisible. I pushed the shadows down toward my feet, and allowed it to curl around my legs, consuming them. As I walked, mist only moved, completely hiding my legs. I was actually controlling the strength of my shadow abilities. There was a wave of excitement to them.

Even with this newfound control, I could see there was so much more to it. I felt how it moved within my mind, and I could sense the capacity it had to work with my thoughts. I wondered about it being used in a manner against others and felt its response of not only being something to cloak in for protection, but also that it could cause pain towards others depending on how I wanted to wield it. I quickly closed the idea of that happening. I wouldn't use it like that, especially now.

I could sense my magic went even deeper, though. A shadow power that could be unleashed, greater than I ever had conjured. It was frightening, but I didn't necessarily feel scared of it. I tried to make sense of the feeling, and decided to save anything more for a secure and watchful setting with Bergen. I beckoned the shadow back within me with the same easiness as my other magic, and sighed in relief. A twinge of exhaustion came from what I had just done, the magic I've used, and I knew it was enough spell work for now until I could build the stamina to use it for longer periods.

I arrived at the Quarter Moon Village just as the first sprinkling of rain came down. It wasn't far into town for me to hurry to the inn's entrance as the sporadic drops shifted to a drizzle. The village was one of the few, named after the phases of the moon, that separated the surrounding towns from Briaroak. The buildings in Quarter Moon Village were all made of pale gray stone, crescent shapes were adorned in framework around windows and doors. Small white picket fences had the same moon shape cut into them. The inn was decorated in the same fashion and had a cheerful, welcoming feel.

A kind old woman greeted me inside the inn, assisting with my lodging, and gave me a list of rooms available. Her white hair was tied up in a high bun and the wrinkles of her face were those of countless smiles and continued positivity. I could see just how much she loved caring for others, and I felt like it was confirmation why Bergen had me come to this village.

The room was small but it still felt like a home. A small bed was tucked against the wall across from where I sat, and a desk was placed on the wall nearest my chair in the corner. The window looked out to the other small buildings of shops and homes. The steady tapping of rain on the ceiling was soothing, and I welcomed it.

My stomach growled aggressively after a few minutes of relaxing, and I decided to change into an oversized sweater and some clean leggings before heading down to the inn's tavern to see what supper would be for the night. I pulled my hair down from the tie I had it in and moved the long waves over to one side of my shoulder. I liked seeing the streaks of sun-kissed auburn throughout the darker strands.

As I made my way downstairs to the dining area, my stomach nearly tumbled. I couldn't decide if I was just that hungry or if it was something more, almost as if I was being led into the tavern of the inn. The wonderful smell of a roast and vegetables filled my senses as I walked through the open entryway. I took in another deep breath of the aroma, and before I could finish exhaling, I froze.

Tucked into one of the corner tables on the other end of the room, I saw the familiar silver hair tied half up, accentuating the attractive angles of his face. I took in those broad shoulders and arms for a second when Tyran turned, looking around the room as if he were trying to find someone.

CHAPTER 9

I HID.

I don't fully know why, but I didn't know what he'd do if he recognized me. I tucked myself to the other side of a cabinet in the room that had various decanters of alcohol on display. I tried to remain out of his view as much as I could and peered around the wood frame of the cabinet when I thought it was safe. Luckily, one of the tavern maids was speaking to him, and he didn't notice.

"Can I help you?"

The voice nearly had me jumping out of my skin. A bartender was nearby, and I hadn't thought how awkward I probably looked. He stared at me for a moment to make sure I wasn't a threat.

"Oh, I'm sorry. I—" I couldn't think of what to reply.

He looked out at the dining room and smirked while going back to polishing the bar top, "Someone catch your eye? Take a minute. You're alright."

I felt my cheeks go hot at the absurdity of my stunt. Gentle tugging appeared once again from within, as if it were pleading with me to bring it near a part it had long missed. I closed my eyes and took in a deep breath to steady my thoughts.

I didn't need to hide. I had no reason to. We were in a public neutral area. On top of that, I had too many unanswered questions to just ignore him. *I need to talk to him. He's a Necromancer, and—*

I couldn't finish my thought as I remembered Viggo's warning and his own experiences.

He could be dangerous.

No. I pushed the doubt away. I needed answers. For many things.

Be confident. I told myself, as I willed a level of confidence within that I hadn't felt before. I stepped from my hiding spot and walked more into the room. Tyran was wearing a similar white shirt and dark trousers to what I first saw him in. A black jacket hung on the back of the chair next to him. He had just received his food from what it looked like, as I made my way over to his table and sat down.

Panic. My mind went entirely blank, and I sat there wide eyed staring at him.

My shadows were swirling in excitement and anticipation of something. The spoon of soup was halfway to his mouth as Tyran paused and looked across the table to meet my wide stare. For a moment I thought I could see shadow swirling in those hazel eyes, but when he blinked it was gone.

"Yes?" He spoke before he put his spoon to his mouth and kept eating.

"I, uh, What are you doing here?" I sputtered.

"Eating," he said with a twist of sarcasm.

I scowled at him. The panic I felt lessened and was replaced with annoyance.

"I mean, what are you doing *here*?" I asked more sternly. I seemed to have to ask the same question twice before he'd end up telling me the answer.

He continued chewing and gave me a lazy smile. I would have melted at it under other circumstances. His hazel eyes were easy to look at. Blues, greens, and brown flecked throughout brought such faceted beauty to them, and then I noticed the hints of red to them as well. Small and only if the light caught right, but they were there. *Such a dangerous, attractive face,* I thought as I waited.

Beyond his handsome features and the strong form I was attracted to, he could be dangerous. He could be a killer. He could be hiding so much, and if I let my guard down around him, I could end up a victim. I had heard how they could manipulate and mind control you, even speak to you when dead. I would need to be smart in how I approach him.

"I think you owe me a few answers first," he said after tearing a piece of bread from a loaf that sat on the table, and I begrudgingly accepted.

"What are *you* doing here?"

Fair enough, I wondered if I should lie or not, "I'm on my way to deliver some items to the Briaroak Village."

Not a lie, but also keeping specifics private.

He nodded, still staring at me, as I waited for him to have more to say, but he only took another bite of his bread before my stomach growled in torment loud enough for him to hear.

"Have some," he offered half the loaf to me.

"Thank you." I said, grabbing it without hesitation and tearing a piece of my own.

"What magic do you practice, Wren?"

I found it to be odd, but not out of line to ask. I also really liked how he said my name.

Mages were well known by their spells alone, but he hadn't seen me cast anything, which is what made the question odd. For all he knew, I could be like Viggo, where magic may not be defined as an ability to cast, but I could fight and train like a warrior. I wondered if Necromancers could sense magic within people.

"I am a Mage," I finally said after eating more of the bread. My stomach was settling, but the shadows swirled with continued excitement. "Now you tell me why you are here."

He shifted in his seat and cleared his throat. "Spending a few days away to relax and see the sights."

I hummed at him in disapproval, and he laughed.

"You don't take holidays once in a while, Wren? I suggest you do, they are refreshing."

I could only roll my eyes at him and wondered if I should find a table and finish a meal alone, but he wasn't finished.

"Sometimes it's nice to get a break from the pressures of home," he said, looking into my eyes. I could see he was slightly guarded about the truth he was telling. "Overbearing family and all."

"The clearest answer I've had from you yet, Tyran," I said, leaning back in the chair, hoping the lightness of my response eased any of those guarded feelings.

He let out a soft laugh, shaking his head at my attempt at humor as the tavern maid came over and I ordered some of the delicious roasted vegetables I had been smelling.

A large plate of chunks of potatoes, carrots, onion, and broccoli in a fragrant sauce came no sooner, and I dug in. I offered some to Tyran in thanks to the bread.

We ate in silence for a moment. I was pretty hungry, and the veggies were delicious. I caught him looking at me as we ate. Staring actually, and checked if I had spilled something on me, but hadn't. It wasn't in reaction to me eating; he was noticing my features, my eyes, hair, and anything else.

"Are you checking me out?" I blurted out before I could stop myself.

His eyes went wide, and I shot my hands over my mouth. My whole body went hot with embarrassment, before we both suddenly erupted in laughter. He put his hands up in feigned innocence.

The release of tension made it much easier to talk as the night wore on. We finished our meals and ordered tea and evening coffee while we got to know one another.

"Tell me about Necromancer magic," I said after taking a sip of my warm drink. A part of me wanted to see if any of the children's tales were true.

"Let me guess, you want to know if I talk to the dead? If we serve a higher evil power? Death himself? If we can summon demons and control minds?" he asked, sounding more exaggerated with each suggestion.

"Well, yes, but I'm going to assume the spooky stories we were told as children weren't exactly true, then?" I replied with a shy smile.

"No, not really." he said, smiling back at me. "We are ushers of the dying, helping them pass. We are transferers of life, and a window between the realms. We can speak to the dead, and a few less noble do travel to the smaller villages and prey on those who recently lost loved ones, having them pay to send last messages, to which most of us find it revolting. Some of us can cast runes for protection, and travel." He paused, "Then of course you have the darker side of our abilities. Curses, life absorption, manipulation of the dead... All of which we don't choose to use; it's dark magic, but as a Necromancer, you are bestowed with the gift, or burden, of the ability to use both."

"Unless you are Rhonin." I said without thinking, and regretted how openly I put his name out there.

He sighed, "Look, what he's doing isn't something that all Necromancer kind agrees with. Especially as Baron of the town."

My eyebrows shot up. The *Baron* of Reapford was behind this?

"How is he doing this all and still protected? He still governs your town, I presume?" I pressed further, lowering my voice to keep our conversation more between us. The tavern was almost empty by now, save for a random check in from the tavern maid.

"He does, and not without causing fear to anyone who would want to oppose him." Tyran clenched his jaw tighter. I could see what Rhonin was doing really bothered him. "We aren't taught to use dark magic. Many of the Necromancers haven't even seen a book containing dark magic spells, but those that have…" His gaze met mine again, "If you make the choice to use it and find the power to be enticing, it's not easy to avoid the allure, and as you delve deeper, it bends your mind to its will."

"And that's what Rhonin is choosing?"

He nodded, lowering his gaze again.

"I want to stop him. He will do more harm than good to anyone."

I shuddered at the thought. I wanted to ease the tension that was built again after asking about Rhonin, and from Tyran's responses, he seemed genuine in what he said.

"So, you don't have a Wizard then?" I asked, thinking how a Baron would assume their role with a Wizard also taking on town responsibility. It wouldn't happen.

"No. When Rhonin assumed his role as Baron, he quickly got rid of the position, saying that Necromancers shouldn't need anyone else beyond their own kind."

"But Wizards commit to the magic within the towns they serve."

"Yes, but again, Rhonin seems to think that being of a pure lineage is greater than a Wizard's abilities. He decided a council of pure-blood Necromancers would be better," Tyran said with an exasperated sigh. "It's yet another thing I disagree with him on."

"Do you know more about the bandits, then? If they are controlled by Rhonin, does anyone other than him know how to find them?"

I reminded myself to tread carefully, asking about this information. Reminding myself of Viggo's distrust of them and what he experienced. My shadows continued to stir around him though, and I knew it was telling me something different.

"Rhonin tried to hide the fact that he controlled them, initially. He went as far as to stage a robbery in our own town. He had them attempt to burn our library, and had two of our own Guard killed." Tyran nearly shook with anger, "He swore to his people he would hunt down the ones responsible, and yet did nothing toward finding them. Didn't put in orders with the Guard or push the subject further. I began digging around on my own and discovered what he was doing."

"Who are they?" I nearly whispered.

"He reanimated the Butchers of Drog."

I hadn't heard of the Butchers of Drog, but I knew Bergen and Viggo would need this information. "Why do you trust telling me this?"

Tyran looked at me for a while before speaking. I fought the urge to blush at his gaze, and for a moment caught what looked like shadows swirling behind his eyes.

"I don't know right now, but something is telling me it's the right thing to do."

My shadows swirled so interestingly, almost as if it found something of importance. I wanted to ask him if he felt something like this too, but I couldn't think of how to even properly bring it up without sounding like a lunatic.

I could feel my body growing heavy after the long day of travel and the full belly of food I now had. Tyran picked up on my fatigue after my second long yawn and offered to walk me up to my room. I hesitated, but we said goodnight at the top of the stairs. Before he walked down the hall to his room, he asked when I'd be leaving in the morning. A small twitch of hopeful excitement that we could have more time together rose in me.

I shut the door behind me before I saw him make it to his room. Exhausted, I pulled off my sweater and crawled into the small bed against the wall. The rain was still pouring down and pinging against the window. I sighed, happy to know I'd sleep well to that melodic drumming.

Images of Tyran swirled in my mind as I went over our interactions tonight. As much as I had enjoyed his company this evening, the weight of discovering Rhonin's control over this group of bandits, and that they had a name, was overpowering. I needed to let Viggo and Bergen know, and thought about sending a messenger cat right away, but then there was the matter of trying to explain where I got the information from and I didn't think I had it in me to tell Viggo I interacted more with a Necromancer, and enjoyed it, through a letter.

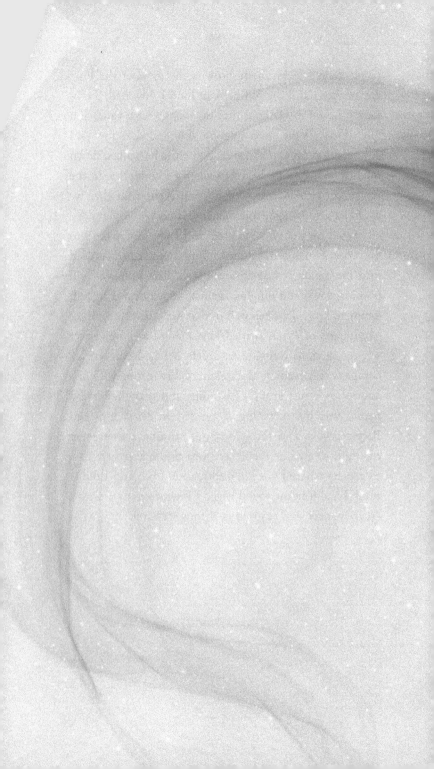

CHAPTER 10

*S*HADOWY TENDRILS DANCED *around me in pure, lighthearted fun. I willed it to envelop me, making my figure wholly shadow, and then slipped them back into laces and bands that weaved around me. My attention drifted out into the darkness as tendrils from elsewhere moved towards me in curious search, from one and the same. I reached out my hand and lightly touched the mist of the other that greeted me. I could feel the familiar tingling sensation down its tendril, and I let the laces of my shadow roam the darkness to meet the other.*

A soft gentle touch was felt in response when my shadows met with the other, and I smiled. I allowed for their extension of mists to explore. Wrapping around my legs, my thighs and abdomen. Slow and careful to not invade anything too personal I noticed. I saw the vision of my own shadows forming around the other, around their fingers, and hands, moving towards their arms and broad shoulders. Both were so light with our touch to one another as we enveloped each other's bodies in shadow, leaving only our faces to be seen. I stroked the mist around me and felt the form beyond, moving my hand up towards their face. The shadows moved in and took shape.

Tyran. I lightly slid my hand from the side of his cheek down to his neck and back up to a lock of hair that had fallen to the side of his face. Mist filled my vision, and I could feel his hand brush from my temple down to my jaw. His thumb moved across my lips before resting against my cheek. It was a comfort I hadn't felt before as I drifted to sleep. Our shadows stayed.

Thunder boomed and woke me in the morning. I listened for the rain, only hearing a seldom tapping at the window, and steadied my pounding heart at the sudden noise. The rumbling settled me quickly once I realized it was the storm.

I yawned and stretched my arms up while flexing my toes to get rid of the last bit of sleep that remained. My dream was still fresh in my mind, and I felt like I slept incredibly well. I wasn't sure what to make of the dream exactly, and who was at the other end of the shadowy tendrils, but I figured it was of my imagination. I knew Tyran's presence in my dream was only a result of my thoughts before falling asleep. Right?

I stood, giving myself more room to stretch, and looked out the window of my room to see if there would be any sign of the storm letting up soon. Morning light peeked on the horizon of the village showing a break in the clouds, and I sighed happily, knowing I wouldn't be trudging through rain all day. I pulled my hair up high with a tie, changed into some fleece-lined leggings, and pulled on a chunky navy blue sweater. I collected the items I was going to bring to Briaroak.

I lightly stepped down the stairs and greeted the innkeeper with a cheerful good morning, as smells of a delicious breakfast were already in the works in the tavern area. The innkeeper gave me the options of what was available, and just as I turned to get myself some food, I saw Tyran make his way down the stairs. I noticed he had a pack on his back as well. A part of me pinged with sadness, thinking he wouldn't be here when I came back this evening.

"Good Morning, Jurna," he said to the innkeeper, not yet looking at me. "I smell something wonderful in the kitchen, I can only imagine that's thanks to you."

Jurna smiled widely at his compliment and thanked him for the sweet words.

"Care to join me, Wren?" he said, turning to me. I could see something was on his mind.

After waving farewell to the innkeeper and letting her know I'd be back in the evening, we placed our things down at a table next to a window and walked up to the bar.

Plates and silverware were placed on the bar top with an assortment of breakfast pastries, fruit, eggs, and oatmeal, laid out for guests to serve themselves. I grabbed a pastry and a tangerine as Tyran piled his plate with eggs, and oatmeal topped with fresh berries. We sat down and I expected him to eat right away, but he stared at me, still with that look lingering in his eyes.

"Are you alright?" I finally asked, not sure of what else to say.

"How'd you sleep, Wren?" he asked.

I felt a twinge of my dream stir in my mind but pushed it down and shrugged my shoulders in response.

He stared for another moment before looking down at his food and started eating. The magic awoke more as we sat together, and I felt the familiar sensation from my dream. A rush of worry went through me, as I thought that maybe my shadows actually appeared again when I was asleep and dreaming of him. Maybe he had seen them when he left his room for something? Or did I actually send them to him?

I steadied my face as I took a bite of food and kept quiet. If I had sent them out, though, then whose shadow was visiting me? Tyran was looking out the window at the clouds breaking up. Beams of sunlight shone down in spotlights on the roads and buildings of the village. I watched him for a moment before he looked at me again.

"Are you leaving today?" I asked, thinking again of the pack he had with him.

"I thought I'd join you, if that's ok. I've always wanted an escort to Briaroak," he said, still a bit off than the warm tone I was used to getting from him.

"Oh, yes. I mean, sure that's fine," I said with a pause, "I'm not sure what they'll think if I bring a guest with me, you might have to wait while I get some things dropped off."

I knew I had to deliver the texts to Agatha, and I was sure I was probably the only name on the welcomed list to expect from our town, and walking in with a Necromancer of all people. I'm sure that would raise some eyebrows.

He shrugged at me the same way I did to his question, added with some dramatics, and I let out a quiet scoff.

"How'd you sleep then, Tyran?" I asked, pushing the unspoken subject.

"Hmm, I slept well," he started, "almost like I was in the arms of—" He didn't finish after seeing my face.

I knew my mouth was open for a moment, and my eyes wide. I quickly looked down to avoid drawing attention. He *had* seen my shadows. They must have creeped out of my room towards where he slept. It's a wonder that no one else saw them. I didn't know where to begin. The utter shock of last night hit me. The tender touches I shared with him, but he had done the same. I realized I hadn't taken a breath yet and finally took one in for a moment to center myself.

"What magic was that, Wren?"

When I looked back up to him to try to figure out a way to answer, I saw shadows swirling faintly in his eyes again. My body tugged at the recognition of it not only from the magic, but it finally made sense in my mind. I could feel my shadows moving and churning under my skin, wanting to touch the shadow magic that resided in him.

"It's an ancient magic," I said softly, "and I know you have it, too."

He looked out the window, not answering, and I could see his body tense at the discovery we both had just made. I realized it wasn't my shadows leaving my room at all, and relief washed over me.

"We are connected, somehow, by this magic," I whispered, lowering my eyes as he kept his from me.

I wondered if he even knew he had this magic within him, too. That he could wield it and use it at will. If there had ever been a time it had slipped from him like I'd experienced. Perhaps I was just weak in that sense.

Tyran kept his gaze from mine, making my mouth run faster.

"I have to get going soon if I want to be back here before night. I'm not sure if you still want to join me. I wouldn't blame you if it was too much right now. I'm sorry about the dreams, I don't know what I'm doing, really—"

"Wren." He finished one last bite of food before standing up and collecting his pack. "Let's go, shall we?"

CHAPTER 11

Ｔʜᴇ ᴀɪʀ ᴡᴀs still thick with moisture from the rain, and the smell of dirt, plant matter, and Aura drifted around us. I always imagine rain as the cleansing of old that clears for the magic that permeates our world. We walked side-by-side out of the village gates and toward the northern road. It would be hard to keep clean from the muddy roads that were ahead, but I tested for firm patches of dirt, avoiding the puddles and softer-looking spots. It was an intricate dance of steps and small leaps from one part to the other, and within a couple minutes Tyran was laughing at my attempts at avoiding the mud.

"You look like a cat," he said, the earlier tension having dissipated.

"I don't want to get too messy," I said to him as I maneuvered another area, stepping into the grass and back to the road.

"Oh, you're going to get messy," he said amused, "You'll barely make it to town leaping around like that before your legs give out."

I stuck my tongue out at him and continued the large steps and half-leaps. It wasn't more than a few exaggerated movements later that I was deceived by a chosen spot. I gritted my teeth at the squelching of mud as my boot sunk into the sludge. Flecks flew into the air, hitting my pants and arms.

Tyran walked by with a stifled look of smugness.

I pulled my boot up and shook off what I could before walking with less animation and accepted the addition of muck that clung to me.

We spent a few more minutes in a quiet stride as I thought over everything I knew about Tyran. A lot of what I had learned so far was very much what Bergen had said, and hearing just how far dark magic can lead you into such… madness. It's what I imagined of the Necromancer General that Viggo lost his partner to. Lastly, his honesty confirmed the good I thought I saw in him. No sign of aggression or manipulation. Nothing to gain or take from me.

"So you've told me a lot about what Necromancer's magic is," I began my attempts at breaking the silence, "Want to hear about what Mages do?" I asked in a teasing hush, "I bet I could light a candle faster than you."

He couldn't help but crack a smile.

Most everyone knew of Mage magic. We were the most common of the magic schools, and Gaelfall was the largest town from what I was taught. Many knew of our ability to use the basics of fire, frost, and small variations of shields and wind control, sure there's more to tell about the intricacies of it, but his growing smile made my heart flutter at the fact that I hadn't completely lost his interest.

"Honestly, I'd like to hear more of this magic we spoke about this morning," he said, turning back to me.

I paused beside him as we stood facing each other. It hadn't been clear just what he thought about the dream last night, and maybe he thought I had intentionally known what I was doing. It made me wonder if he felt like there was an invasion of privacy.

"I don't know how it found you, last night. I was dreaming too, if you think I may have had more of an idea of what I was doing." I finally spoke, unsure of how to clear any mixed feelings about the interplay that occurred.

"It wasn't just last night." he said, and I remembered the first time I sent my shadows out when thinking of him in my dream.

I couldn't avoid the redness warming my cheeks.

"Can you do that while awake, too?" He asked with sincere interest.

"Not like how the dreams are, no." I said, thinking for a moment if I should show him part of the magic that I could manifest. It might make him run in fear from me.

"I've only been able to use it in my dreams." He finally spoke as we started walking again. "I hadn't thought of it other than being just a dream, and now that it's finding you… if it's something that is actually real…" he trailed off, giving me a sidelong glance, as if asking for something.

I wrestled with the choice again, if I should show him the shadows, the vines of dark mist I could create. If he could use them too, he shouldn't find it terrifying. If anything, maybe it could help him wield his own powers. I certainly wasn't in any position of being a teacher, I had only just had a breakthrough in controlling it while venturing out on this little adventure, but maybe showing him what I did know could help. This shadow magic was rare enough that it pulled us together.

I held out my palm and Tyran watched as I willed the shadow to appear in small wisps, like tiny dark flames at first, then form into the shaded bands that curled as they took form. We watched as it weaved through my fingers and around my hand and wrists, allowing it to move up my forearm and back down. I let the bands combine and split, making the tendrils of shadow larger and smaller. The mist enveloped and covered my fingers, making them nearly transparent against the horizon where I held them. Then with a small breath out, I willed the shadows to slowly dissipate and my hand was left where I held it out.

Tyran stayed still next to me and asked me to do it again in wonder. I had to snicker at his request, moving that magic through me, and feeling it happily responding to him, and the same type of magic he had within. The shadow appeared quicker this time and more formed as I moved it again around my hand. Thicker plumes of mist crawled around, exploring my fingers. Tyran moved his hand slowly toward mine. I quickly retracted the shadows to nearly vanish before he caught me.

"Don't. Can I?" he asked, the wonder and sincerity still in his eyes.

I gave him a small smile and kept the shadow there, only growing slightly. I wasn't sure what it would do if he touched it and didn't want it to cause harm if it was the darker plumes that were previously present.

Tyran put his hand a few inches above mine, and the shadow rose like the flickering of fire up to meet their new visitor. His breathing shifted as we both felt that familiar connection from our dream. I started to see his shadows form around his hand, and the transference of our magic moved between the small space we created. The gap between our hands closed, whether that was from me, or Tyran, I wasn't sure, until we interlaced our fingers and the shadows moved in a dance with one another.

Looking into Tyran's eyes, I saw his shared excitement and awe at what we were experiencing. It sent lightning through me, and I had to look away before I burst into something embarrassing that I wouldn't be able to control. I knew there was some connection to this magic and my emotions and I didn't want it to affect the power of it like what had happened to Bergen in the basement of the library. I could feel him slide his thumb over mine, as I looked back to him, his gaze on me.

You are a dark star. I heard his voice clearly in my head. The break in our silent awe startled me and I pulled my hand away, immediately making our shadows evaporate.

"What did you say?" I asked quickly, still stunned at what I heard.

Tyran looked bewildered, "I didn't say anything."

"I heard you!" A sharpness to my tone.

"I know I didn't say anything," he responded, he looked as though he was protecting something.

Liar. I thought.

"I am not a liar!" he said with a look of objection.

Neither of us could believe what was happening. Were we able to hear one another speak without saying what we were thinking? I didn't know if he could hear my thoughts now as I tried to think of anything that would explain what had happened. Communicating through the magic, perhaps? Or maybe through the connection we had holding hands, but he had heard me call him a liar after I pulled away. Maybe we absorbed magic from one another? The idea of him hearing my thoughts, how I thought he was deliriously attractive, made the panic grow within me.

"I... I think I should go on alone," I finally said.

"I don't know what that was," he protested, but I had already started walking away.

I tried not to think of anything until I was some distance away from him. Not only would it have been an embarrassment if he knew even half of the times I had looked at him and swooned, but I still hadn't told him exactly why I was going to see the Witches, and I wasn't sure if that would somehow compromise anything that Bergen and Agatha were working on.

It took me a while to settle down and think more clearly about how the communication worked. What if it was only what we wanted them to know, as if you were actually saying the words to one another, but chose to leave unspoken? I couldn't be certain, and would have to confront that with him if he was going to still be at the inn tonight.

CHAPTER 12

I MET TWO WOMEN at the front gates who were a part of the Battalion. They took my name down and with a snap, I was cleared for entry. The Battalion wore thick black robes for armor with embellished stars imprinted on the shoulders, elbows, and lower hem. A black hooded linen cape was attached at the neck.

Briaroak Village was breathtaking. A mixture of celestial elements and flora blended seamlessly into one another. The buildings were crafted of white-painted wood cladding, and red-shingled rooftops. The eaves of the buildings had ornate carvings of flowers and stars. More stars and planets magically floated above streets offering light in the evenings, and the plant life grew with a vigor that was hard to achieve anywhere else. Oak trees lined between homes and cobbled roads with moss that hung down and twinkled with dew in the light. Colorful blooms of marigolds, dahlias, and chrysanthemum filled the air with a soft musk of fragrance.

The road curved slightly toward the center of their town, to what I imagined would have been a gorgeous towering library. Scaffolding and a frame of a building stood in the center, many of the village workers were busying themselves with the rebuild. I walked beyond the construction zone, following the path until it split into two directions.

To the far end of the street, I could see stables set up, and what looked like large foxes within the corrals. The faint noise of chitters and fox calls floated down the street, and I tried to squint to get a better look. One of the great creatures stretched, and I nearly stumbled backward.

They had wings. Large feathered wings that looked like they went more bat-like at the tips. I began to absently walk toward them, wanting to touch them and learn more about this wondrous animal, but fought the urge when I noticed I was right next to the building I needed to be at. I'd have to ask Endora and Viggo about them.

The small two-story building that could have once been a private home, sat next to the line of stables that went further toward the flying foxes. There was a small note on the door giving instructions to come in without knocking. I turned the warm brass handle and slowly walked into the building.

The oak floors creaked as I walked down the entry hall to the first open doorway to the right. It was a large room that stretched to the back of the house. Bookshelves lined the walls and were filled with all sorts of literature. In the middle of the room, a long table stretched from one end to the other, piled with different papers, history, and other works which were awaiting their final home within the rebuilt library.

I went to leave the room and look for someone when a woman came in behind me. She gasped as we both jumped back, and she let out a laugh at the sight of our introduction.

"Hello, Wren. My name is Agatha," she said as we moved back into the room.

She was as lovely as her voice sounded. I don't know why, but I always imagined someone as old-looking as Bergen when I thought of her, but she was gorgeous. Her age barely showed, mostly in the strands of gray curls that accentuated her dark hair. She had soft olive skin, only a hint of fine lines appeared, and the dark liner across her eyelids made the liquid amber color of her eyes stand out. Her lips were full and painted a deep burgundy that matched the robes she wore nearly perfectly.

"Good Morning, Agatha. I apologize for the jump scare!" I politely started. "Your village is absolutely lovely. Thank you so much for allowing my visit."

"You are welcome here, dear. I have heard who your father is, and your close relationship with Endora. As they are of our own, that includes you being welcomed here as a second home."

I could hear the warmth in her tone as I thought of Endora's broad smile she would have if she came back here.

"I brought you the requested books and scrolls… I need to warn you, they are sorted in the same fashion Bergen organizes in," I joked while taking the scroll case from my back.

She let out a soft laugh. "Chaotic?"

I couldn't help but smile back in agreement.

We sat at a clear spot at the end of the table to go over everything Bergen sent along. I pulled aside the papers she didn't need while she looked through the stacks of other papers and quickly organized them into better working order. She thumbed through the parchments and read quicker than I had ever seen anyone do. Books flew open, and she found a place in them where she would take a moment to slow, then would find another spot on another manuscript and move back to flipping through the books again.

"Rhonin has proven difficult to track." Agatha said as she skimmed through the pages.

"We haven't been able to keep a good track on his bandits either." I said, remembering the name Tyran called them, I didn't want to give that out until I told Bergen first.

"They are searching for something in particular. The ancient texts they have stolen seem to lead to something made from the Warlocks. I'm almost certain we will have the answers here... somewhere." She said as she tried to make sense of the small stack of papers left to sort.

I was in silent awe at her skill, her face showed moments of enlightenment and knowledge, then moved to furrowed brows while finding another piece of information. Her voice softly made inaudible narrations to what she was learning.

It didn't take long before something began to pull at my shadows. A calling. Familiar to how it felt when I was near Tyran, but not quite the same intensity. I stood up and began walking around the room, examining more of the texts that had been saved.

Another draw of magic beckoned as I neared the back of the room. There was an opening that led into a hallway. The walls were bare, save for a picture of a landscape that hung between two closed doors. Sconces were lit with magic flames, similar to the style of the celestial orb lights outside. I wanted to follow where my shadows were leading me, but didn't think I had the right to just explore the house freely while Agatha worked.

I took one last glance, looking for anything that would tell me what was calling to me, but nothing stood out. I returned to Agatha's side and sat once again.

Agatha looked up at me finally after some time. I couldn't quite place the look she gave me, but it was almost as if she were assessing me, or something about me. I felt my cheeks flush wondering if I was being too bold to explore the room while she worked. She looked back to one last book, then closed it, sitting up against the back of the chair.

"I would like to send a book back with you to Bergen, if that's alright." she said.

"Oh, yes. It won't be any trouble to deliver it." I replied politely.

Agatha nodded, still with the assessing look. Not one of mistrust, but as if she were trying to solve something. She stood up and went to a shelf nearest her.

"Bergen was here the night your library was attacked and had helped me restore these books." I saw the line of books on the shelf she was speaking about. Many looked incredibly old, some just bound paper. "I'm about to give you one to take to him. Please take care of it. If we lose this one, we can't replace it, as it was already once restored." She turned and held the book to her heart a moment before handing it to me.

"I will keep it by my side at all times until I get to him." I assured her.

She handed the book to me, and I carefully placed it in my bag.

"I can see why Bergen has taken you under his wing, and why he sent you, now. You are special, dear. Something brews in you that others would destroy for. Be careful." she said as I stood up to place my satchel over my shoulder.

"I think I have a lot to learn with Bergen on my return." I said.

"I'm almost certain it won't be the last of us seeing one another." She smiled warmly, but her eyes showed a hint of unease, "I have a feeling, if confirmed by Bergen after this, that we will need to warn not only the Warlocks of an incoming attack, but the Red Kingdom as well."

"What do you think the Red Kingdom will do to help?" I asked.

"They won't be helping. They'll need to protect themselves if what Rhonin seeks is there." Agatha paused while looking at me, "While we have done all we can to separate ourselves from their reign, we're far from being able to fully secede like many would want."

I saw the glimmer of unease change to a look of conviction at her last words.

I knew Bergen had worked tirelessly to remove any need for the Red Kingdom's influence beyond the taxes and exports we send them by ship, and to have Agatha involved and feeling the same way shouldn't be so much of a surprise, but I couldn't help but feel a cold creep up my back at the idea of fully pulling away from the Red Kingdom.

With a nod of farewell to one another, I made my way back out into the village. The cool air kissed my face, and the smell of burning wax and incense carried on the light breeze. I imagined how wonderful a harvest celebration would be here.

It was a little unsettling that she might recognize the shadows within me. I wondered if that's why she was looking at me the way she had earlier. She and Bergen worked closely together with research, and it wouldn't be too far off for him to mention my abilities to Agatha. I felt like I should have been told though, if that were the case. I also felt like I couldn't ask if she knew, in case Bergen had kept it between only us. I added it to my list of what I'd speak to him about when I returned.

There was one more stop today, and I tried to orient myself to the town center to know where to find the shop that I was headed to for Endora. She had a cousin who opened a shop in town with various herbs, spices, and teas, along with containers for elixirs, potions, vials, and other such things.

I walked by the construction and again took in the library being rebuilt. It would soon be beautiful once again. The care was already showing on the faces of the people, much like what I saw in our people. They all looked so hopeful to see it finished once again.

I followed the cobbled roads to where Endora had told me the shop would be. Before I opened the door, however, a voice spoke to me.

Please tell me you at least made it to the Witches.

I gasped and looked around.

I'm here. How much of my thoughts do you hear? I asked, still a little startled at how clearly I could hear Tyran.

Only now... and you calling me a liar, he said, sounding slightly wounded.

I let out an audible annoyed sigh at his tone, but also one of relief. At least there was some sort of understanding to this form of communication. I didn't respond to his feeble attempt for an apology.

The door to the shop creaked open and I walked into a fantastic space filled with the scent of cinnamon and cloves. A small bell rang when I crossed into the different displays, alerting the shopkeeper of a visitor. A beautiful woman came from behind a doorway.

She looked like she could be a younger version of Endora. The mocha skin and soft brown eyes matched, save for the soft shimmer of shadow she had on. The only difference beyond age was that instead of tight dark curls, she had straight silky hair that cascaded to her waist, and shined in the natural light that came through the picture window of the storefront.

"Welcome," she said in a warm voice.

"Hello," I was nervous. It was like I was meeting part of my family. "My name is Wren, Endora sent me to gather some supplies." I stumbled over the last bit, unsure of how much she knew of our relationship.

"Oh my Stars! Wren!" she gasped, "I'm Jaradae! It's so wonderful to finally meet you!" She ran over and grasped me in a hug. "Endora has told me so much about you! Viggo is doing well, too?"

I beamed, "Yes. We are well, all things considered."

She poured some tea, and we sat in a conversation area, talking about how things were going in Gaelfall, and what they experienced in Briaroak after the attacks. It was a refreshing change to feel so welcome in a new town.

I hardly noticed the shift in sunlight until the lights flickered on by whatever magic was set in the shop. I realized I'd be walking in the middle of the night if I didn't leave now, and reluctantly moved the conversation towards having to leave. I asked about the things Endora had requested, and she happily obliged, offering additional gifts to take with me.

Jaradae was so welcoming and offered a room for me to stay in above her shop, but the pull to learn more from Tyran was still there, and I knew it would be a long night of questions and frustrations if I did not go back to the inn. I also didn't want to make a full day's walk tomorrow just to get back to Gaelfall. We hugged our farewells and she made me promise to return when I could, this time with Endora.

"Hey, be careful on your journey. There have been reports that a monster has been coming close to the roads." Jaradae said out the door as I started down the path, "They think it's the shifting seasons and they are looking for an easier meal."

The hair on my body bristled, wondering if it was a monster, or if it could be the bandits.

I thanked her as she paused, "Wait, take this with you, something that can help." She reached back into her shop, and returned quickly with a small talisman. "May the wind always carry at your back with this."

I smiled and set a pace that reminded me of the march that I had done with Viggo and his group of Sentinels on our way to the Hidden Forest.

CHAPTER 13

A COOL PURPLE TWILIGHT filtered through the trees as I moved down the freshly dried path. I could see the shadows stretch farther as time went on and had to keep my mind on getting past them before it was dark. They cleared to grassy fields halfway through the journey to the Quarter Moon Village, and I knew I'd have a better opportunity to see anything prowling around there than having a creature stalking me from the treeline. I didn't even want to imagine what sort of monster it could be, and the idea of the bandits was too horrifying to think about.

The chill of the night was settling in and I hugged my arms against my body, even with the increased pace.

Keep going. Keep walking. I told myself as the road became fully covered with the shadows of the evening. I rubbed the talisman between my thumb and fingers, trying to ease my anxiety. If it didn't help speed my journey, at least it could help to ease my tension.

Stars began appearing and twinkled ever so dimly above me in the deeper blue sky. Rustling high in the trees had my senses on full alert, but it was only the gentle breeze. I decided I'd save running for when the clearing came into view.

A snap sounded nearby. I went near silent, listening intently. My vision narrowed on a bush at the side of the road stirring. My heart pounded in my chest, as a small ground squirrel came running out on the path and to a burrow on the other side.

Breathe. Slow breaths.

I picked up my pace again, trying to settle my nerves. It would be best to listen to the sounds of the insects and crickets singing their night song. If anything too dangerous lurked, silence would be the enemy.

Where are you? His familiar voice had me nearly jumping out of my skin.

I shouted a curse.

I'm almost halfway back to the village. Why?

I was going to dinner and thought of inviting you, but I'm more concerned that you are still out there in the dark. It's not exactly safe traveling alone out there. He said.

I could feel his concern, but I was still annoyed at how he made me jump.

So I've heard. I'm fine, I snapped, frustrated that I had to hear the warning again. *I see the clearing up ahead, I can take care of myself.*

My focus shifted back from being consumed with interacting with Tyran, that I hadn't realized I was now walking in silence.

Total silence.

I froze, and a chill ran up my spine. I wondered whether breaking out into a run would allow me to escape whatever it was lurking, or if I should hide and wait for the insect song to resume before sneaking back to the road.

A low growl gave me my answer, and I ran.

I could hear it leap from the trees and slide across the soft dirt, still wet enough, that its weight caused the mud underneath to be exposed. It was not the bandits, which I thought would be a relief, but this was nearly just as bad.

I could feel the power in my legs as I kicked off the ground into a full sprint, trying to gain as much ground from whatever was behind me. I needed help.

I need help.

Help.

I kept my body propelling forward, focusing on the road ahead and steadying my breath as I tried to remember the feeling of the running I would do for exercise. This was much different. The thudding of paws and heavy breaths could be heard not too far behind me as I gritted my teeth, pushing my legs to move faster. A growl came again, and I could feel it take a leap behind me. I only had a moment to react.

Fire shot from my hand as I reached behind me creating a wall of flames that rose well above my head. I paused, glancing back as the orange glow lit the eyes and head, then the body of what was chasing me.

A fur-covered black beast stared at me. Its body looked like a wolf, its head more like a bear, and sharp canines protruded from its muzzle. Two bony tusks came out from its jowls and its tail whipped around behind it, more reminiscent of a large rat that split into sharp whips at the end. It stopped behind the flames for a moment before letting out a ground-shaking roar and leapt over the flames. The beast's claws were like razors as it came crashing only a few feet behind where I was.

"Think. Think!" I shouted to myself as I continued hurtling myself into the clearing. It would have been a relief to have made it here, but now that didn't matter. I pushed myself forward and felt hot, jagged breaths behind me. Another split second was all I had once again, as I turned, shooting a blast of freezing blizzard air in a frontal cone towards the monster's face. The blowback of the subzero temperatures I cast chilled the air, as the beast let out a pained scream from my spell. It backed up from my attack. I again made the horrible choice to turn to see it shake off the ice that clung to the fur on its face, before I sprinted back into a full run.

I'd never seen a beast like this. Fighting it, let alone using my spells defensively on another person or creature before was foreign to me, and uncontrollable panic rose. The monster moved with more power, as it regained its galloping gait, and leaped once again in my direction. It would hit its target this time if I didn't do something, and I pulled the dagger from my satchel, turning to slice as I dove into the high grass to the side.

Its claws reached for me, extending out as I met it with my blade. A yelp of pain emerged, and I hit the ground.

My last thought of survival was lighting the field on fire and risking burning myself as well when I heard another shriek of pain from the beast. A pale green light flashed through the grass as I moved to sit up and see what other manner of horrors met me.

Tyran stood with his back to me as he battled the monster. He had a sword in one hand and was casting out what looked like pale green bone spikes that slammed into the monster's side, slowly working their way below its skin, causing the beast to writhe and twitch where they hit. Another shriek of pain and it lashed out at him with its massive claws.

He swung the blade forward and severed the beast's paw. I covered my mouth at the sight while splatters of blood rained down, hitting us both. It was only another blink of a moment when I noticed Tyran cast a rune that encircled the beast in the faint glow of purple and green mist that rose from the ground.

The beast writhed in pain, captured in the rune while trying to escape, but met invisible walls. Tyran made his move and plunged his blade into its skull. A guttural groan came out, and the beast slowly went still. I watched Tyran as he placed a hand on the monster, his eyes glowed a faint green like I saw in the forest, and chanted an incantation that I didn't understand.

I steadied myself and slowly stood up. My stomach ached with the adrenaline that coursed through me. My lungs burned at the running I had done, and I had to pause to make sure I wouldn't need to retch. Unable to move, or even think about what all just happened, I almost didn't hear Tyran as he spoke to me.

"Are you hurt?"

He came over to me quickly as another wave of nausea hit me. I had to bend over, placing my hands on my thighs, still not quite catching my breath.

He looked me over and smeared the beast's blood that had splattered on my skin, making sure it wasn't from a wound of my own. I went to wave him back, knowing that I didn't want him too close, but he caught my arm to help me stand straight. I looked at him for a moment and saw the worry in his expression. My heart fluttered a whole different way than the stress of what happened, and I had to tear my gaze away to steady myself once more.

"How did you get here? How did you find me?" I said as I swallowed back the last feelings of sickness, and thought of his eyes as they faded back to their hazel. "Did you help it pass over?"

"I heard you yell for help. I runewalked to the outskirts of the trees, and that's when I saw you leaping into the grass… and slicing at that Ursendir," he said with a hint of being impressed, "And yes. It's part of… a personal oath to my magic. I will help any animal pass without pain in the final moments of death.".

I wasn't so sure that monster was worth a painless death, but it struck me what he had done.

"Rune… what?" I wiped the sweat that formed on my forehead, "And that thing is called an Ursendir?"

"It's a way of quick travel for us." Tyran spoke, still assessing if I was okay.

"I hate that thing," I finally said, not knowing how else to resolve what I just went through.

He laughed and shook his head in disbelief.

What am I going to do with you? His tone was endearing, but I didn't want to read too much into it after tonight.

"Walk with me, please." I said, answering him out loud.

"I've got a better idea," He placed a rune on the ground, and held out his hand, "Come."

The whirling of wind twisted my hair up and around us as we walked this in-between. Everything was a shade of gray and within seconds, we were at the front door of the Quarter Moon Inn. Runewalking was a rush.

"Does every Necromancer know how to do that?" I asked, fixing the lock of hair that was sticky with remnants of the beast's blood.

"No, it's a more powerful line of spells. It's usually only taught to the higher status of pure blood lineage. I don't normally use it within Reapford."

He opened the door for me, and Jurna's expression told me everything I needed to know about our appearance… and smell. She quickly pointed us upstairs to two washrooms each at either end of the hall where our rooms were and asked that we spend all the time bathing that we needed.

Shutting the door behind me, I went to fill the bath with water from the boiler that was continually lit in the corner of the washroom. Steam from the water rose into the air as I quickly removed my dirty, bloody clothing, and sunk into the warm liquid. I slid my back down so that my ears were below the waterline, stilling myself to feel the gentle peace of the water's quiet.

I was wondering…

His voice rang into my head and my eyes went wide as I shot up, looking for him in the room.

Wicked Necromancer! I shouted back to him as I returned into the warmth of my bath. I could hear his audible laugh down the hall.

Seeing as you seemed to be the one who started all this, what do I get for saving your life tonight?

I couldn't believe the brazen tone he had.

Ok, for one, I didn't start this… I objected.

You are the one who found me in the forest, you found me here, in your dreams… It seems to be a pattern. Pure amusement lingered on his words, and felt near outrage at his boldness.

You seem to be the one who can't stop talking to me.

Fair enough, but I did save your life.

I'll buy you dinner, I said wryly.

I was able to finish washing in peace and made it to my room to change into some comfortable warm clothes without seeing him. My hair was still damp as I pulled it into a bun atop my head and made my way down to the dining hall. Tyran was talking to Jurna about the encounter we had and assured her that things were taken care of. I met them both, and she smiled widely at us, as if she were even more pleased seeing us together.

The aroma of another amazing meal filled my senses. We ordered our late dinner at the bar and found ourselves at a table in the back corner of the tavern. I looked at Tyran sitting across the table from me. His hair was down, still slightly damp, and faint wet spots formed on the broad shoulders of his white shirt. The top buttons were left open in a v-shape that showed a hint of what could be a scar or tattoo across his chest, and his sleeves were rolled up, showing off his impressive forearms. I looked at his hands and thought about how it felt holding them earlier today, and how he gently rubbed his thumb over mine.

"How many of those things have you killed?" I asked, trying to clear my head of the imagery I was creating.

"Hmm? The Ursendir? A few. Only the ones that end up going after what they aren't supposed to," he replied nonchalantly.

"So, is that your job? Are you a hunter of sorts for your Guard?" I asked.

His eyes met mine, and he gave me that lazy smile I melted over. "Not exactly. Being a part of the Necromancer Guard doesn't cover hunting. We are assigned to work within a role that suits their abilities. I happen to be more of an investigator, making sure we establish a balance within our town and surrounding areas, but having to take care of a monster or two does happen to fall in that area."

"Which is why I suppose you were asking for payment, then?" I snipped in fun. "Because I'm not from your town?"

He gave a teasing, ironic look, "I'm just doing my job, but I won't turn down an offer of thanks."

"So valiant," I dramatically said, smiling back at him.

Dinner came quickly, and we both dug in before speaking again.

"So what is it that you do, Wren? I've seen you with a tracking party, and then on a delivery mission. How do those connect?" Tyan asked after taking a drink.

"Actually, I work for our library, directly under the Wizard of our town." I finished swallowing my bite before continuing. "Although, it seems my tasks have shifted by some degree after the recent attacks. I'm thinking my role might be in limbo as to what it will officially be."

He picked at his chicken before taking another bite. "Hmm, I'm just thinking of when the next time you're going to run into me again will be."

"Oh, are you going to miss me?" I feigned excitement in a high-pitched tone. The question was true, though. I wanted to know.

He smiled and shook his head at my theatrics.

I'll just have to see how far away this works.

I couldn't help but smile shyly at him. His persistence in communicating with me made me feel so giddy. While jarring at times to suddenly hear his voice when I don't expect it, I don't think I'd want anyone else other than him to have the ability.

I had to pull myself away from the ease of staring at him and that damned smile. I looked around, making sure we couldn't be overheard, and lowered my voice, "So you don't know exactly what Rhonin is looking for, then?"

Tyran shifted in his seat and I thought I saw a hint of a guarded expression in his eyes before he responded. "I've only gathered that he is trying to use Aura in a way that can cause great harm. Who or what he's after for that, I'm not certain yet."

The conversation with Agatha today was still fresh in my mind. I knew it would be better to wait and tell Bergen everything first, but I felt like Tyran needed to know more as well. Whether it was our shared magic that made me trust him, or the fact that he was so different from what I was told about Necromancers, I knew he would be more helpful than anything for our search in how to stop Rhonin.

"I met with the Wizard of Briaroak today."

Tyran didn't respond, and I saw the smallest tensing at the corners of his mouth.

"She mentioned that Rhonin might be looking for a particular object. That we may need to warn not only the Warlocks, but the Red Kingdom as well." I paused, "It sounds like you were on the right path as to what he's looking for."

Tyran nodded, "Thank you for sharing that."

I wanted him to trust me, and trust that we could figure this out, but it wouldn't be easy to work with Viggo and those close to him. I needed to figure out how to get them to be open to Tyran. There was an uneasy silence as Tyran looked away, thinking things over before meeting my gaze, "I think I know what he's after."

"Oh?"

"The Warlocks are known for their relics. A common one they use are obelisks for channeling magic. Various materials are used for different purposes. He's probably searching for a specific obelisk that will help him somehow contain or channel Aura." Tyran whispered, lost in thought at trying to solve what an obelisk like that could be.

I held in a gasp, trying to mask any outward emotion to avoid drawing attention to our conversation. "I need to get this information back to Bergen." I reached out and grabbed his hand, giving it a light squeeze. "Thank you for trusting me, too."

The inn's tavern started to fill with more village people as the night went on, and music had started by the time we finished our late meal. I thought for a moment to ask Tyran if he wanted to stay and dance, but the exhaustion hit me, and I knew I wouldn't be able to dance more than a song or two. His yawn told me he was probably thinking the same thing, and we stood up to walk back to our rooms. I was grateful that we would be on the other side of the music that reverberated from the tavern.

As we made it to the small landing at the top of the stairs, I stopped for a moment, not wanting the night to end just yet. I knew I'd be leaving back home tomorrow, and the small discussion of when we'd see each other again hit me. I really liked being around him, beyond the fact that he was so easy on the eyes. I was still so interested in learning more about him, the Necromancers, and what we were going to do with this magic we shared.

More importantly, he saved my life tonight. I tried not to think of it that way, because it sent a weird chill to my heart that I had come that close to death, but it was true. I would have been Ursendir food. My magic moved excitedly as I waited at the small landing. He faced me and met my gaze.

"I need to say thank you. For something else." I said in a soft tone. "You did save my life tonight, and I'd feel awful if I didn't at least say something."

His expression changed to something more tender. His hazel eyes sparkled in the dim light that caught them.

"When I heard you call for help, I could only think of finding you, and tearing apart anything that was going to harm you. I was worried the bandits had…" he trailed off, "I'm glad I saved your life, too."

I put my hand on his chest ready to playfully push him back as I laughed at his slight twist of humor when he reached up to hold my hand in his.

We lingered, looking into each other's eyes as I felt that small, familiar flicker of his magic. Staying hidden between us, the swirling of smoke and tingling sensation of our connection filled my body and senses. He moved his thumb over my hand again. I could feel myself, or him? It was me, getting closer as I tipped my face up toward his.

My lips softly brushed against his. I gently pressed, and felt him respond with the same care. A light kiss once, twice. Moving from bottom lip to top and back until I felt his breath catch. The magic intertwined within us and he kissed me deeper, pulling me into him and wrapping his other arm around my waist. I tangled my fingers into his hair and pulled him towards me as our mouths opened and we drank from each other. His strong body was warm against mine as we held that magic between our hands, and between us.

We slowed back to a soft kiss after a couple moments and Tyran touched his brow to mine, as I let my hand slide down from his hair and over his hard shoulders and biceps. He moved his free hand up to my neck and under my chin, gently kissing me on the side of my jaw near my ear.

"Goodnight, Wren." he whispered.

Chills moved across my body in waves as our twisting shadows returned to one another. Tyran smiled as he turned, finally letting go of the hand we held against one another, and strode down the hall to his room. I stayed stunned, lightly touching my swollen lips before I went to my room as well.

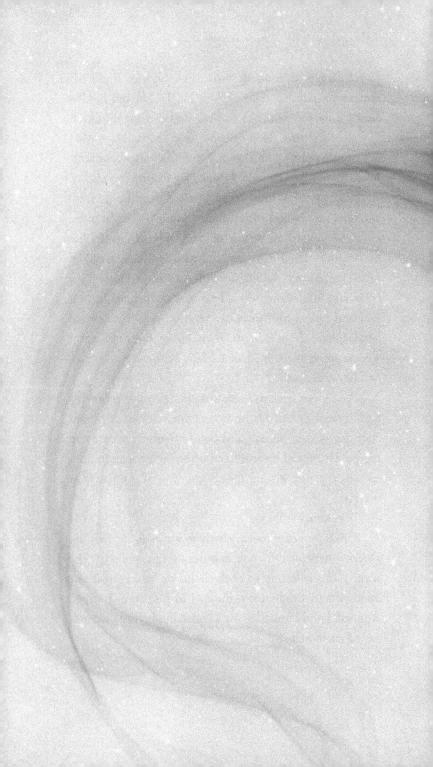

CHAPTER 14

THERE WAS A quiet ambience of the surrounding fields as I walked home. The winds picked up once again, and another threatening system of storms moved slowly through the sky. I would be back to Gaelfall before the rain, but I couldn't shake the chill I felt through my body. I knew it wouldn't be solved by layering on more clothing, either. It was the cold left from where Tyran had been.

I woke up that morning thinking I'd have one last meal with him before we parted ways. I took more time getting ready, wearing the last change of clothes I packed, and let my hair down in a tumble of waves from it drying in the bun I kept it tied in the previous night, even lightly lining my eyes with a brown kohl pencil. When I glided down the stairs towards the dining room, he wasn't there. I picked at a pastry and sat waiting for him, thinking he may have been tired from yesterday. I certainly felt the soreness from the attack he saved me from. It wasn't until

I had finished breakfast and grabbed my things to make my way home that Jurna told me he had left in the early hours. I gave her my thanks for the lovely stay and left disappointed.

For the couple days that I kept my mind out of the negativity and self-doubt of what it commonly sank to, I felt a small twinge of defeat. He definitely had kissed me back, that was for sure. Was I bad at it? I hadn't ever thought to ask anyone about it. No one complained before. It certainly wasn't my first kiss, and I highly doubted it was his. But why didn't he even try to, I don't know, speak to me however we do within our minds? I knew he would have known I'd be up and on my way by now. I tried to convince myself it was most likely some pressing matters in his town that caused the quick leave. Why couldn't he take a moment to say something?

Ugh. I thought to myself, *Get a hold of yourself.*

He did save my life last night. He wanted to tear apart what was going to hurt me. I could feel a warmth creep up through me at the strength of those words. Maybe he just needed time. Maybe I needed time.

Gaelfall greeted me with a sense of peace as the familiarity of my environment surrounded me in a happy welcome. The first thing that came to my mind was how much I missed training with Viggo and wanted to head straight to the Sentinel training grounds as soon as I dropped off the book to Bergen. I thought about how I was going to tell Viggo about the Ursendir attack, and it quickly became clear if I told him about the attack, I would have to tell him about Tyran.

I would have to look at him and tell him I spent time with a Necromancer straight after he opened his heart to me about the pain he endured at the hands of one of their kind. I couldn't do that to him, and yet, I had no other choice. I needed to tell Bergen even if it means Viggo finding out the source of my knowledge.

Bergen was outside speaking to the Sentinels that guarded the newly restored front doors of the library as I walked up the stairs to meet them. The plain light gray linen robe he was wearing told me he had either just come to the library, or was heading out to run errands.

"Wren! Welcome home!" he said, pushing up his glasses as I smiled at him and the Sentinel.

The library rebuilding had already begun, the sounds of construction droned on in the background as we talked.

"Good morning! I have some light reading for you from Agatha. I thought I'd drop it off before I meet with Viggo for training," I said cheerfully.

He nodded, and we entered the loud space of the library as I dug through my bag for the book. Its deep blue canvas cover had rich brown leather accents along the binding and corners. It would have been mistaken for a new book by the cover alone, but the pages looked yellowed, wrinkled, and aged. I passed it to him and he gave a look of familiar surprise.

"Thank you, I'll be sure to send this back to her soon. It's one of the few we recently replaced," he said, rounding the hall into his office.

"I need to talk to you about a few things I learned while on my travels." I said, not quite knowing how to bring it up without having to dive into everything right away. "There's quite a bit to unpack if you have time?"

"Oh, yes. We definitely can," he said, still distracted by the book, examining the work they had done to restore it.

I sat on the chair set to the front of his desk as he took his seat. "Agatha filled me in on some of the information you have been seeking about Rhonin, as well as indirectly noting that I have something special about me… does she know about my shadow magic?"

"Oh, yes. She's known since you were young. She can be trusted." He said nonchalantly.

I wanted to scold him for not telling me, but the news of Rhonin was far more pressing. "She mentioned that Rhonin is hard to track, and that he's looking for an object that possibly the Warlocks and Red Kingdom night have?"

Bergen began tugging at the corner of his beard. "Mmm… I thought this much. This book Agatha sent along goes over various relics and sigils that can lead us to what he could be seeking."

"Well, I have a theory…" I started, "Not my theory, I happened to meet the Necromancer who was in the Hidden Forest at the village. He seems to think it's an obelisk that Rhonin could be seeking."

Bergen straightened in his seat at my revelation. "Interesting. It sounds like you are trusting his information, then?"

"He is against what Rhonin is doing, and he didn't have to share a lot of what he told me, but he did. I do trust him." I said, I didn't know if I should tell him that

Tyran also held shadow magic right away. It felt like Tyran would need to be open to it first.

Bergen sat in thought for a moment before smiling, showing his deep wrinkles, "Well, it seems like part of this task was already a success then. How did it go using magic without supervision?"

"Surprisingly well," I said, happy for a shift in subject. "I think I found the balance with Aura and my shadow magic." I said, stopping once again, realizing it was going to be hard to shift the subject from Tyran and our shared shadow magic. "I found out a few more things that I can do with my magic, but I need to clear some things up first before going into it all."

"I'm interested in hearing more about that. I'm sure there's a reason for the hesitation." He said, "But I want you to know you are free to say all you need to about it. The more we know the better we can understand your magic, and how to keep you safe."

"I know." It was all I could say. I wanted to go into further detail, but I knew I had to protect Tyran's choice as well, even if I knew I could trust Bergen.

Oona was stationed at her desk when I came in. She was a little upset that I didn't think to interrupt her conversation with the contractors the day I left to say goodbye, but was quickly over it as we caught up with everything that happened over the past couple days.

I told her about seeing Tyran, and while omitting the shadow magic connection, I watched her emotions range from shock as I told her about Tyran saving me from the Ursendir, to squealing over our kiss, and then joined in on the frustration of him being gone in the morning. I knew she wouldn't mention it to Bergen, which also meant Viggo wouldn't hear.

It was really fun to relive some of the excitement of that evening with her, and I thought about maybe working up the nerve to say something to him through our link. Not now, but if I didn't hear from him, maybe I could work up the courage tonight.

It didn't take long to find Viggo in one of the training rings, working with a couple of Sentinel recruits. He let out a gruff laugh as he saw me standing outside the fence entrance and then barked some orders at the two before coming to meet me.

"Look at you. Coming straight from your travels to train," he marveled.

"I figured I had a couple days away, might be good to knock some of the rust off. Though, I might have to fight these guys for your time," I joked back with him as we hugged.

I pulled out the borrowed blades and set them on an armor rack nearby.

"How did it all go? Hoping that you didn't have to cross anything to warrant using those," he asked lightly.

My breath caught for a second as I fought back the urge to tell the truth of everything. I could only offer a smile back to him that things were fine. He didn't pick up on anything being off, and my smile seemed to be the only answer he needed.

"I'll see you tonight with Endora. She'll love seeing what I brought from Briaroak." I said, and Viggo happily nodded before being called away for a meeting.

It was cold enough that we sat in front of the fire after I showed Endora all the gifts I brought back from her cousin's shop. The light it brought to Endora's face made me momentarily forget the serious realities that were beginning for me. Viggo and Endora talked about how beautiful it was there, and about how amazing it would be to visit together soon.

We finished the evening sharing some chocolate Jaradae gifted us. I still couldn't work up the nerve to go into detail with Viggo of who I spent time with at the Quarter Moon Inn, and went upstairs to change into pajamas. My large bed never looked more appealing.

As I tucked myself into the plush comforter, I thought about Tyran. I hadn't heard from him all day and again wrestled with whether he was choosing to not talk to me, or if he had tried and maybe we were too far away from each other. I rolled to my side and tried to close my eyes, but the images of him and the memories of the past couple days wouldn't leave; How he laughed at my sad attempts at humor, that lazy smile, and that he truly had saved me. How his eyes sparkled. That kiss.

I let out an exasperated sigh and rolled to my back. Fine. I told myself I would try to say something if I hadn't heard from him by tonight.

I miss you.

I waited for a response, and after a few minutes of silence, rolled my eyes at my weakness and tried to clear my mind.

I thought you'd say something first.

His voice was quieter, but his amused tone was as loud as ever.

Wicked Necromancer. I sneered back to him.

My heart was bursting through my chest at his voice. I couldn't keep a wide smile from my face. I wanted to ask him about this morning, and why he left so early, but his response was enough for tonight.

I miss you too, he said, and I could hear the sweetness to the words.

I was exhausted, and I kept those words and his voice in my mind as I fell asleep.

CHAPTER 15

*O*UR SHADOWS INTERTWINED *as they easily found one another within the dream. The tingling sensation moved down me in waves as I felt Tyran's form appear in the darkness. He reached for me and pulled me close into his shadows. I wrapped my arms around his waist as he put his hands on either side of my face and lifted it towards his. The inky wisps that had taken our forms heated in the same warmth we had when we were last together on that small landing of the inn.*

We kissed deeply as I moved my hands over the strong lines of his back, across his broad shoulders, and back down. He ran his fingers through my hair and down to my lower back where he pressed me tighter against him. We kissed for what felt like hours, exploring one another within the magic that held us together. I couldn't get enough of his familiar smell of bergamot and ginger, and the taste of him that made me so incredibly weak, and yet craving more of anyone than

I ever wanted. I heard him sigh into our shared space as we kissed, "My Dark Star."

I didn't want to wake up. Even after the dream slipped into nothingness where Tyran and I remained holding each other, and I truly had slept so incredibly well, I didn't want to open my eyes. The dawn light filtered in, and I knew it was slowly becoming later and later as the seasons were changing. I tucked in my knees to my chest as I lay on my side in my bed, keeping my eyes closed. I heard Endora close the front door as she left for the day and with a small sigh of realization, I slowly stretched my legs out of the side of the warm blankets and felt the cool air of the morning wake my senses.

Giving up on my feeble attempt to sleep longer, I yawned and made myself get out of bed and change into training clothes. I layered a tank top under a long sleeve shirt, as well as a hooded sweater that reminded me of what the Witches' Battalion wore when they were hooded in their cloaks. Endora had gifted it to me, and I wouldn't be surprised if it was from Briaroak.

I walked downstairs to boiled eggs, fresh fruit, and granola for breakfast. I saw the potion bottles and different herbs I brought freshly washed and hanging up to be dried and stored for later. I couldn't help but smile at the care Endora had taken with them. Agatha had welcomed me as one of their own because of my relationship with both Viggo and Endora, and it made me happy how comfortable I felt with them even when I couldn't use their schools of magic and potion creation. They were true life healers.

I opened our front door, and saw Newt the cat laying at our entrance, basking in the sun, with a message attached to him for delivery. I gently scratched his stomach before he could playfully claw at me, and picked the note off his harness. A sprinkling of treats and he was purr-crunching once again in appreciation. It was from Viggo. He hastily wrote that his watch had detected a disturbance near the Hidden Forest, and that they were heading out to track it down. The scribbling of his words let me know he was in a rush to get this out before he made his way to the action. The last bit I could barely make out, but it said to the effect that I was to train on my own and he'd be back as soon as they learned more.

Panic quickly mixed with frustration that rose through my body at the realization that I wasn't there to help. Why was he even training me, if he wouldn't even wait for me when I was here at home?. If it were anything like the Ursendir, I suppose I may be more of a hindrance, but the feeling of being left out led to a weird feeling of annoyance and irritation.

Even my steps carried the bitterness I felt. There was a heaviness in them as I thought about what I would do to train without Viggo around. I knew the sets and workout rounds to make, but nothing sounded remotely appealing without him guiding me. The looks from other townspeople told me my face expressed my frustration.

I made it to the dirt path of the training grounds when I saw one of the Sentinel soldiers who had joined us on the first expedition for the bandits. Without hesitation, I asked if she knew where Viggo was headed to track this disturbance. She ran her hand through her short blonde hair as her blue eyes darted around at the other soldiers while telling me about the intel they received from the Watch, and where they planned to track.

There had been a report of partial remains of different monsters and beasts at the forest's edge that appeared to be intentional, possibly ritualistic. A trail of the recognized enchantment magic similar to that of the bandits was found, but the foot tracks of what they were following weren't that of just one type of creature; They were from all the creatures that had been slaughtered.

I thanked her and immediately went to put my armor on and armed myself with a sword strapped to my back and a dagger hung at my side. I grabbed a bag of food rations near the armory and marched out of our town through the now golden fields toward the first treeline on the horizon.

I didn't give myself any logical amount of time for doubt to even strike my mind until I was a couple of hours into my journey of trying to catch up with Viggo. It was then I realized just what I was doing. Walking alone, with some sort of creature, or thing, who tore apart monsters on the loose. Possibly bandits. And I'm trying to meet up with a group of Sentinels who would probably be the ones who ended up protecting me more than anything. My heart raced, and I knew if I kept ruminating, I'd panic and turn to run back home.

Taking what I felt was the more direct path to where the reported location of evidence was, I looked around for any sign of recent travel from the Sentinels or creature. The outcropping of trees beyond the Hidden Forest swayed and moved in rhythm to the tall grass as I strode through, stopping to listen for voices or anything unnatural. I knew I'd have to walk through the trees, and if anything it probably would offer better protection than being out in the open the way I was, but I had to steady myself before entering, thinking about the last monster that had come after me from out of a treeline.

It was much cooler in the canopy of timber and leaves. I slowly stepped, keeping as quiet as I could, and searched for the best place from which I could survey my surroundings. Boulders jutted out of the ground and stacked up to higher vantage points. I found one that would be the easiest spot to rest and keep hidden. I climbed up the makeshift steps of shale stone that jutted out, worn down by wind and rain until I reached a flat surface near the top. I started to get hungry, and pulled out a loaf of bread from the rations.

The songbirds and small chittering of the squirrels let me know it was highly unlikely that I was going to find much in this grove of trees, and I'd need to move on after my meal. I looked toward the north where another grove was located, near the base of some rocky foothills. I would need to move soon to keep up with Viggo's team, so I brushed the last bits of crumbs off my pants and left for any critters to enjoy. I climbed down from my safe spot. It wouldn't be too far of a walk to get there, and I should be able to get home before dark if I can't find them. I wanted to factor in swinging by the library to let Bergen or Oona know I was safe, just in case.

Before reaching the trees of the foothills, I noticed how the air shifted ever so slightly. Not the air, necessarily, but something was different. Heavier. I hesitated entering, wondering if I should just turn around, but the voice in me that kept me going pushed more. I cleared my thoughts and moved into the second grouping of trees.

A deeper cold than the last grove met with me as I moved farther into the shade. More rocky formations and boulders towered up, and I told myself that the elevation change had caused the chill and heavy feeling surrounding this space. Climbing up the layers of shale that jutted out every few steps, I continued with the idea of it being best to have the high ground. It was also quieter walking on the smooth stone than the twigs and leaves of the forest floor.

The wind shifted in the trees and a putrid smell of dead animals that had been left for some time filled my senses. Something deep in me told me I needed to leave, and fast. My body reacted almost immediately as I searched for a place to hide. A small alcove carved into the rock was the only thing close to me, and I took that as the only option, pressing myself deep into it while listening intently.

Labored breaths and uneven stepping made their way into the grove. I wanted to shut my eyes as if it would help me hide more, but I had to keep them open to see what it was. The smell became overwhelming, and I tried to pull my sweater over my nose to keep from gagging.

The creature made gurgling sputters, grunts, and groans that were completely unnatural. Something dragged across the ground as steps lumbered forward, and I wondered what it could be. A soft breeze moved across the wall of shale stone into the small space where I hid, curling back out towards the beast. I went completely stiff at the horrible luck of that breeze as the creature stopped moving and sniffed my scent. My hand shot up to cover my mouth from the scream that wanted to escape.

A haunting wail rang through the forest as it moved towards the rock wall within which I hid. The creature came into sight, and I saw parts of fur, skin, hooves, paws, and claws hung from the massive body of the monstrosity, nearly as big as the boulders I hid between. Its head was crudely melded together of bone, ripped flesh, and brain matter. Within the raw flesh of the creature, different eyes were haphazardly placed. Its mouth hung down in a wide set open jaw of rows of teeth, as if from different monsters.

I finally saw the appendage it was dragging as it swung the massive paw at the stones I hid between, cracking the gigantic boulder, and nearly knocking me from the wedge of space. Slivers of shale poured down on me. I shrieked and could feel tears forming.

It smelled the air again, searching for me, and I knew I wouldn't have long if I stayed here. I had to do something. It wasn't more than a few seconds later that it moved again, and I willed my shadows around me.

I hadn't tried to have it completely consume me beyond the dreams, but the smoke obeyed my pleading demands as it enveloped my whole body. The transparent mist clouded my vision as it covered my head. The monster shrieked in surprise at my disappearing act and began smashing at the rock to get to me. I blasted out a freezing ball of ice at it and made my escape as it briefly stunned the giant creature. I fled to the trees ahead of me as I heard it slamming its heavy appendages against the rock again, realizing it hadn't been aware of my escape.

My vision still faintly showed the shadows around me, which were obscuring me from the creature's view.

Another sound rang out, this time familiar, and my blood ran cold at the recognition. Viggo's voice boomed over the snarls of the awful monster as he and his Watch advanced on the creature. It slowly turned from tearing apart the alcove I was just in. Every part of my body knew I had to help them, as I ran to the shouted commands that Viggo gave as they readied their weapons against the monstrosity that now groaned and sputtered in their direction.

The creature lumbered towards them, and two Sentinels ran up to begin an attack sequence. The beast swiped one of its appendages as they dodged, only to slice them in half with the claws of another arm that they hadn't noticed was poised and ready to strike. I let out a cry of panic, seeing their bodies torn apart so easily as the vile monster made its way closer to Viggo.

Viggo showed no sign of backing down, pulling two swords from his back and getting into a defensive stance, one that I had practiced with him so many times. His remaining soldiers stood around in tactical placement, a pair stood ahead of Viggo, and three more stood at either side of him, ready to move on his signal. The beast let out another wet, choking wail, and suddenly charged, sprinting in their direction.

The next two Sentinels it met dodged its swipe and maneuvered a slicing blow with their weapons. The beast didn't respond to the pain and returned an attack, swinging around two of its extra appendages, crushing the Sentinels into one another. Bones cracked and their bodies went limp on the ground.

Viggo was next. I knew he wouldn't back down with the three others near him who I recognized as his closest members of the Sentinel Watch. They were no match for its power. The thought of seeing Viggo fall victim to this putrid monster caused me to nearly burst.

Anger and pure hatred for this horrible thing ran through my veins as I felt my magic and shadow call to me, beckoning me to use it defensively in a way I told myself I wouldn't do without fully understanding it. I didn't have time to wrestle with that choice and willed my shadows, moving me stealthily, to appear between Viggo and the beast. My shadows retreated from enveloping me and moved back into the many tendrils and vines that weaved off my shoulder blades. I spread them out, creating a vision of unholy wings at my sides.

I felt the power of my tendrils, realizing that I could form them into something darker, denser, and more solid. Small forms of onyx spikes appeared, becoming more solid, then dissipated back into shadows.

I didn't know if I'd have time as the beast turned its attention toward me. I had to keep willing them into these onyx spikes. Growing longer, and larger with each moment, I shot one forward, and it smashed into smoke against the body of the creature.

"Damnit!" I screamed through gritted teeth, assessing that I had one more chance.

The ground shook with each heavy step as I focused on solidifying my shadows. I needed to keep them solid as I shot them forward. One last attempt was all I had as I sent them toward my target.

Multiple spikes whistled through the air before piercing its flesh and exiting through. The beast screamed once, and I had to cover my ears at the sound while it fell to the ground, unmoving. Thick black blood and putrid liquid spilled from its wounds as my shadows melted away.

Viggo swore before I could turn around.

"What in the world was that, girl?"

"I had to help!" I didn't know what else to say.

"What was that? How did you…?" Viggo couldn't finish as he walked over to inspect the fallen beast, which continued to bleed out vile and puss. "You… You… I've never seen that from you." He looked back at me, his tone still high.

"I didn't know I could use it like that," I said, hoping he wouldn't be completely terrified of me.

I didn't know what else to say. I was also astonished at what I had just done. I used my shadow as a cloak, and then as a weapon. I was afraid of the cost of that magic, but I couldn't sense anything beyond its normal churning within me. What had I just done?

"You damn well saved our lives from that Abomination," Viggo said, finally breathing out in a more even tone.

"Do they have a name?" I asked.

"It's Necromancer magic. Dark magic. They only call them Abominations. Mixtures of beasts and creatures reanimated and controlled." Viggo angrily glared at the dead body.

The rest of the Sentinels attended to the dead, making a pyre for them and leaving a marker of where they fell. I felt the rush of adrenaline leave me and broke out in sobs at their lifeless bodies. The shock of what I just witnessed, seeing them actually die in front of me was too much.

Viggo had me go sit away while they stood and chanted a warrior's verse, ending with the familiar 'May the Valiant Prevail' before lighting the fire.

As I watched the flames dance up into the sky, I snapped out of my haze. If this monster was made from Rhonin using dark magic, then I would need to talk to Tyran. Fast.

I marched with Viggo's Watch, knowing we had four fewer Sentinels coming back with us as twilight spread over the evening sky. There was an edge to our walk home, and I noticed the unease of the Sentinels watching me after they witnessed the magic I could use.

Viggo told me to go straight home, and that he would check in after informing the families of those we lost. He also told me sharply that we would talk about the stunt I pulled being out there alone tomorrow. I knew I probably had that coming.

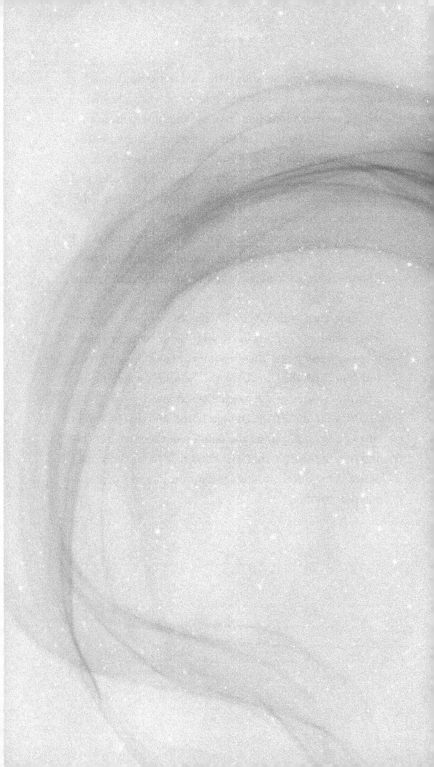

CHAPTER 16

*C*AN WE MEET *somewhere? I need to talk to you, and soon.*

My hand was placed on the handle of my front door, but couldn't bring myself to go inside just yet. I knew I wouldn't be able to sleep until I talked to Tyran, and it didn't seem like this would be easily talked about through our shared magic.

Yes. Do I need to come to you? His response was quieter, like he was far away.

We need to meet out of town. I didn't want to have Tyran in town and run the risk of Viggo finding out that way by seeing us together.

Quarter Moon Village was too far to walk, especially in the dark. It would need to be just far enough outside of town to stay hidden.

How far can you runewalk? I asked.

I can come straight to you. Is everything alright? His response was a little louder.

I'm going to head out of town and have you come to me. I'll explain more then. I said, not waiting for his reply, and headed toward the closest northern gates.

Gaelfall had a wall that surrounded our town, mostly for protection for the importing and exports done to the Red Kingdom, and gates that were regularly patrolled by the Sentinels. I knew I'd have to sneak past them, and hoped keeping the hood of my cloak up would suffice enough as someone passing through the night.

Once past the northern gate of our town, I walked far enough out of view of the guarding Sentinel, and hid in a small outcropping of trees.

A fluttering of wind came from behind, and my shadow magic swirled excitedly as Tyran appeared next to me. I panicked immediately, pushing him into the darkness against the wall, trying to hide him as if he were a shining lantern to be discovered.

"How did you know where I was?" I asked in a hushed tone.

"I followed the shadow magic. I recognize its pull toward you, now."

"We have to find a spot to talk that won't be interrupted by our Sentinels, if they saw me out here my Dad would lose his mind."

"I've got a place." Tyran smiled and placed a rune on the ground.

We stopped at a small village I hadn't visited before. I looked around at the unfamiliar setting and tried to piece where it could be. Dark black wood buildings, like stave churches, rose around us, some only a couple stories, and others stretched higher. I almost thought they were charred buildings in the dark, large posts at their corners, and palisades of wood reached up to support beams to the other levels.

It made me wonder if this place had been attacked and was left abandoned until I noticed the glowing light in the windows of a few of the towering buildings. Taking in more of the village, I noticed the black shingles on the overhanging roofs were glittering like stars under the light of the moon.

"Where are we?"

"Welcome to New Moon Village," Tyran said, as he guided me to the front door of the inn.

The lovely smell of cedar and pine welcomed us, along with a tall, pale man. The tavern was filled with travelers and village locals. Music played while people talked and danced. I knew this place would not be appropriate for what we needed to discuss.

"We'll need somewhere more secluded."

Tyran gave a hint of a smile and nodded.

He asked for a room, and we were led upstairs to one. A large bed with a silky black duvet was placed at the center of one wall. A dresser, desk and chair against the others, all in matching ashen wood.

I dropped down on the foot of the bed and laid back, taking a second to organize my thoughts of what I needed to tell Tyran. I needed to figure out how I could say what I needed to, and make sure he didn't hide what he already knew about this type of weird reanimation or creation that occurred. Tyran leaned back against the shut door, giving me that lazy smile as I looked from the ceiling toward him.

We stared at each other, and my shadows went wild at my drifting thoughts before I realized that I definitely looked like I was expecting something else, and quickly sat back up. The heat in my cheeks appeared quickly, and I let them cool before getting into the conversation. This one would not exactly have a light flirty tone to it. His smile remained on his face as he pushed off the door and walked over to the chair, turning it around to face me. The words took a moment longer to come to me.

"I took down an Abomination today." I said, sounding much blunter than I wanted it to.

"You what?" Tyran stared at me in disbelief for a moment.

"I used my shadow magic…" I trailed off, then decided it was easier to show him than to describe what I had done. I opened my hand and allowed the shadows to shift some space above each of my fingers before turning them into solid spears, like claws floating out of each nail. Darting out into the open space of the room where we sat facing one another. "Except they were much larger, and many more of them."

A look of pure surprise and awe crossed Tyran's face as he watched my spikes move from the solid opaque black to mist, before finally retreating into me. He bit his lip, looking at the ground a moment as he processed it all.

"Why would Rhonin make something like that?" I asked.

Tyran thought for a moment, his eyes searching the ground, "He's got to be setting up something. He's been out of Reapford for the day, and I was checking in with those I trust in the Guard, hoping they knew of his next moves."

I knew it was time to ask him to meet with Bergen and Viggo. To see if he'd actually work with us toward stopping this. The hard part was knowing if he'd go against someone of his kind so openly.

"I think it would be good if you met our Wizard and went over the details we've learned. Working together could help us stop Rhonin before any more lives are lost. We don't know where the bandits are yet, but together I think we have a better chance at stopping them all."

Tyran slowly nodded, realizing that it was our best option. The more we could work together, the better. There was something like sadness in his eyes before he took another breath and cleared it from his expression.

He moved closer, putting his arm around me as I leaned into him. That wonderful smell of citrus and ginger spice nearly had me melting. I knew he was the best link to find the bandits and hopefully end this whole mess that consumed our towns, but the worry of how my mentors would react still lingered. Bergen would understand, but I couldn't get past the hurt it would cause Viggo.

"Tell me again how you took down that Abom," he said playfully as he laid back on the bed.

I sat straighter and turned in his direction, unsure of the closeness and where this all was going. I wanted to follow him, his smell was intoxicating. The bed was soft, and being so close to him again was making me weak. "Have you explored your shadow spells much? What you can do defensively and offensively yet?" I asked, slowly laying on my side next to him, but still keeping conversation our focus.

"I haven't. I've been back at home and around people that I don't know if I can trust with what this is," he said, looking at me then smirking, "Want to train me?"

I hesitated, trying to think of how to approach asking him to train with Bergen and me. "Did you know people were hunted for the magic we carry?" It sounded so out of place, but I needed to know where to begin with explaining to him what little I knew of our shadow magic.

Tyran nearly startled back from the blunt statement of a question. "I hadn't thought of that, but now that you mention it. I guess this is linked to the Originals?"

I nodded. "Bergen will go over the history lesson with you if you'd like. He said that we need to protect this magic, and he helps me with my training. It would be good to have a partner."

"I'm looking forward to it, I guess?" Tyran joked.

I moved up, reclining on my elbow as I took in that beautiful face of his. Assuming things could somehow be smoothed over, I wondered if Bergen would be willing to train Tyran, too. My experience with this shadow magic told me that the power wasn't easily trained beyond what the wielder wanted of it, but we undeniably responded well to sharing the same magic. Maybe honing our skills together could be advantageous. This pull and connection I have with Tyran through our magic was something deep and complex, and I wasn't sure if I'd be able to understand for quite some time.

Tyran moved closer, stroking the loose strands of hair as we laid there in silence feeling the closeness of each other. My heart raced, thinking about being so close to him again, but it was in dreams where we had held each other. I wanted to feel that same touch with him. Here.

"Tell me about your family." Tyran said.

I paused, I guess it was as good of time as any to go into that all. I moved closer to him, succumbing to our magic and his intoxicating features. I loved how his hair nearly glowed in contrast to the dark duvet. He pulled me in closer to him, tucking me under his chin. I wanted to squeak in joy but stifled it thinking of where to begin with my parents, and now Viggo and Endora.

"Viggo is my adoptive father. He is head of the Gaelfall Sentinels. I was three when I was found by a wonderful Witch named Endora, who happened to be the orphanage matron, she still is, but also is a caretaker for me, and mostly Viggo." I smirked, "It was hard, growing up as an orphan. I didn't fit in with the other children, and was the target of a lot of their taunting and abuse." I said, trying to block out the memory of the pain I experienced there.

I could feel a smolder of anger flicker in his body at hearing about the taunting and abuse I sustained.

"By the time I came along into Viggo's life, due to throwing a fireball through the wall of the orphanage…"

"You what?!" Tyran interrupted.

I couldn't help but smile sheepishly, "Yeah, the bullying hit a peak, and it was the first showing of my magic coming in."

"I'm honestly very impressed." he smiled, "Did you ever know your real parents?"

"I barely remember them. Just that they were on the run, and I later learned they were killed the night I was found. We have now realized it was probably because of the shadow magic."

The pain hit my heart. With everything going on, it's been easy to forget about that part of me, but it still was something I yearned to know more about. Tyran had pulled back to look at me, and I thought I would cry at his sweet expression of sympathy.

"I never met my mother. She died giving birth to me." He said softly. "I grew up with my father, who was more concerned about his status and our pure bloodlines, than putting effort and care into raising a son. He's pushed me to do things I can't agree with when it comes to Necromancy. It infuriates him to no end that I won't give in and be his puppet."

His face and those sparkling eyes showed one of shared pain. One of broken families and not having a choice in the matter, and one of wishing it were different.

I loved Viggo. I could never repay him for his unconditional support and affection, but if I would give anything to find my parents alive. I could sense Tyran felt similar about his mother.

"Is that why you spent time in the Guard? To escape your father and his treatment?" I asked.

"Yes." Tyran smirked. "It was more because I had always looked up to the Guard when growing up; seeing their strength and fearlessness when it came to protecting our people and upholding our code. However, it became a good reason to not only escape his relentless push to follow his path, but also to anger him further by seeing the friends I made and the people I chose to hang out with."

I gave him a curious smile, waiting for him to go on.

"He hated that I hung out with Necromancers from lower houses, and that I didn't choose to align with keeping an inner circle of high-status purebloods." Tyran's eyes flashed with enjoyment. "I became fast friends with someone from a lower household, his parents were more than happy to toss him to the Guard when he was eight to have one less mouth to feed at home. The face my father would give every time I invited him over, or trained with him… I think I hoped it would help change my father if he saw our friendship, but that was a naive wish as a child."

Tyran's eyes shifted slightly as he finished speaking. I put my hand on his cheek, only getting slightly nervous after it happened. I wished there was some way I could take those moments of lost hope away from leaving a mark on him, wishing he could have known the love I felt growing up. My nerves finally got the best of me, and I moved my hand away before Tyran grabbed it and held it to his chest.

We stared at each other once more, Tyran brought my hand up to his mouth, giving me a soft kiss on my fingers, "Warn me if you ever plan shooting a fireball in my direction?"

I rolled on my back, laughing as he moved over me, smiling, and kissed me.

I didn't plan on spending the night with Tyran at the inn, but when I woke to sunlight shining over the ashen desk, Tyran's arm was wrapped around me and his warmth pressed into my back while his soft rhythmic breathing let me know he was still sleeping.

We hadn't spoken any more last night after kissing, allowing ourselves to be completely focused on each other through our touch, our movements in sync, and the overwhelming sense of wanting to tip over the edge, and our magic intertwined, seeming to make a commitment that strengthened something between us in that moment. But we restrained ourselves from anything further and took in the moment of our physical touch. It was everything of our shadows meeting in dreams, and so much more. I wanted these moments to stretch for as long as they could, and to give into everything now would be so greedy.

He stirred, lightening the weight of his arm around me when I moved to face him. His bare chest showed the rune tattoos carved in black ink on each of his muscled pecs. I traced my finger on the points of the inner stars and moved along the rings and intricate designs they created. I marveled at seeing them last night in our blur of kissing and removing each other's clothing, but forgot to ask about them when I realized he was about to see me in my underwear as well. Fortunately, that insecurity was shut out quickly by his reaction and I wasn't able to think of much beyond him. They were hauntingly beautiful against his pale skin, and I wondered what meaning they had to him.

Tyran breathed out in a low tone as he woke up. He slowly opened and closed his hazel eyes adjusting to the morning light, and I saw those red flecks of ruby gems in them reflecting the sunlight. That mind-melting lazy smile grew across his lips as he felt my fingers tracing along his tattoos. My heart raced, and he pulled me tighter into him.

He kissed my forehead, and I smiled up at him as we stretched against one another, becoming more aware of our day ahead.

"I don't suppose we could spend another night here before meeting with your friends, could we?" he asked, only half joking.

"Mmm, leaving the room is going to be torture, whether it's today or tomorrow. Sadly, I feel like I might have a search party for me if they don't hear from me this morning," I replied, as a twinge of anxiety hit me, knowing that I hadn't actually returned home when Viggo sent me there. If he checked my room, he'd know I was gone.

"I guess meeting your Dad and staying with you will do. We'll just have to find a way to sneak away," he teased, and my body jolted at the thought of doing half of what we did the night before in the same house as Viggo.

"Oh, we will come back here if that's the case," I said, as we both laughed.

There was something about this moment with him that struck me. Something different from other relationships, then the other intimate encounters either of us have surely had. There was a shift in our touch, the way we looked at each other, the way we connected. Our magic connected deeper than ever, and I was head over heels for him. It soothed and empowered me at the same time. Tyran spoke, as if he were thinking the same things.

"I think I knew in the forest that I wouldn't ever be the same after meeting you," he said while gently moving his fingers up and down my spine. "And I don't think it's the shared magic between us alone that makes me feel that way. You see me in a way that others don't."

"I think I was in denial of my first dreams when I found you. That they weren't telling me of the person I needed to find. After I found you, I think it has been your pure heart that I see that lets me know I'm safe with you." I said.

He pulled me into him, "I will always protect you, Wren."

There was such a truth to his tone, I couldn't look away from him. I knew at that moment I'd protect him if any Sentinel soldier tried to come after him. I would kill them if I had to. I would battle my people to protect him, it was such an odd feeling of truth. It was dizzying, because I wasn't sure if it was just the magic protecting one another or if it was something more.

Being with Tyran would hurt Viggo, but I had to tell him, and I had to try to get him to see the person Tyran was. That he led a group who were trying to keep balance and peace within his people. He was a part of me now, and I wasn't about to spend time apart if it wasn't needed.

I kissed him again, wanting to give in to the temptation of his smell and touch. "I think we need to get dressed before we end up spending all day in here. You have two of the best mentors I know to meet today."

Tyran smiled and watched me slide from the bed. I blushed a little at him, seeing me fully in my underwear again without covers to keep me concealed, and quickly looked for the clothes we threw off around the room.

We walked down to the tavern for breakfast. The cedar and pine still filled the air, and I realized their morning options were incredibly limited compared to what we experienced at the Quarter Moon Inn. We decided against the options available, and I told Tyran we'd have brunch in Gaelfall. Tyran runewalked us back to where we met the night before.

We met two of the Sentinel soldiers at the top steps. There was a flicker of guarded fear in their eyes before they moved back into a steely stare ahead. I nodded at them, but neither would acknowledge me like they usually did any other day that I entered the library.

I cleared my throat, not sure what to say at their reaction as each Sentinel grabbed the handle of the great doors and opened them. I knew that word had either traveled about my shadows or Viggo was on a rampage after I didn't return home.

CHAPTER 17

TYRAN'S GAZE MOVED slowly from the rows of books we walked past up to the architecture of the building; the high cathedral ceilings, the skylights throwing sunlight down towards us, and the ornate carving of the support pillars and beams, many still in a dilapidated state of repair.

Oona hadn't noticed when we entered. She finally looked up as she was going to take a book somewhere, but dropped it on the floor when she saw who I walked in with.

"Hello Oona!" I said, slightly strained, but trying to stay cheerful.

"Wren!" she squeaked out, still frozen and barely breathing.

"It's okay, this is Tyran." I said, hoping it would break her of her shock.

A moment of processing passed, and she snapped from her stare.

"Oh my Stars! Nice to meet you, Tyran! Welcome to the Gaelfall Library. It usually looks much better than this," she said as a large smile spread across her face, then looked back at me again with that same shock. "We need to talk. I heard about what happened yesterday. Your father is looking for you…"

"It was not what I was expecting, but I'm totally okay," I reassured her, not letting the worry show that word had spread of my magic, not to mention Viggo's wrath I'd soon face, then said with a wink, "We can definitely talk more later."

She quickly looked to Tyran, then back to me, and a different type of smile came over her face at what I was possibly getting at. She picked up her book and put it back on the desk, before tucking her hair behind her ears and let us know Bergen was in his office.

"Bergen is our Wizard, and my magic mentor. I want you to meet him first as he's more open to Necromancers, and will definitely be more accepting of your reason for tracking these bandits." I said, only a slight sharpness to the last part, as we walked down the hall. "Well, and as for Viggo, I need to handle him first before I surprise him with you."

"The other mentor is your Dad?" Tyran questioned with wide eyes.

"Well, I don't think I'm considered a Sentinel trainee, but he's as close to a mentor as I have for that sort of training," I said, trying to stifle the sudden shift of anxiety both of us now had.

Tyran collected himself and grabbed my hand, giving it a squeeze of reassurance before we walked inside.

Bergen was sitting at his desk, which was piled with papers and books. Not unusual, but it looked like there were some very old texts I normally didn't see splayed out on its top. His sage green robes were embellished with gold thread and pearls forming into ivy that laced through the trim and edges. His glasses were on, and he had a finger on a line of a book while he pulled at the side of his beard with the other. His staff sat at the corner of the room, the raw crystal that sat into the carved roots glimmered in the natural light that shone through the window. My nerves hit me as the usual view of the training grounds appeared from the window.

I was about to speak when Bergen held up a finger, asking for one last minute as he finished the paragraph he was on. Tyran stayed close to my side, and I wondered if it was because of his own insecurities of being here, or to let me know he was with me. The quiet seemed glaringly loud before it was broken by Bergen.

"I'm glad to see you in one piece, Wren," he started. "You brought a guest, who do we owe the pleasure?"

"It's nice to meet you, I'm Tyran," he said with a slight bow of his head to Bergen.

"Ah, Tyran, I believe Rhonin has a son by that name," Bergen said.

Tyran stiffened and nodded.

Bergen gave a nod of knowing.

I froze, my thoughts escaping me as the questions rose. *Excuse me?*

I was going to tell you last night, but... I couldn't.

Do you even know what this means?! I was already stressed over how to tell Viggo, and now I'd have to factor in that he happened to be the son of the man responsible for our library burnings. My shadows moved with the conflicting emotions that twined in me.

Remember, I'm here and not with him. I'm not on his side, and would never want what he's trying to do. Tyran's gaze met mine as the silence in the room became clear.

Bergen remained calm in that way he does, and I knew I'd have to say something.

"I've brought Tyran here to go over the information that we received from him, as well as something more." I glanced back at Tyran. "We share something. Something you've seen in me, and I think it would be best if we could work together, training our abilities and spells."

Bergen went back to tugging on his beard while he looked at Tyran, as if he was assessing the magic within him. His gaze went far off, the way he does when he is remembering something from a book.

"A Shadow Mage and Shadow Necromancer, of complementary forces. Ones who work together, and not against." Bergen was at a near whisper as he spoke. He paused for a moment again before standing up. "Tyran, if I am correct in my assumption as to who you are, I understand the risk you are taking being here, and I'll be honored to help you both in the mastering of your skills."

"Thank you," Tyran said.

"The head of our Sentinels will need to be made aware so that you can freely enter, Wren, I expect you to escort him while in town and our library to our training space."

"I'll need to talk to Viggo first before anything, and he'll need to hear about what Tyran and his Guard have been working on," I said.

Just as I was finishing speaking, Viggo came into view of the window, stomping down the path towards the entrance of the training grounds. Dust kicked up behind him, and immediate panic shot through me like lightning.

"As a matter of fact, I might have to go meet him now. I didn't turn up for training this morning, and technically didn't go home last night," I quickly said before turning to Tyran. "Stay here in the library. I'll be back"

"Take a seat, Tyran, I'm sure you'll get a front-row view from the window," Bergen said as he sat back down at his desk.

I gave Tyran a light touch on the back of his arm as I ran out to meet Viggo.

Viggo reached the entrance of the training grounds before I caught him. His face was red, as if he had caught a bad sunburn that made his strawberry blonde beard look lighter than usual. I wanted to apologize, but I knew it wouldn't even be the beginning of what I needed to be apologizing for and I had to save those words for what counted most.

"Aye girl! Just where in this damned world have you been?" he yelled. "You want to disobey orders, put your life at risk, then when told to go home, you disappear and don't show up for practice the next day?" He stared at me, and I watched the beads of sweat form on the top of his head and move down his neck.

"I need to tell you something, but I need you to listen to me," I finally said, I needed him to calm down, but what I said only seemed to fuel his fire.

"You went alone into a dangerous situation without getting the full information. You knowingly placed yourself in harm's way, and don't even get me started on the stunt you pulled with those shadow magic spells you used. That was reckless using it the way you did!" he waved his hand around him.

"Dad!" I shouted. "You need to listen to me."

I waited while he breathed a few times, then closed his eye and sighed. Concern hit me that he may have thought I was in danger for showing my shadow magic around his Sentinels.

"I need to apologize to you for what I did yesterday, but I need to apologize for more than that, and I need you to hear me clearly with what I'm about to say," I said softer.

Viggo looked at me, his bright blue eye still held anger, but it had already subsided some.

"I hurt you when I didn't listen to you, and I'm sorry. After I was out there trying to find your group, I thought about the risk I was putting others in, and while I did end up helping you out in the end, I know it wasn't expected or told of me to do, and I'm sorry for that."

I had to take a moment before starting in on what I knew was about to hurt him most.

"I didn't go home last night because I met with the Necromancer I saw in the Hidden Forest the day we were tracking the bandits." His face twisted, but I had to get it all out there. "I saw him for the second time on my journey to Briaroak Village and confronted him to find out what he knew of Rhonin and the bandits. He told me who the bandits are and he agreed to work with us."

Viggo was seething with rage. I could see his hands shaking as he spoke barely above a whisper to me, "They are liars. They will manipulate you and then kill you."

"You hate them because of what happened, and the last thing I want to do is continue to open that wound, but that isn't who they all are." I tried to explain, but he kept shaking his head in disbelief that I would try to defend Tyran. There wasn't a way to even tell him he was Rhonin's son.

"They don't teach dark magic. They prosecute those who do, but something happened and their texts fell into the wrong hands with the bandits, and now they are trying to make things right and find who did this."

He looked back at the training grounds, and I thought for a moment he would tell me to never come back, but he turned and looked at me again.

"Trust me, Dad. If you don't want to trust a Necromancer so readily, trust me in this. Let me have you meet Tyran." I said.

The wind picked up and the formation of rain clouds showed on the horizon, heading our way. Viggo stared at me, trying hard to keep his breathing under control. I knew I didn't have much more left to say if he wouldn't agree to work with us. I knew I might have damaged and hurt him by not telling him about Tyran.

"Wren, I'll trust you. I've watched how you've found a purpose in doing something that matters to you, and I can't deny that." I looked down. Feeling the weight of what he said as he continued. "You are making decisions and doing things based on what feels right to you. Not by hiding, or only relying on the direction of others. You are trusting what's in you. What has always been a part of you."

"It's still hard. To keep myself on that track. To trust myself. I just know what we are doing now, and what we must do, working with Tyran is important. For our town, and for his." I said.

Viggo looked at me in silence long enough to make me uneasy. He wasn't happy with the decision he was making, but he was respecting my asking for trust. "I'm not going to be able to treat that Necromancer with any sort of friendly respect, but I'll meet with you all at the library after lunch."

I could feel my eyes sting with tears. I wanted to hug him, but I knew we would need time to understand the severity of harm this may have caused between us. I could only whisper, "Thank you."

Tyran had been slightly paler than his normal self when I walked back into the library. Bergen had a smile and said how it may have been a little upsetting to Tyran seeing Viggo and me hash it out. Bergen laughed while telling me about how Tyran had offered to go out and assist in the conversation, and I couldn't do more than offer a nervous smile at the imagery that could have occurred. Bergen knew we would be fine, but I felt bad for Tyran having to see the reaction Viggo had to what I told him.

Bergen and Tyran took some time to talk while I decompressed from everything. They went over the formation of his shadow abilities; when he first felt that it was something different. Tyran told him how he thought it was dark magic when he was young and made it a point to keep it fully suppressed. He hadn't felt much from it for years until we met in the forest. They talked about the texts and history they kept in Reapford. Bergen made it known, more than a couple times, that he would love to visit their library to understand them further, but Tyran let him know his father would most likely not be open to it under the current circumstances.

It made me smile to see them get along. Bergen held his position as Wizard of our town for a reason; for his knowledge, and education, but also for his ability to interact and welcome those who wanted to learn more. Seeing this side of him toward others outside of our town made my heart swell. I wanted to hold Tyran's hand and feel that bond between us, to feel what he was experiencing, and let him feel how I did about this moment, but I couldn't work up the courage to do so in front of Bergen.

The door to Bergen's office was shut, and I knew it was probably to keep Viggo from storming down the hall towards us while we ate. We entered to find Bergen at his desk and Viggo standing near the corner of the room behind Bergen. Two more chairs were set in front of Bergen's desk for us.

Viggo kept his back straight, arms crossed over his barrel chest, not meeting my gaze as Tyran and I took our seats. I knew this was hard for him, and it pained me to see him so out of his normal self. Tyran kept his body language cool, nearing the same indifference he had earlier.

"I understand there may be some tension being together in the same room, but I want us to recognize the reason for this and the ability to work together." Bergen began, more diplomatic than I had ever heard him, "Tyran, it is recognized that you are putting your allegiance to your people on the line by involving us in matters that are usually kept within your kind, and Viggo, it is recognized that you are putting aside a distressing past experience and allowing yourself to hear from Tyran's perspective."

"I'm only here to help our people of Gaelfall," Viggo said sharply.

Tyran gave Viggo a return look of indifference before speaking, "My father, Rhonin is responsible for the attacks to the libraries in Briaroak, Gaelfall, and even attempted to cover his tracks by attacking our own in Reapford."

I saw Viggo react to the new information of Tyran's relationship, and hoped he would stay against the wall.

"He has reanimated the Butchers of Drog, who have been leading the attacks and is looking for what we believe to be an obelisk to help him control Aura in a way that could harm the people of Caldumn, but I'm not sure what he plans to do beyond that.

"It means that your kind can't be trusted," Viggo started, but Bergen raised his hand to silence him.

"I am not your enemy. We aren't the enemy. I am choosing to be open to you about everything with the offer to work together and make this stop," Tyran said, but it only seemed to further enrage Viggo.

"Do we know if he's obtained the obelisk?" Bergen asked, raising his voice enough to end what could have started.

"My contact in the Guard doesn't believe he has that yet. He wanted a group to head toward the Warlock

Camp, to scout out their town, and it didn't sound like he was pleased with what they returned with." Tyran said.

Bergen sat back in his chair thinking for a moment. "It's becoming more clear what we'll have to do. The Red Kingdom needs to be warned of what Rhonin's plans are."

"Do they have obelisks there?" I asked.

"The Red Kingdom will have their own relics and obelisks from the Warlocks that reside to the north. If Rhonin didn't find what he was after in the Warlock Camp here, then he will be heading up to them to get what he's after."

"I've sent word to those I trust in the Guard, and they will let me know when they see Rhonin on the move." Tyran said.

Before Viggo had the chance to respond with some more angry accusations and words, Bergen spoke. "It appears we are at a good stopping point, we can figure out more as Tyran receives more information from his Guard."

I quickly agreed, standing up and opening the door behind us to give the room a fresh renewal of air. Tyran stood, adjusting his jacket, and told Bergen he would get back to us as soon as they knew more. He stared at Viggo, not saying anything before turning to the door. I looked back at Viggo as well, following Tyran out the door, and saw his anger lessen when he met my gaze.

The rain lightly fell as we left the library through the side door. My stomach twisted at the thought of Tyran leaving so soon, and remaining quiet made me uneasy. Tyran's hazel eyes looked darker than I had seen them, as he thought through everything he just laid out before Bergen and Viggo. He really had opened himself up so much, and now he had to trust someone who hated him and his people.

I laced my fingers into his as I said, "I'm thinking Mages aren't necessarily welcome in Reapford, and I don't think your father would be pleased with you walking hand in hand with one, either."

"I have a habit of breaking the pure blood expectations my father tries to keep," he said, letting a small smile slip at my attempt to change the mood. "But no, my town wouldn't just gawk at an outsider, and I don't want to cause more of an issue than what is about to rock them once they find out who is breaking our code."

Tyran gave a pained look before sighing at his admission of guilt. I felt our magic tugging at one another as we kept walking through town. I wanted to help him feel better, and I wanted to show him where I lived before heading to the nearest gates for him to runewalk home.

"Do you ever go to the coast?" Tyran asked.

"Not usually. I'm not really a fan of the sand and smell." I smirked.

"The ships have to be something to see."

I shrugged. "Sometimes I can see them through my window, but only the large ones with the tall sails."

Tyran gripped my hand tighter and moved me closer to him as we walked toward the road leading home. I nearly talked myself into inviting him inside, but I knew that would just make it harder for me to let him leave.

Very few people regularly traveled to the eastern entrance to our town, as most of the buildings here were homes and farmland. It was refreshing to walk together without any stares or whispers. We finally stopped just past the gates beyond where the Sentinels stood watch. I pulled myself into him, hugging his strong frame into mine, smelling him, and wishing he could stay. I listened to his steady heartbeat as he kissed the top of my head.

Let me know if you need company in that bath, tonight.

Wicked Necromancer. I sweetly shot him as I tilted my face towards his.

I'll see you in our dreams, my Dark Star. He kissed me as he spoke.

I watched as he took a few steps away and gave me his heart-melting smile as he cast a rune at his feet and was gone.

CHAPTER 18

"Let's start light and first see what you've learned to do, then move on from there." Bergen said, and we began our magic training.

The dimly lit room of the basement in the library still had a faint hint of smoke smell to it as we stood on the threadbare rug I had so many times before, only this time, Tyran was next to me. The stone walls kept the chill in the space, and I pulled my jacket tighter around me before starting.

My shadows moved easily from me as they wrapped around my body in twists and turns of inky smoke. I kept them close to my body, watching Tyran. My shadows begged and pleaded to be closer, touching him. I watched as the shadows slowly crept from Tyran's hands, moving up around his forearms of the jacket he was wearing, as if they were exploring their outside world without the support of mine for the first time. Tyran kept his gaze on his tendrils of mist as they continued up his arms and around his impressive chest.

We moved on to creating a barrier with our shadows, allowing it to form around us and protect us like a dark barely transparent shield. We each took turns, and Bergen would use his staff to send a shockwave in our direction to see if the shield would hold. The more we worked on it and became comfortable, the easier it was for the shadows to become translucent.

From the shielding, we went to work on shadow cloaking ourselves, and I smiled at the memory of when I first showed Tyran our magic, allowing my fingers to go transparent as he watched. I stood to the side as he moved his shadow tendrils around and watched as they consumed him slowly until he was a figure of shadow exactly as in our dreams, then they billowed into transparency.

As we trained, Tyran showed such an increase in his power and ability. He picked up naturally on his shadow magic and it easily bent to his will. Satisfied with our work, Bergen moved us along to begin our defensive abilities. I shot my solid shadow spears into the empty wooden crate, shattering the planks.

Tyran's defensive spell was much different. His shadows formed a circle around his target, much like the runes I've seen him cast, and the flickers of smoke rose high, while a sound of shrieks came from the shadows. I felt a gravitational shift at the center of his spell. A broken chair shook in the middle of the rune as particles of matter formed into solid skulls, swirling around, shredding and chipping away at the wood. I shuddered at the howling noise that continued until he called his shadows back.

We ended our training by talking about any news from the Necromancer front, which wasn't much yet. Tyran spoke of his friend, Gunnar, who was keeping tabs on Rhonin's whereabouts and had only heard of him sending a messenger owl out, which very well could have been for the north.

We both were pretty spent on our magic, but took some more time talking with Bergen about what happened when I used my magic defensively. I still felt that deep thrumming of a magic so powerful that it scared me to think of what it would look like unleashed. We planned to work on methods of emotional control and what forms we could bend the shadow into for protection and defense.

The days wore on, and training continued. Viggo warmed back up to me after a short time, and we were back to sparring and bantering between each other with the added bite that my shadow spells freaked him out. He didn't ask about Tyran much, if at all, and I didn't bring the Necromancers up when training beyond any news that needed to be shared.

Tyran and I spent as few nights as we could apart. Any time we had to be separate we communicated with one another through our magic link and nearly crashed into one another in our dreams. The man was not only gorgeous, I couldn't get over the features of his face, his strong body, but his heart was pure. The moments he took to help animals cross over to avoid pain at death, even the

Ursendir. What I realized I loved was who he was at his core. For some crazy reason, he chose me to open his heart to and shower me with his affection.

Endora was aware of my lessened presence at home and requested that she meet this man, eventually. I had to not only prepare Tyran for that but prepare myself for it as well. I was nearly twenty, and it wasn't like I was too young to not make these decisions, but I still respected her wishes for me.

After a few exchanged messages with Agatha, Bergen gathered us to go over our next steps.

"We're going to the Red Kingdom," he said, as he laced his fingers together in front of him.

The crisp air of the day and lingering threat of more rain felt nice after our magic training that day. Viggo met us outside of the library, standing together on the dormant grass, I pulled the petals off a late-blooming marigold as Bergen spoke.

"I've sent an owl. Turns out cats don't like climbing mountain sides, and rams had a high chance of eating the attached parchment," He said with a wry smile. "They've allowed us to visit. I've included you, Tyran, if you'd join us."

"I would like that, thank you." Tyran said.

Viggo snorted, still not able to fully speak to Tyran yet.

"Are we sailing there?" I asked, a little worried about what it would be like on a ship.

"Fortunately, no. I have it on good authority that one of the ancient lifts that we thought had been destroyed long ago is still in working order beyond the Warlock

Camp. We have been granted access to use it." Bergen smiled, "I've always wanted to go on an adventure to the north."

Tyran and I walked down the steps of the library into the cold air of the now dark night. I wrapped my arms around my sides as Tyran pulled me close to him as we walked. I didn't want him to go. He was supposed to head back to Reapford and pack, spending the night before returning. My heart was still pounding at what we were about to do, and I couldn't bear the thought of him spending the night away.

"Stay with me tonight?" I asked.

"At your home?" "I know you have to pack and talk to Gunnar and the Guard, but could you come back?"

Tyran looked back at me with a smile in his eyes and gave me a squeeze of approval at my request. My heart settled into a flutter of happy calm as I kept myself tucked in under his arm. He lightly kissed me before saying he'd return soon, and runewalked back to Reapford.

I nearly skipped through the door of the cottage and didn't even know where to begin to prepare him for meeting Endora. Viggo said he would be spending the night at the Sentinel camp, going over our plans for tomorrow, and while she wasn't expecting him, I knew she wouldn't say no to the opportunity.

Endora was in the kitchen and immediately eyed up Tyran when I opened the door to his gentle knock. Necromancer or not, she wanted him to know she'd be watching him, and his intentions with me closely. Tyran was polite and respected her weariness.

We ate dinner together in front of the fire and Endora loosened up as the night went on, seeing how happy I was with Tyran here. He was also earning points for being a perfect gentleman towards Endora while she pelted him with questions on how we met and what he did in Reapford. He even entertained her questions about his father and what he thought about him spending so much time away.

When it got late enough, and she realized I wasn't about to send him back to his town, she laid down the ground rules.

"You sleep on the couch, and so help me, Tyran, if I hear you lumber your big muscly self up those stairs at any time of the night, I'll be at Wren's door in a flash." Endora threatened, and we took her word for it.

She brought an extra set of blankets down and a pillow for him and let us stay downstairs to say goodnight.

I pulled the blanket up around us and settled into him on the couch. "Thank you for staying. I know it won't be the most comfortable night, but I'm happy you're here."

"You know, Endora might be someone we can use against the bandits with that look she gives," Tyran said, and I laughed.

"I'd rather not know what sort of wrath she can unleash when angry enough," I said, shaking my head at him.

The fire popped and crackled as we enjoyed the quiet together. I couldn't help but think about what it would be like actually heading to the north, and visiting the Red Kingdom. From the history lessons and stories, it was a large place with all magic kinds living together. But even as wonderful as that sounded, it came with its own set of problems. One being their fanatical devotion to Ismael, one of the Originals who they believed would return. Worshiped like a god, and yet Tyran and I carried that shadow magic they worshiped him for, and yet hunted the lines down because they came from Jareth and Marion. They saw Jareth and Marion, the other Originals, as murderers responsible for stopping the grace they believed Ismael was trying to bring to the people.

"What do you think it'll be like in the Red Kingdom?" I finally asked.

Tyran let a long breath out as he moved me into his lap, tucking me under his chin.

"I think it'll make me grateful for the freedom we have where we live."

I thought about what Agatha said, of wanting to secede. "Has Reapford ever thought about separating from the Red Kingdom?"

"I don't think we could even if we wanted to. Not with the control Rhonin has at the moment."

"What do you think they would do if they saw our magic?"

"I don't want to begin to entertain the thought of that," Tyran let out a soft chuckle that vibrated in his chest. I melted more into him. "It would be dangerous no matter if they worshiped the magic or saw us as a threat."

I nodded.

I made every effort to go upstairs to bed later that night after spending as much time as I could with him before I knew Endora would be huffing and puffing at her open door. I changed into a sleek nightgown and brushed my teeth before closing my door. Within a few minutes, Endora had closed the guest room, too. I tried to sit on my bed, but that pull to be with him when he was so close was enough to drive me crazy, and it wasn't from the magic.

I slowly opened my door so that it wouldn't creak and tiptoed down to Tyran, where he laid on the already too small couch for his large frame. I slipped under the blankets and he pulled me in between the couch and him, holding me close. I breathed him in and slowly stroked at the silver hair that fell around his face as we fell asleep in each other's arms.

CHAPTER 19

A N EXASPERATED SIGH from Endora woke me as she came downstairs to see us asleep on the couch. I sheepishly smiled and got up as Tyran stirred and went back to sleep. Whether he truly was sleeping heavily, or secretly knew what was going on and didn't want to wake up to the look Endora was giving, I didn't blame him. I tiptoed into the kitchen and she gave me another warning look, but didn't say more about it.

We quietly worked together to make a breakfast of oatmeal and fresh berries. I also cooked eggs, knowing Tyran would probably have eaten a pot of oatmeal himself, and figured some additional protein was welcomed by him. Endora sat at the table after serving herself some oatmeal and lightly drizzled it with honey.

"You know your father would burn that couch if he knew Tyran stayed the night. I think it wise for us to keep that between us." Endora whispered.

I could feel the heat rise in my face, "Thanks. I know it's hard to accept him, but he truly is different."

"He certainly has manners," she said with a smile.

Tyran began to stir. His arms stretched up, and I watched as he slowly sat up, looking at us from the back of the couch with a sleepy look on his face. Endora couldn't help but chuckle at his grogginess and shook her head.

"Come get some breakfast. Eggs, oatmeal, and fruit," she called to him as she rose from the table and put her empty bowl in the sink to rinse.

Tyran lightly kissed the top of my head and sat next to me as Endora dished up a large plate of the eggs and oatmeal for him. The sweet smile he gave Endora as he gladly accepted the platter nearly made me fall off my chair as she patted his shoulder and walked to grab her things to head out for the day. Before she left, she gave us the same warning glance as last night, letting us know we were also to be quick to get moving on with our day.

"I'm thinking her serving me breakfast and giving me a pat is a good sign?" he said, taking a bite of eggs.

"It's something, that's for sure." I said with a shrug, still fighting the urge to throw myself at him.

As we walked quietly to the library in the chilly morning, I thought about my birthday nearing, and just what I'd want to do to celebrate. The same night of the Aurarius Lights, where golden stars rained down from the sky. Even when I didn't have much of a celebration in the orphanage, I always thought that the sky was at least celebrating my day.

I was looking forward to spending it with Tyran for the past couple weeks, and thought that we could go to the New Moon Village where it was so dark, and the stars so bright, to watch it. Now, though, I wasn't sure we wouldn't be in the middle of hunting down bandits. At least I'd be with him.

Bergen met us at the entrance of the pathway to the Sentinel training grounds, waiting for Viggo to join us. The sun offered some welcoming warmth, knowing that the higher elevation meant that we would have much cooler temperatures.

"I wonder if we'll see snow." I said to no one in particular.

"I'd like to not, if that's alright with you," Bergen smiled. "Even with a large cloak, robes are not ideal for cold temperatures."

I stuck close to Tyran, and saw Viggo start down the path.

"Tyran, would you mind using that rune ability of yours to get us to the outskirts of the Warlock Camp?" Bergen asked once Viggo met with us.

"I'm not allowing him to touch me." Viggo snapped.

Tyran sighed, but didn't say anything.

"Dad, it'll take days for you to get to us, allow for this just once. It's really not bad."

Viggo grunted, and I realized it would be the closest we'd get to him agreeing.

Bergen spoke quietly to Tyran, "Take Viggo first so he can calm down by the time we all get there."

Within a moment, a rune was placed on the ground and glowed in a now familiar green and purple hue. The light reached up and shimmered in the dust that kicked up from the soft whoosh of air as Tyran grabbed Viggo and they disappeared.

My heart raced at the passing time, hoping that the two of them weren't fist fighting, or worse, before even making it to our destination. Tyran returned unharmed only a minute later, and I let out a small sigh of relief. Bergen went next, and then Tyran came back for me.

When we arrived, the immediate smell of soft floral and fresh pine filled me. I looked toward the mountains we were now incredibly close to.

"The Great Northern Sierras are simply spectacular," Bergen commented as he gathered his pack and began walking, "Come, the Warlocks know we will be traveling close to their lands, and won't bother us. It should only be a few hours' walk."

We followed a worn path until the trees became denser, blocking the view before us until we came into a clearing.

"Holy smokes." Viggo spoke his first words since we arrived.

I smiled. "Same thought."

The ancient lift before us was enormous.

"How old do you think this is?" I asked

"Over a thousand years? Honestly, I'm having second thoughts." Viggo said with a nervous laugh.

"Oh hush. The lift is constructed of fossilized wood along with Aurasteel. It's nearly indestructible." Bergen said as his pace picked up, more excited to check out the massive contraption.

We entered the large wood ramp that led to the base of the lift. The lift itself could easily hold twenty or more comfortably. Large chains rose from the pulley and wheels that allowed for movement. A series of large carved stones used as weights were hanging at various heights, linchpins keeping them in place.

Bergen started to pull at the pins, as a loud creaking noise shuddered through the sheer mountainside. The pulleys and wheels sprang to life, squeaking and spraying off dust and dirt that had long since caked them from lack of use.

I jumped back at the sudden movement, grabbing around Tyran's waist as if I could somehow pull us to safety if it collapsed.

"I should be the one protecting you," he laughed.

"I don't know if I can do this." I said, tucking my head into his back.

Viggo came over to my side, "Aye, girl. You're a fighter. Remember that, besides, we'll need you to shield us in your shadowy webs if we fall."

"I'm really not one for joking right now." I groaned. "Is it too late to take a boat?"

Viggo chuckled and moved up toward Bergen. That moment had my heart jumping for a different reason, however. Viggo had actually looked at Tyran while laughing at the moment, and didn't shift to a glare. It was small, and could easily be brushed away as nothing, but to me, it meant everything.

We'd been ascending for thirty minutes before I made the poor choice to look over the edge of the large platform we stood on, letting out a shriek at the height we had climbed.

"I told you not to look!" Viggo laughed as I stumbled back to the middle of the platform.

I shivered, partly because of the height, and the other of the cold that surrounded us at this height next to the mountains. Tyran rubbed the sides of my arms as I stayed close to him.

"The mist below has practically wiped out the view of the forest," I finally spoke, realizing this was much too high for my liking, "The Red Kingdom can stay up here."

A different kind of shriek from my own rang through the air.

A dark outline appeared, quickly growing in size as the creature flew toward us at an alarming speed. Wings of a dragon. Scaled and leathered. The head and tail were of a predatory cat, with a mane of fur, and its body was more of a mountain ram, with hooved back legs and large, taloned front arms.

"What in all that is blessed is that thing?" I exclaimed.

"Chimaera." Tyran quickly said before the creature blew out a breath of fire.

My shadows swirled into a near-transparent shield, keeping the fire from touching us as it dived toward us. Tyran had his shields up just as quickly as mine, and Viggo pulled a sword from his back.

The beast tore through the sky, setting up for another attack as we continued to move upward. I quickly checked just how close we were to the top, and noticed we still had quite a distance to go.

"Why does something so beautiful have to be so deadly?" I gasped, as the Chimaera soared back in our direction.

"I'm not willing to see if we can tame it." said Viggo as he parried a swipe from it.

Tyran sent out green bone spikes in its direction, while Bergen launched an attack with his staff, blasting a concentrated boom of air toward it. The beast dodged the blastwave, but was hit with a bone spike in its side. It called out angrily at the slow penetrating shard that continued to dig deeper. The beast dove below the platform, and we lost sight of it.

"Did you harm it that bad?" I asked.

"I didn't think so." Tyran said, "One shouldn't have been fatal, and they only go so deep before dissipating."

I considered nearing the edge to peer over, but it would have been a poor decision to do so. The beast sailed up from where I would have looked, tearing at the wood of our platform before landing with shocking force where we were trapped.

It swiped at us with its sharp talons, and Viggo's blade met it with its attack. The beast growled, but its talons were strong, and weren't cut through. Shadowy tendrils moved out from behind me, as I weaved them out around the creature's arms and legs before solidifying them into shackles. The beast cried out in shock as I twisted the shadows, causing it to fall on its side.

The beast bared its teeth and flapped its strong wings against being held down before Viggo moved on it, bringing his blade up over my head to deliver a death blow.

"NO!" I shouted.

Viggo stopped immediately at hearing the pain in my voice.

"Please! I won't be able to get over killing it and having its body left on the lift like this." I begged. I wasn't sure where my empathy was coming from, but the Chimaera was such a stunning creature.

"Wren. This thing will kill us if we don't first." Tyran tried to reason.

"Trap it. Please, anything. It's too beautiful." I knew I couldn't keep my shadow spells in the open, we had talked so much about keeping them hidden, especially from the Red Kingdom.

Tyran nodded and placed a rune of entrapment, much like the one I saw him use on the Ursendir. I breathed a sigh of relief, as I slowly pulled my shadows back.

The Chimaera hissed, and slowly returned upright, attempting a lunge against the wall of Tyran's rune. A growl of frustration escaped low in its throat as it sat back in a defensive position, watching us with wild feline eyes.

"What do we do now?" Viggo asked

"We'll need to release it when we can get far enough away from the lift." Bergen thought aloud.

"You have a lot of faith in my magic." Tyran. said, while giving me a half-joking smile.

"What is the Red Kingdom going to think when we arrive with a Chimaera trapped?" I almost laughed.

Viggo shrugged, and I couldn't help but hug him and shake my head at how ridiculous this would look to anyone we come across once we reach the top. I hoped they wouldn't see it as a threat. I looked up and saw the top of the lift coming closer in view.

A tense remainder of our climb into the north later, and the lift came to a slow before finally stopping. We hadn't talked much, mostly staring at the beast as it grumpily growled at any movements we made.

"As odd as it is, this Chimaera really is fascinating to watch. I understand what made Wren hesitate in wanting us to kill it." Bergen said with a soft chuckle.

"I need you to head into the trees before I remove the rune." Tyran said, as I noticed the weeping pines that blanketed the edge of the rocky peaks. "Hide in there and don't come out until it's long gone."

"You better be right behind us, or you know I'll be coming to help you." I warned.

I took in the rest of the lands that lay before us. The peaks of the mountain we just ascended gently rolled into a grassy field with pine trees gathered in small clumps of shelter. It was cold, and frost still clung to the shadows as I looked around for anyone who might be waiting. We were the only ones that I could see before my focus returned to watching Tyran set the Chimaera free.

As we moved off the lift, I couldn't help but inch closer to the beast still within the trap. Its gaze remained wild, but I could almost see a hint of fear behind it.

"It's beautiful." I gasped.

"Wren, you will be the death of me, I swear." Tyran chided.

Viggo lightly guided me away from it by placing his hands on my shoulders, "This way you creature sympathizer." I noticed he and Tyran looked at one another again with the briefest of friendly gestures. My heart leapt.

As soon as we made it to the treeline, and tucked into the drooping branches of the pines, Tyran lifted the rune spell that kept the creature trapped. The Chimaera rose and stared at us, deciding if it should continue its hunt or escape with its life. I felt Tyran's hand lightly touch along my back as he stepped into the treeline to meet us while we watched the creature stretch its wings. I could swear it gave us a nod as if relinquishing its attacks, and took off back into the sky, diving into the air below the craggy peaks we stood on.

"I don't think he'll be as forgiving on our way down. Let's hope we don't meet again." Bergen said.

"Noted," I said, and turned to investigate the unfamiliar territory we stood on. "How far is the Red Kingdom?"

"I would have thought they would be here to greet us." Bergen said, looking around.

"Maybe we scared them away by bringing the beast along with us," Viggo smirked.

Before I could turn to smile at him, darkness surrounded us. I reached out and felt Tyran's hand for a brief moment before it was ripped from mine. A soft gasp escaped my mouth and I yelled out for Tyran, Viggo, anyone. Hands came over my face, and I tried to fight off what took me from behind, only to be met with a starry deep black and lost all ability to move.

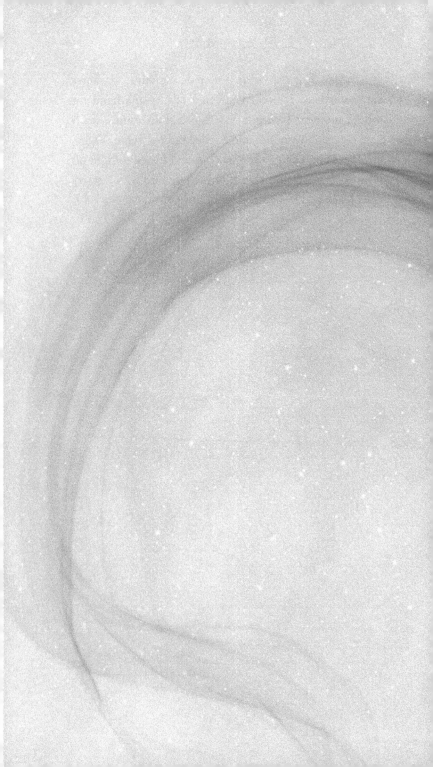

CHAPTER 20

Dark spots still lingered as I blinked a few times to the light that filtered in from the cover over my face. I could hear the chuffing of an animal that carried us along on what seemed to be a cart or open carriage. I reached my hands out and felt someone's leg, and their hand met mine. It was Viggo I quickly recognized.

Are you awake? Tyran's voice called.

Yes. Who are they? I tried to reach out with my other hand and felt the wooden side of the cart.

I wasn't able to see them before they covered my face. I can't use my magic. He sighed.

"What is the reason for this?" Bergen's voice rang out, "We come on the invitation of the Red Kingdom. Release us at once. Remove the magic dampening spell, immediately!"

I tried to create a fireball in my palm, and could feel the sluggish resistance to it appearing. It felt as though I was trying to light something through thick mud. I moved my hand up and felt for the cover over my face. It was magic as well. I could feel my features as if nothing were there.

Viggo released his hand from mine, and I could feel him slowly move away. The wheels of the cart that carried us creaked to mask his movements from anyone who wasn't watching.

Suddenly, there was a loud thud and someone shouted out. I could hear armor clinking together, Viggo was attacking someone blindly. A new voice called out.

"You deserved that. You weren't paying attention to them. Get that warrior back up there."

I listened more and tried to make out how many were around us by their footsteps. At least four, maybe more. Viggo struggled against the ones that pushed him back into the cart.

"I'll do it again! You've made a death wish, and I'll see to serving it out!" He threatened.

"You'll do no such thing. As guests of the Red Kingdom, it would be your death wish to assault a soldier of the King." The voice boomed. He sounded old, and something radiated from it that felt different. Dangerous.

"I am Bergen, Wizard of Gaelfall. Please remove our shrouds and we will do no harm"

The shroud dissipated around our faces, and I squinted to adjust to the light before searching for Tyran. He moved quickly from the front of the cart to meet me when we saw one another. Bergen sat near the front, adjusting his robes and Viggo was nearby quickly taking in the number of Red Kingdom soldiers that were marching beside us.

I looked back up to the front and saw the familiar dark fur of the creature that pulled us, and nearly dove into Tyran's arms.

"That's an Ursendir." I startled back in shock, trying to escape being so close.

"It is. Hell of a time domesticating them." One of the Red Kingdom soldiers next to me responded.

I paused, slowly looking back at the Ursendir, harnessed and lumbering along with the soldiers at its sides.

"Absolutely awful way to treat a guest." Bergen mumbled.

"Yes, well. We don't take lightly to warnings, even if they are coming from the visitor. Can't be too careful." The dangerous voice spoke again.

I looked over Tyran's shoulder and saw him. He was a Wizard, wearing crimson velvet robes that matched the capes of the soldiers. Ornate designs were embossed around his cuffs and collar. When I looked up beyond his faded sandy brown beard, I nearly gasped. I thought his eyes were a shade of violet, before he blinked and they went to a deep blue. My eyes must have still been adjusting, I thought.

His smile sent chills down my spine as he met my gaze. "Hello, I am Gerald, the Red Kingdom's and King's personal Wizard."

The Kingdom came into view after an uncomfortably quiet remainder of our travels. Its large fortress walls of stacked stone carried upward nearly as tall as our own library. As we arrived at the iron gates, a birdcall was made and a loud thud echoed before the doors started to open.

I always thought there would be something so awe-inspiring or magical at seeing this place, but it felt dark. The gray stone walls were heavy. The guards and soldiers all stood watch as if anyone could become an enemy. Even the townspeople that milled about were scurrying past, staying low and keeping themselves covered in linen cloaks and hoods.

Mud and dirt and shabby buildings were all I could see as we moved toward the stables and exited our cart.

This isn't anything like I imagined. I said

I have a feeling we are in the lower sectors. The poor and those who the Kingdom doesn't necessarily benefit from.

I looked at Tyran. It hurt to think that people weren't cared for in the way we took care of our own in Gaelfall. We ran things in a manner that uplifted and supported one another. Not to push away and hide those that suffered. It made my stomach turn.

As we were escorted through the Kingdom I noticed how things changed. The buildings went from being run down and shabby to clean and stately. The people dressed more elegantly. They paraded through the streets in gowns and dress tunics, and pants, along with fur lined capes to keep warm.

The inner castle walls were heavily guarded, and another set of gates put us in the King's courtyard. The gardens were immaculate, and roses bloomed in the cool temperatures. Topiaries and soft gray cobbled paths meandered through the lovely landscape.

"Come, you'll be meeting the King in the Great Hall." Gerald said as he ushered us up the large steps to the large wooden doors.

The castle loomed high above us, taller than any building I'd ever seen. The bossed stone walls stretched up with corbels and other carved filigree. Arched windows were adorned with beveled leaded glass designs, and large crimson banners hung down from the tops of the castle's various elevations.

The inside was just as large, with marbled floors and the continuation of intricately carved archways and support pillars. Long rugs of the same red led us up to a dais with a throne that was more elaborately carved than I could have imagined. Everything about this place that I thought would hold wonder, just hadn't. It made me want to support seceding from their reign even more than ever.

Gerald walked up the dais and stood to the side of the great throne, making his tall figure look small in comparison. "Please bow to the ruler of Caldumn, King Tormond."

I looked up from the curtsey bow I held as the footsteps came closer. The man that entered was almost as chilling as the Wizard, Gerald.

King Tormond wore a large fur cape, and was adorned in the signature crimson velvet of matching tunic and pants. He held sharp features with a strong pointed nose and dark, piercing eyes I would hate to have staring me down. He was pale, looking more unhealthy than a natural color for him. Dark hair curled around his crown and just past his ears as he sat at his throne, watching as we held our bows.

"Rise," he spoke. "Who is the one responsible for the message sent?"

"I am, your highness." Bergen said, standing tall.

"Speak, Bergen of Gaelfall. What threat do you warn of from the South?"

"The south of Caldumn has been experiencing attacks on our libraries and stealing of important texts from a Necromancer by the name of Rhonin. We believe he is after an item that will cause great harm to the lands and the people of Caldumn if he isn't stopped."

"And what is this item he's after?" The King said, leaning forward in his chair.

"We believe it to be an obelisk. Something that can harness Aura, and we've learned that the Warlocks in your Kingdom hold the one that can do just that." Bergen clasped his hands together in front of him, "We are concerned that Rhonin, after scouting out the Warlock's Camp and not finding it there, will make an effort to steal the one you have."

King Tormond glanced over to Gerald, something exchanging in that glance, before turning back to us. "I see. Tell me Bergen, what makes you think we need the warning? What makes you think that the Red Kingdom would have a weakness in place, where Rhonin could steal our obelisk?"

Bergen opened his mouth to speak, but words didn't form.

"It appears you have a few cracks down there in the South. I've given you my trust in allowing our trade without more of my armies stationed in your towns. You might not protect that which you should in the manner that we handle things here in the Kingdom, but I can assure you, no one can steal anything from us."

Gerald held a smirk, "It appears the distance from the Red Kingdom has made you forget just how powerful we are. Which is another reason for showing you our power while we escorted you here. No one would think to cross us."

I could feel my brows furrow, and quickly smoothed my expression, not wanting to cause an issue, but the undertone of dismissiveness stung, along with the jabs at not being able to protect our libraries and texts that were taken. I could see Viggo tense next to Bergen, feeling the passive insults as well.

"With much respect, your highness, we know you are well equipped and protected, but I know my father, and he won't let guards, or gates keep him away." Tyran said, and I startled at his voice, "Rhonin has been using dark magic, reanimating the Butchers of Drog to burn and capture what he needed in the South."

The King's attention rose at Tyran, "The son of the accused? This doesn't bode well for how things are being run in Reapford at all."

It was then Tyran's turn to open his mouth, and unable to come up with a response.

The King let out a light scoff, "I'm going to look past this warning, and not punish you all for the waste of time you've put my Kingdom through. If anything, it sounds like you may need some assistance from us down south, not the other way around. Do I need to worry about our imports being at risk now?"

I felt my anger as heat rose from my gut up to my ears.

"We'll be able to take care of ourselves and your continued taxes," Viggo snipped. "Our Sentinels are ready for any advancing attacks, land or sea. We will handle what comes our way without help."

King Tormond stared at Viggo for a moment, "I do hope you'd be ready for any storm that is forming." But before Viggo could respond to the blatant threat, he smiled, "Come now, I am not only your King, but your host for the evening. You've journeyed far, and I offer you stay within our castle before returning home. Make yourselves comfortable. I will have my people show you to your rooms."

With that, Gerald had us bow and the King left.

The castle was cold. Heat seemed to escape quickly even when sconces of torches illuminated the walls. I walked with Tyran down the hallway from our dinner that evening. The King hadn't joined us, and we were only momentarily checked in on by Gerald. It made it clear that we were definitely being given more welcome than they wanted to have us here.

The pork roast and vegetables smelled divine, and I may have had a meal alone in the soft buttered bread rolls, which left those uneasy thoughts of the king to fall into the back of my mind. As we moved into the corridors that led us to our bedrooms, a series of paintings caught my eye.

Three shrouded figures, the largest in the center, wearing a crown, while the other two bowed at his feet. A sword and scythe were crossed over one another between them. I noted the small placard below titling the painting: *Praise be to He who is Immortal.*

The next painting was of the same figures, but of the two who bowed now were upon the third, piercing its heart with the sword, the other mid-swing with its scythe. The placard titled: *The Betrayal.* I grimaced at the way the painting showed the waterfall of blood pouring from his wounds.

The final painting in the series showed the middle one larger than before floating and illuminated in light, as the other two were on their knees caught in a freeze frame of being torn apart from the power that emanated from the third. Its title: *The Rebirth of Ismael.*

"Oh. Wow," I said, "These are the Originals."

Tyran came to my side, "They don't like Jareth and Marion?"

"They betrayed Ismael. The one who found them and offered them immortality." Gerald's voice came from behind us.

I started as I whirled around quickly to see him watching us from an alcove.

"Let me tell you the real story of the Originals."

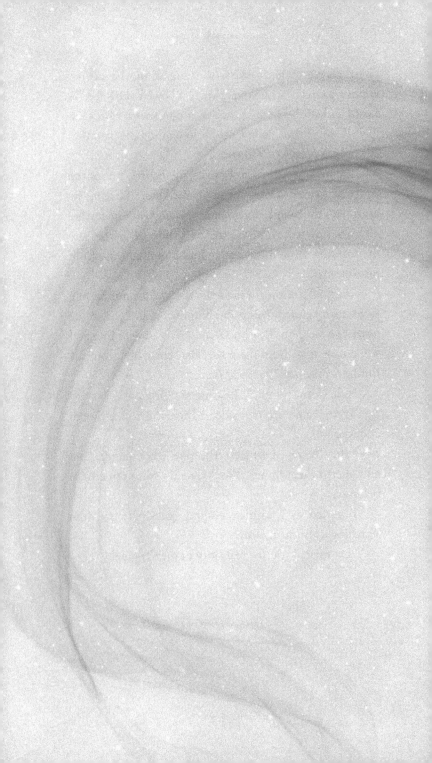

CHAPTER 21

CCOUR RECORDS BEGIN with one of pure shadow magic. A gift that appeared through divine intervention. Ismael's history was the first recorded. A hundred years later, there are records of two more. Marion and Jareth appeared with that of pure shadow magic. It is unknown if they were born of it, or gifted. Ismael felt their presence, and sought them out, forming the three Originals." Gerald slowly moved to our side next to the paintings, "When the three Originals began their reign, they ruled together as equals. They helped to establish our relationship with Aura, and through that fostering, we established our different magic kinds."

I knew of that part, and nodded, unsure if this would be another repeat lesson, but something in these paintings told me his view was quite different from our versions.

Gerald began to walk, beckoning us with him to a pedestal that held an empty parchment laid out flat. He waved his hand over it and a map of Caldumn appeared.

Of what Caldumn was before the Red Kingdom established the southern territories as they were now. Our towns hadn't existed. It was a feeling of familiarity and yet so unknown seeing it so different. I leaned in, wanting to examine it closer.

"Over time Ismael wanted to further our knowledge and use of Aura. Marion and Jareth feared it, and wanted to limit the exposure of what we could do as people."

We watched as the Hidden Forest came into view before our eyes. The map shifted as if time flowed through it, showing how things changed over time and how towns and villages became more established. The magic of the map thrummed against the pedestal and I grabbed Tyran's hand tight as I continued to stare.

"During that time, Ismael found something that went beyond the use of Aura balance. He saw the amplification of magic, and what could be done to create a power greater. This concerned Marion and Jareth, knowing that if given the chance, Ismael would no longer need them to achieve greatness with all magic kinds."

My back straightened. This is where our stories shifted from one another. I looked at Tyran for a moment, and he also had the same knowing expression I did. We remained quiet and allowed Gerald to continue.

"After seeing Ismael's desires for our world, Jareth and Marion couldn't continue to take part in his plans. They were weak. Fearful of Ismael's vision. They tricked him and led him into the Hidden Forest where he was slain by them."

I watched the map zoom into the middle of the Hidden Forest where the Originals battled. Charcoal-drawn figures appeared, and a thrum of magic continued as we watched the two versus one battle occur.

"Ismael fell, but not without the prophecy of returning to our lands to reestablish what they prevented him from doing. It's said that once shadow magic returns to our world that Ismael will be reborn, and able to fulfill our destinies."

"What is our destiny?" I asked, still peering at the map as it faded into a blank page once again.

Gerald met my gaze as I looked up at him. That spine-chilling smile crept over his face again and I swear I saw the flicker of violet appear in his eyes. "Time will tell."

"Shadow magic has been hunted down. If it's believed that Ismael will return, why were they killed?" Tyran sounded indifferent, but I could see how he tensed.

Gerald's smile faltered, "Those who carry shadow magic are the descendants of Marion and Jareth. Before they perished, they passed an essence of their magic on. Followers of Ismael believe the release of their magic will help call to Ismael from the beyond."

This was getting into religious territory that I wasn't about to understand. I also didn't want to lead on that Tyran and I have that shadow magic that Gerald seemed fine with having hunted down.

I pretended to stifle a yawn, "Thank you for taking the time to tell us this."

"I didn't expect the South to have the history correct. Stories float up here how the belief might be more in line with Marion and Jareth down there."

"We value Aura and the balance that is within our world. I don't know if that's a religion per se, but we are taught that Marion and Jareth were the ones that fostered that belief."

Gerald snorted at my reply and turned down the hall, "Sleep well. We'll escort you to the lift tomorrow."

I couldn't sleep. It didn't feel safe. The bed was uncomfortable. I was alone. I had checked in with Viggo who was staying in the room across from mine. He had been more quiet than usual during our stay, but he would be long asleep by now.

I sighed and tossed on the uncomfortable bed again. It was a beautiful room, very much in the familiar design of the castle, but it wasn't our home. It didn't feel like what Caldumn was to me up here.

Are you awake? I asked.

I was met with silence.

There was no reason to stay in bed if all I was going to do was toss and turn, and so I decided I'd do a quick few laps around our sleeping quarters to see if it would tire me enough to go back to bed. I slowly opened my door, not wanting it to creak and wake anyone when a large figure appeared at my door.

I almost shrieked, but saw that familiar silver hair glint in the moonlight, and let out a breath in relief. I put my hand over my heart, smiling at Tyran as he silently laughed with me.

"I checked if you were awake, you didn't respond." I whispered.

"I was down the hall, and decided to just come to the door instead." he smiled, "Can't sleep either?"

"Not here, no." I sighed, "Want to go for another walk, this time without a creepy Wizard hovering?"

He nodded and held out the crook of his arm.

We walked past the hallway as the moonlight shone across the floor through the windows. The torches were still lit but dimmed to a warm glow for the evening by magic. It felt more beautiful in the quiet dark like this with Tyran than any other time so far in this place.

We took notice of the various works of art on the walls. Many of the castle itself, and many of King Tormond. The Originals series was one of a couple others depicting Ismael as practically a god. I began to wonder if they really did worship him. It made me think more about just what happened to cause Marion and Jareth to kill Ismael. What sort of danger to our world would he have been putting it in for them to have to go to such measures?

I was lost in my thoughts before I recognized Tyran's voice as he lightly shook my arm, "Why haven't we seen any guards?"

"I… I hadn't noticed." I said now looking around.

We had wandered out of the guest halls and were near the great hall now. Surely there would have been guards stationed out here. A faint noise came from a narrow corridor past a statue of the King, almost hiding it from view.

"Did you hear that?" I asked, moving toward the sound and the dark corridor.

"Wren, we need to go back. Something isn't right." Tyran said.

As he went to turn around another noise echoed through the dark space stopping his movement.

"What if they need our help?" I almost whispered.

Tyran nodded, "We need to wake Bergen and Viggo at least, if we see any others we'll let them know what we've heard."

Bergen sleepily opened the door, clutching his sleeping gown, "Yes?"

"Hi Bergen, sorry to wake you, but something is going on, and we need to check it out. We think some guards are missing and we heard some noise coming from a hallway."

"Are you certain they aren't on break? I'm sure it gets boring around here. Rhonin would have been more than a half day behind us."

My senses told me it was more, "I'm not sure. Tyran wanted us all to check it out."

He let out a large yawn, becoming more awake to what we were saying, "You two have the right idea. Let me put on my robes, I'll meet you in the hall."

Viggo was quick to answer, adrenaline already coursing through him at my knock, "Sorry Dad, something is off and we need to check it out."

"This place has been off since we arrived." He said as he reached for his dagger.

"Were you even asleep?" I asked, noticing he was fully dressed.

He didn't answer and nearly walked straight into Tyran as he moved toward Bergen's room.

He stopped and glared at him, "If this has anything to do with Rhonin and you knew about it. I will kill you first."

Tyran only held up his hands, but the cold stare back had me hurrying over to separate them. Thankfully, Bergen was stepping out as well, still caught in another yawn as he met with us, "Viggo, save that for who's storming the castle."

I shook my head.

We followed our steps out to where we heard the noise. Viggo and Bergen became more alert as they noticed the lack of guards on duty as well. The halls were empty save for our soft steps. I pointed toward the statue and the corridor that was nearly hidden beyond it. We hadn't heard any more noise, but Viggo took the lead and walked into the darkness.

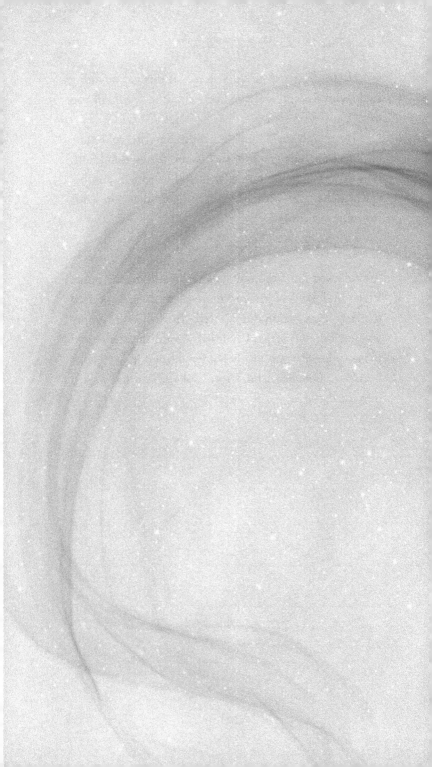

CHAPTER 22

THE AIR GREW thick as we made our way through the small entrance to stairs leading down. An iron lock laid on the floor next to the open door that appeared to have been picked, and Viggo immediately went into a defensive stance. "Something doesn't feel right about this. Even if they broke in, there should be guards or someone to inspect this by now."

Bergen nodded and pushed open the door to look down the winding stairs with torches lit brighter than the others in the main level of the castle.

Tyran and Viggo were the first to go down the stairs. Viggo gave Tyran a silent look of mistrust before he went first, noting that Tyran was following closely behind. Bergen started down and I followed last. The steps were carved out of the same stone that the walls were made up of, and as we continued downward, the chill soaked through my light cloak I wore over a large tunic and leggings I quickly threw on.

The air still hung heavy in a weird contrast to the cold. It felt almost stuffy to breathe, and yet I couldn't help but pull my clothing tighter around me. We reached the bottom of the stairs to another open door and a lock was picked next to it. The room it led to was dark, and Viggo grabbed the torch closest to bring with us as we moved into the space.

"Where are we?" I asked, peering over Bergen.

"I believe these are the castle's catacombs. They most likely lead around the whole kingdom through a series of tunnels and rooms. Much of this would have been guarded." Bergen replied.

"There weren't even signs of a struggle." I said as we slowly made our way through the first room.

Large arched pillars of stacked stone led around the open space, leaving plenty of hiding spots for things to jump out at us. I could feel my anxiety rise each time Viggo took a quick turn around one of the pillars to make sure we were indeed alone down here.

"I think they used this for more than burying their dead." Tyran said, as he made an opposite turn from Viggo around a nearby pillar.

The space ahead of Tyran was enclosed with metal gates at the openings. Inside there were tables and chairs set up to what looked like a place of worship, or holding a seance. Sheer fabrics hung tattered, and billowed at the slightest movement of air. I shuddered.

"I don't like that room." I said, turning away quickly.

Just as Tyran went to place his arm around my shoulder, a muffled, dragging noise halted our movement. Viggo went still for only a moment, picking up on the direction and distance before waving us forward. We moved quickly, while trying to keep our steps light to avoid too much noise on our end.

We weaved through what felt like numerous rooms and passageways before picking up on a voice.

"It is close. The chamber's walls are thrumming with its magic." The raspy voice floated in the space between us.

I bit my lip trying to focus my breathing techniques. I worried my heartbeat was loud enough for them to hear. Viggo looked around the alcove we were hiding in once the footsteps faded away.

"I saw two. One looks like a Butcher of Drog, the other is taller and cloaked. I assume that was your father." Viggo turned to Tyran, moving on him quicker than I could react.

His dagger moved up to Tyran's neck, "Tell me why I shouldn't cut you now."

"I'm not with them. I'm here with you." Tyran glared back.

Bergen was quick to speak, "Viggo. Let the boy go. He could have led us to his father by now, and he hasn't."

"Dad, please. Listen to Bergen." I said.

Viggo held the blade a moment longer before pulling back and letting Tyran go.

"If it was Rhonin and his bandits, then we need to act fast." Bergen said, now leading the way. Viggo followed Bergen and I grabbed Tyran's hand giving it a squeeze.

"I'm sorry." I whispered.

"You shouldn't be. It's not your fault. I don't blame him either." Tyran said.

"He shouldn't have done that."

Tyran smiled and squeezed my hand in return as we followed Bergen and Viggo.

The last series of corridors led us to a fully enclosed room. Alcoves were carved out of the stone walls with pillars holding various items. A faint glow of purple shielded many of them, and I realized we had entered the space where their relics and artifacts were kept. The room had an additional door that went into other various rooms that held items on pillars.

"They should be in here, stay quiet." Viggo whispered.

I could see the obelisk in the next room before we even crossed to the center of the current room we were in. The pillar stood in the middle, and the obelisk floated a few inches above it, rotating slightly.

"There." I said, as I began moving toward the room.

A loud clanking of metal echoed through the room and I nearly jumped back as an iron gate came slamming down over the entry into where the obelisk sat.

A cloaked figure walked out from the side of the room with the obelisk.

"There you are, I thought we would see you all here after getting word I wasn't the first person to use the ancient lift recently." He said.

Tyran straightened at his voice, and my assumption was confirmed as the figure pulled his hood back, revealing his face. He had white hair, much like Tyran's, but kept it styled short, along with a tight, manicured beard and dark eyes. Tyran must have received his hazel color from his mother. He looked sharp, and while there were some recognizable features that Tyran had from him, he was wholly different.

"Rhonin." Bergen said, "You need to leave at once. We've informed the King and they are sending guards at any moment." He bluffed.

"I don't think that will happen. My bandits have made quick work of anyone in our way, and as you can see, I'm in here, and you're not."

Viggo began pushing at the gates, trying to lift them, but they wouldn't budge.

"And here I thought my own son would keep better company. Always choosing those less than our pure lines. I'm insulted, Tyran." He said with a tsk.

"These people are more than what you'll ever be, father." Tyran sneered.

"Yes, well, we'll see what tune you'll be singing once I have the obelisk and show you what real power looks like." Rhonin said and turned toward the floating black relic.

Viggo began beating on the gate once again, trying to move it, before Bergen said, "Stand back, I'll try to break it open."

Viggo moved as Bergen took his staff, and charged a blast of air toward it. The crashing sound of air and metal met, but the gate held. A dampening thud had us moving closer to inspect it.

"They've shielded the gates against magic as well. Similar to the dampening spell we were placed in during our arrival." Bergen said.

Tyran sent bone spikes toward the gate, aiming them toward the openings only for them to meet an invisible force and begin their slow dissolve, as they couldn't penetrate further.

Rhonin let out a scoff, "Try what you want, you won't be able to muscle or magic your way in here."

I thought about shooting my shadows through, and looked to Bergen, "I could—"

"No." Bergen cut me off and whispered, "We can't risk him seeing what you have."

We were helpless as Rhonin cast a rune around the pillar, negating the magic shield it held, and grabbed the obsidian obelisk. I could see how he felt the weight of it, moving it in his hands, as a smile crept over his face, "It appears I have what I need. Now, I'll leave it up to you to explain to Tormond what happened to his precious stone. I don't expect he'll be pleased with you at all, even with the warning."

Viggo growled, and slammed against the gate again.

"You'll not make it far, Rhonin, we will come after you." Bergen threatened.

"I'll look forward to it, Wizard." Rhonin said, and looked to Tyran and me, "Once you're done playing around with lesser kinds, I'll be waiting for you. You should feel so lucky I'll look past this tryst you have going on."

That stung, and I flinched at his words, Tyran however, launched himself at the gate now.

"I'd never choose you. I've never wanted to be anything like you."

"Such a waste." Rhonin said, before turning to leave through the door beyond.

We made our way back up the stairs and through the corridor before noticing the guards were rushing around calling out orders.

"You! Where have you all been?" One soldier called when seeing us move around the statue.

"We need to speak to King Tormond. There has been a theft. We witnessed Rhonin and the Butchers of Drog carry out the act." Bergen said.

Gerald had rounded the corner as Bergen finished, "I think we have a few things to speak about."

There wasn't much of a choice as the guards surrounded us and led us to the great hall where we met with King Tormond before. The sun was rising and the glow of the morning light filtered through the windows, as the footsteps of the King entered the room.

"How dare you try to come here under the ruse of helping, only to work with that thief!" He accused.

"Your highness, with all due respect we came to warn you, and tried to stop him, but the gates and magic dampening you put in place prevented that." Bergen tried to reason.

"I find it rather convenient that they happened to be working for you, but Rhonin was able to get through without issue. Perhaps realizing the fact that you have one of his own kind with you wouldn't be such a giveaway."

"I'd like to know the same thing." Viggo said before Bergen could respond, "Where were your guards?"

"Are you saying this was our fault?" Gerald said, stepping forward.

Viggo shrugged, and Bergen put his hand on his shoulder to keep him from continuing a verbal assault,

"We only came with hopes to stop him. He was able to steal the obsidian obelisk, and we must work together to assemble a party to look for him before he takes it back to the South."

The King gave a sarcastic smirk, "We will not take orders from you. Especially in my presence. How little you think of our power when you are the ones that brought the issue to us, clearly the South has been unable to govern themselves in a manner that would continue to benefit them. I have half the mind to move my armies in and relieve you all from governing your towns."

Bergen stood straighter now, "We apologize we couldn't have been of more help, but we must take leave to find Rhonin and stop him. We will return the obelisk once we find him."

"You'll do no such thing." The King spat, "You are under arrest for conspiracy against the Red Kingdom."

My body went cold. I looked at Tyran who shared my expression, and then to Viggo who looked ready to fight anyone who came near us. Bergen grabbed his staff closer to his body, and the realization hit me. We were going to have to fight to escape the Red Kingdom.

CHAPTER 23

Aⁿ S THE GUARDS moved in, I noticed Viggo's slight movement, readying to unsheathe his blade. Bergen took one step back, steadying his staff, and the magic began to grow from the raw crystal at the top. I looked back to Tyran

Stay with me. I said, as Tyran's eyes met mine.

What are you going to do?

Just stay beside me, and grab onto Bergen. Follow what I do.

I wasn't sure if this was going to work, but I had to try something to get us out. I only hoped I could cast something quick enough to not have them notice the shadows from my spell.

Viggo was the first to move, slicing toward one of the Red Kingdom soldiers who came forward. Bergen's blast of air hit the guards and sent them back against the great hall's walls.

"Run!" Bergen shouted, as we took off.

We heard the shouting of Gerald and the King as we rushed out of the room. The hall felt entirely too long as we ran for the open doors, guards coming to attention to the commotion. A bolt of lightning shot past me, and I turned back to see Gerald coming after us.

"Quick! Over here!" I shouted to Tyran, and pulled Viggo toward a small alcove in the hall. Tyran quickly responded, pulling along Bergen.

I willed my shadows as quickly as possible around me, enveloping Viggo and I until there was transparent mist.

"Your turn." I said to Tyran, as he caught on and began calling his shadows around himself and Bergen.

I peeked my head around the corner, to see Gerald slowing his steps readying for our next move, "Shut the gates, we've got them cornered here."

His movements were slow, and I saw a guard turning a wheel to bring down the iron bars that were certainly warded and magicdampened.

"We've got to move. Now. Stay close to us." I ordered from Viggo and Bergen and we darted from the alcove into the center of the hall, running toward the lowering gates.

Upon seeing the empty space we once were in, anger flashed across Gerald's face, and he called again for the guards to hurry. He blindly shot a lightning bolt toward us, missing, but I wasn't going to take any more chances. We ducked as the gates came down and almost tumbled down the steps that led down to the courtyard of the castle.

There wasn't any time to relax as we streaked through the lush gardens, making our way to the inner castle wall's gate that was just now being called to close. We cleared it and made it into the upper-class neighborhoods. I could feel my magic faltering, my shield that hid us was taking a lot of effort to maintain along with the running we were doing. I found an alleyway and hid just as my shadow magic subsided.

"We'll need to keep ourselves hidden, the best chance will be in the lower quarters. Split up and we'll meet outside the Kingdom." Viggo took charge.

"I'll go with Tyran." I said, and the protest in Viggo's expression nearly had me rolling my eyes, "Unless you want to, Dad?"

"We'll keep visual of each other, but we can't be seen in a group." Bergen said.

Viggo nodded, and pulled his cloak up tighter around him.

The exit was surprisingly easy, and we weren't looked at twice as we exited. As soon as the drooping pines came into view, and the Kingdom became hidden between the trees, I let out an audible sigh and pulled my hood back.

"We need to get back to the lift as quickly as possible. If it's gone, we'll know Rhonin is already making his way back down." Bergen said as they came into view shortly after, "If it's there, we need to alert the Warlocks and have them keep watch for Rhonin's return. The more eyes we can have on him, the better. I'm setting up a meeting with Agatha. We have enough information to where I think her scrying can be of assistance."

"What can Agatha show us with scrying?" I asked.

"Now that we have confirmation of what Rhonin possesses. The obsidian obelisk, Agatha will be able to scry using the same material as a link. It won't give us all the answers, but it should give us an idea as to where he's planning to go with it." Bergen said as we stayed off the main roads and kept to the forest trees.

The lift came into view after a couple hours of walking. There wasn't any sign of Rhonin or his bandits along the journey, and it appeared the Kingdom hadn't sent out any forces to check on us either. My worries hit as we began our descent on the lift about what the Red Kingdom would do now that the obelisk had been taken. If they were going to wage war, or send more troops to hunt us down.

What bothered me most though, was why it was so easy to escape the kingdom.

"Think we'll find our winged feline friend flying around?" Tyran tried to lighten the mood.

"Maybe we can recruit it to watch the lift. Eat any reanimated in particular that use it." Bergen laughed.

"Too old and stringy." Viggo joined in.

I gave a forced smile, but the weight of everything we just went through was too much. I worried if anyone had seen my use of shadows. If they recognized the magic and what that meant for Tyran and me. I'd already worried about the Sentinels spreading word about what I did to the Abomination, but now the Red Kingdom could have seen. Would we be hunted down? The past weeks have been so different with the way I've had to use my magic, and the danger presented with more people knowing about it was overwhelming me.

The journey down was uneventful and a much needed relief to us all as we stepped back on the lower ground.

The immediate feeling of warmer weather greeted me, even being so close to the Great Northern Sierras.

"Winter is probably so long up there." I said, as we walked down the path toward the Warlock Camp.

Large tree trunks were carved to sharp points and stood on end as a perimeter fence around the town. Stacked slate stone buildings with upper levels made from wood and smoothed stucco popped into view from the open doors.

Two ominous figures approached us as we walked up to the gates. They were nearly as pale as the Necromancers and had their upper torso's bare showing runes of various types tattooed across them. They wore long floor length kilts that covered their feet, and a deep green velvet cape with hoods hung around their neck.

"We're here to speak with Mennew," Bergen said. "I have information that he will find important."

Many of the townspeople walked with hoods covering their faces, and donned long skirts and shirts or full robes. Much of their clothing was of the deep greens or browns, all very much reminiscent of the surrounding nature.

"Wait outside the library," Bergen said to the three of us, "He's a bit particular about who is welcome inside."

Tyran chuffed, and I looked at him in a silent question, "Mennew is more than particular, he's just weird."

"You've met him?" I asked.

"He tattooed me with my runes." Tyran smiled, and I nearly blushed at how much I swooned seeing them. How I liked tracing my fingers along the scarred and etched markings.

Viggo stood next to us, clearing his throat at the closeness he saw between Tyran and me.

Bergen came back out, dusting off his robes to the ash that followed him, "He's working on some additional wards. I'd hate to see the one who tries to get past those."

Tyran runewalked us back to Gaelfall just before I had to nearly catch him before he collapsed to his knees as the exhaustion hit him from the day's magic use. Bergen and Viggo were going to head back to the Sentinels' camp and library to send word at once to Agatha to meet with us about what occurred in the Red Kingdom. I let Viggo know I was going to take Tyran to rest for a while and get some of his strength back. If we in fact needed to fight soon, it was worth him getting as much of his energy back as he could. Viggo only agreed if Endora was around.

We strolled to the cottage in quiet. I kept my arm around his waist to steady him as he leaned into me. I tried not to think about what the next days would look like for us. Readying a small army, suiting up with armor and weapons, preparing to fight something that could be worse than we could even imagine. All of this, and any of it could happen on my birthday. I would be twenty and heading into a battle to help the Necromancers. Helping them to avoid one of their own going mad with dark magic. Helping Tyran.

"We're going up to my room," I said as I pulled him toward the stairs.

Tyran let out a small laugh. "Such demands on my body, Wren." Suggestively half-joking.

"No, you'll be resting in my bed, and I'll be making you some dinner. Endora will be here soon," I said, giving him a sly smirk.

I slowly slid him down on the bed, and he sank into my large comforter with a happy sigh. I sat on the edge of the bed and took his boots off, getting him as comfortable as possible before I went down to cook us a warm meal. Tyran slid his arms around my waist and put his head on my lap.

"I think this will be my favorite place of all," he said.

"My bed? Or my lap?" I joked as I stroked his hair.

"Both," He laughed. "It smells like you in here, like magnolia and vanilla."

I smiled. "Let me get you something to eat before you pass out in this state."

"Thank you for showing me how you care," he said before I stood.

"You make it easy. Very easy to show you." My body went warm.

"Hmm, but you choose to, and that's what matters most."

I could feel my heart wanting to burst as I moved from the bed, and Tyran stretched out on his back and relaxed into my covers.

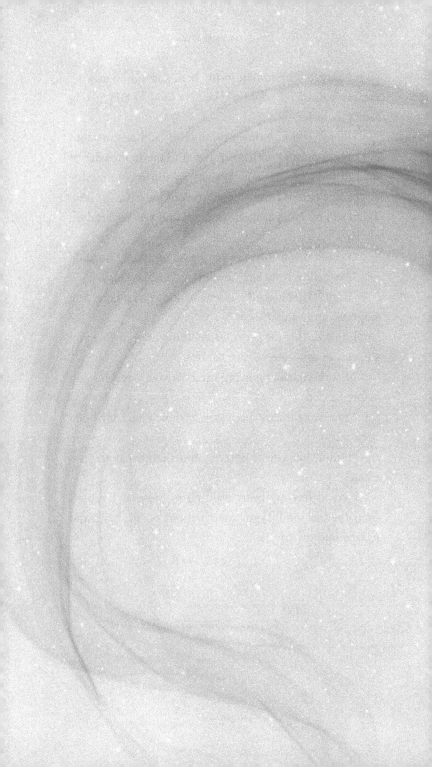

CHAPTER 24

BERGEN GREETED US outside at the foot of the front steps of the library. When walking up the main road, I noticed Sentinels were stationed near every other building, and the people were few and far between. So much so that we were the only two walking the main road. As we approached the library, I noticed Viggo was stationed at the top of the stairs near his Sentinels.

"Good morning, you two, we have a visitor on their way. I thought it would be nice to greet them at the door," Bergen said with a hint of excitement.

"Great. Who are we meeting?" I asked.

"Agatha is on her way, she left early this morning and is flying in on their great Vulpini Bats. I think you'll really enjoy seeing them." Bergen finished as my expression turned into immediate excitement and intrigue.

I remembered the fox-like creatures from Briaroak, and a grin spread across my face.

Moments later a shadow streaked across the sky, and three giant red vulpini with wings of golden red feathers that ended in a nearly black leather streaked across the sky. They circled around and made for their landing on the main road that had been previously cleared for them. The vulpini let out high-pitched barks at the excitement of a new place and began sniffing their surroundings as Agatha, and a Battalion member dismounted, along with someone I had just come to know.

"Jaradae!" I smiled as she brushed loose vulpini hair from her robes.

"Wren! It's so lovely to see you again! I'd have sent word earlier, but this was a pleasant surprise from Agatha." Jaradae said, hugging me in return.

I was in awe of the creatures they flew on up close. Foxes with partially feathered wings that turned more bat-like at the ends. Their eyes were glowing yellow in the light, and I wanted so badly to reach out and touch one. The harnessed saddles they wore were strapped tightly around their midsection, right behind where the wings joined at their shoulders.

"Bergen!" Agatha warmly greeted him, grasping his hands and kissing his cheek.

She wore a charcoal cape much like the Battalion; the hood pinned to her hair to keep it from falling in the wind. Her robes matched the same neutral color and material of the charcoal cloak, as was standard, with Wizards being viewed in public. She greeted me with a hug, and then moved to Tyran, giving him a warm smile.

"Ah, you are the Necromancer. So wonderful to meet you, Tyran," she said with a smooth tone to her voice.

Tyran nodded at her in welcome, and we stepped up to the library.

"Viggo, thank you for the wonderful entrance," Agatha said kindly as he smiled and welcomed her in with his soldiers as they opened the grand doors to our library for her.

Agatha and Jaradae were model guests, allowing Bergen to take them around the library and show everything being repaired down to the type of quartz used. Viggo, Tyran and myself followed a few steps behind, remaining quiet as Agatha and Bergen talked about everything from how they organized their shelves, to who was allowed where within the building, and anything else that wasn't what we were actually all gathered for.

We finally made it into a private meeting room across from Bergen's office and took a seat around a large ebony table.

"I've asked us to come together, because we received new information yesterday about Rhonin and what he's obtained." Bergen adjusted in his seat, "We have a chip of obsidian, the same material that the obelisk is made of. We are hoping you'll be able to track his whereabouts, or what he's planning to do this way."

Agatha gasped at the news. "Obsidian? That's used to absorb and contain. He'll be using it to contain and store Aura." She looked down for a moment, collecting her thoughts, "If my theory is right, he's going to want to use it as a weapon to expend a concentrated amount of magic, most likely to cause harm."

"Like a giant bomb?" Viggo asked.

"That, or anything that can be amplified immensely by the amount of Aura it contains." Jaradae chimed in.

Bergen nodded, "I'd like us to prevent this as soon as possible. The Aurarius Lights are to occur soon, and I have a feeling it would be a perfect time to absorb amplified Aura."

"I don't know how much I can pull from him. He's been hard to track from his name alone, but I brought Jaradae along for help. She has a gift with our scrying where she can visualize the areas that the object or person is in. We can try together to target them," she spoke with uncertainty.

A breath of gratitude from Bergen, and she prepared herself.

"Dim the lights, please," Agatha said, and the lights responded, lowering their lumens.

Agatha hovered her hands over the black tabletop, as Jaradae placed hers on top, calming their breathing, and closed their eyes. The room grew quiet, and I realized it was more silent than ever. The ambient noises, the movements, or breaths of each other were completely gone. The only sound came from Agatha as she chanted into the noiseless room, inaudible at first, then grew in a soft tone.

Light radiated in the reflection of the table under her hands. First it was hues of whites, greens and blues, then they seemed to take form. Agatha continued to chant while Jaradae furrowed her brow in concentration as the forms of light grew into an image that you could see from all sides. Mountains rose, and the dormant yellow-green of a valley below was illuminated in what looked like daylight.

Trees took shape, and we watched as the image continued to form land and terrain outward from its center. Small shooting stars of gold appeared over the now visible field surrounded by trees.

"That's the Hidden Forest. The ancient grounds where the Originals fought," Tyran whispered into the silence.

Bergen nodded in recognition of the location.

Agatha only spent another moment in her trance before she and Jaradae moved their hands slowly down onto the table and the image disappeared. The sound of the ambient noise of the library returned and the lights slowly returned to their previous brightness as we sat in stillness looking at the same spot on the table that had shown the image.

"We can get our Sentinels out there in a day's time. I'll get to work gathering our supplies and we can be ready," Viggo spoke.

"Is he there now?" I asked.

"The obsidian is drawn there. Even when I can't see Rhonin, it's where he will be," Jaradae responded.

"The night of the Aurarius Lights. That's in two nights." I said… remembering the sparkling image that appeared on the table.

"I'm sorry I can't be of any further help, not now, while we are still recovering from their attacks," Agatha said to Bergen.

"Your help today was enough. Once we take care of Rhonin, we can figure out how to best calm the Red Kingdom from our swift and unwelcomed exit," Bergen said and patted the top of her hand.

We thanked Agatha and Jaradae for the help as Bergen escorted her to the Vulpini Bats that laid in the sunny spots of the grass around the library. Jaradae had hoped to stay and visit Endora, but gave me a small package to give her more chocolates and tea. The people of the village had gathered to see them sunbathe and chitter to one another, many laughing and cooing at the unique visitors.

Upon seeing Agatha and the accompanying Witches, the vulpini stood and got ready for flight. Agatha waved to us as those amazing fox creatures jumped high in the air. With the great flap of their leathery and feathered wings, they climbed into the sky and were gone.

Tyran trained with Bergen while I had my combat training with Viggo. We planned to meet up for lunch, and then he would have to send word to Gunnar with everything we learned. I knew we would need as much help as possible, but something felt off to me at how quickly things were happening. It wasn't the same as being alerted and having to react on your adrenaline, but it was a knowing risk, and push towards something that you could have just enough time to think about, but not enough to feel entirely sure of the outcome.

After training, Tyran runewalked us to the New Moon Village for lunch, and some time alone before we had to part ways. Even in the middle of the day, there was this hauntingly beautiful filter of darkness to the buildings and roads. I lingered again at the idea and hope that we could defeat Rhonin, and celebrate here on the evening of the Aurarius Lights. We picked up lunch from a market and rented a room at the inn.

"I don't know if I'm ready for this all." I said, taking a bite of my vegetable pot pie.

He looked at me and tried to give a reassuring smile, "I don't think anyone is really ready when you plan to attack something, but I know given the circumstances, I wouldn't want to be fighting beside anyone else but you."

My face warmed, "I think you put too much faith in me."

"Absolutely not."

"No?" I asked.

Doubt and fear still stirred in my mind, and I wasn't sure if I could shake this like I had been able to in the past. Things felt more real than acting without thinking and preparing, I felt like I had so much more to lose. Tyran watched me carefully, aware of my lack of confidence, and moved our food to the table. He placed his hands on my cheeks.

"I don't think you'll ever know just how beautiful you are when you are open to your shadows," he said. "You burn with a love that is so bright for others, but the power and strength within those shadows comes from you, Wren. Allow yourself to see that. Bring them to the surface and let them out."

I could feel the sincerity of what he said as I saw those red flecks shine in his eyes. My body radiated with heat as he moved his thumb across my cheek.

I knew I had fallen for him wholly then. Not only because of his words that spoke to my soul, but because he was my someone. My person, who could look past my flaws and see my shadows, the self doubt, the anxiety, and still see something beautiful.

I kissed him hard, and didn't stop the shadows from branching out and moving around my body as I climbed onto him. I knew I would only ever want him, and only ever allow him to see me as pure and open as I was about to be before him. Bare, stripped, and his. We melted into one another.

Before I completely gave myself to him and our shadows, I whispered, *I love you.*

CHAPTER 25

IT WAS COLD and rainy as I worked together with Viggo, packing up the essentials we would need for the battle ahead. I sorted through and collected items for med kits, rations, and extra water while Viggo pulled out an arsenal of close combat weapons, extra straps to wield daggers, and sharpening stones.

I love you.

The words stuck in my mind. The complete truth to them as I had whispered them down our permanent link of shadows, and the return of hearing those same three words from his perfect lips, as they kissed every part of me and my shadows, had me over the moon. I knew I showed I cared for him deeply before as we grew closer together, but yesterday I allowed him to see it all, my shadows, my light, and my stars, and he gave his all in return.

We spent hours talking to one another before falling asleep and again meeting in our dreams.

"Aye, girl. You all packed up?" Viggo's voice shattered into my daydream of memories and I nearly knocked over a stack of medical kits I had just finished getting stocked.

"Ah, yep. I think we have it all." I said, trying to close up the packs I nearly toppled, and picked a few up hastily.

Viggo laughed, "You better not be in the stars like that tomorrow, we need you alert and clear as you can be."

"Just reminding myself of what we're doing this for," I said truthfully and swung the bags on my back as we left the weapons armory.

The day was spent training both magic and combat, clearing my mind while Tyran met with Gunnar after sending word to him. I was looking forward to being in his arms again, but the news of whether Rhonin had returned to their town and what the townspeople felt about his actions were in the front of my mind. Tyran wasn't doing this simply because he didn't agree with his Father. There were innocent lives at risk within Reapford, too.

Tyran met with me at the edge of the magic fields near Bergen's home. I was practicing my Mage skills, not wanting to spend another hour in the library's basement, going over my shadow abilities.

Before I could touch the handle, Endora came through the front door. She let out a sigh of relief seeing us and hugged me. I hadn't realized that I probably looked a little worse for wear with the training I'd been through. She held my face for a moment, looking at me with loving eyes, and hugged me tighter.

"I'm alright. I'm okay!" I said laughing, as I could feel her grip tighten again around me.

"I didn't know if I'd see you today, I was going to make dinner and have it ready in case I missed you. I'm just so glad you're home." Endora said, moving back and smiling brightly at me.

"We have more to do, but we are safe for now. Dinner would be lovely. Viggo is going to stay with the Sentinels tonight." I said as we walked with her to the kitchen.

Endora gave me a feeble attempt at a warning glance, and smiled again

She steamed rice while frying some veggies and tofu in a garlic butter sauce, as we made ourselves comfortable around the table.

"It smells amazing. Thank you," Tyran said.

We ate dinner together and spent the evening by the fire. Endora realized that again, Tyran wouldn't be leaving tonight, "Seeing as you would end up on the couch with him anyway, I suppose he'll be more comfortable in your room, but you *will* be leaving that door open."

Tyran nodded with full understanding it being an order rather than a request.

"Good. Rest up tonight." She said with a look that reminded us again she was watching us.

It wasn't much longer until I felt the fatigue of the day as well. I went upstairs to change and wash up for bed while Tyran helped clean the dishes with Endora before she went up to her room as well. When I finished washing up, I noticed Endora had closed her door, and Tyran was back on the bed, pulling something from his pack.

"I wanted to save this for your birthday tomorrow night, but I think tonight will be better," he said.

He pulled me next to him on the bed and handed me a small rectangle box. I opened the black velvet case that contained a white gold necklace. The chain was nearly as thin as a strand of hair and glimmered under the light. Along the chain set multiple six-pointed stars that held white diamonds. The center star was slightly larger than the others and contained a black diamond that looked like swirling shadows.

"It's beautiful," I said breathlessly through my awe.

Tyran helped take it out of the box and clasped it on my neck as I felt the cool metal against my skin and tears formed as I looked into his hazel eyes. They were sparkling. I'd never received a gift like this before. I blinked to fight the tears from falling as he admired how it looked on my neck.

"The diamonds are amazing. The dark one..." I couldn't finish.

"You are my Dark Star," he said. "I see your light, Wren. You show me things I didn't know I needed, and you give it freely. No matter how dark, and through all the shadows, I see you, and I love you."

He pulled me into him and kissed me deeply as tears crept down my cheeks. His tender words, and gift were beyond anything I knew I was worthy of. He healed me in ways that I didn't realize until that moment, and he loved me. I loved him, too.

My dream started out like those with my shadows swirling around me, but instead of finding Tyran, a vision appeared in the distance of a battle. Fog moved around in the early morning air already thick with magic. The smell of sweet grasses and spring blooms were twisted with the coppery sharpness of blood and steel. A soft breeze danced along the field where bodies lay strewn about. All was quiet save for a moan of anguish as the last breaths escaped from anyone still alive.

The people of the south of Caldumn and the Red Kingdom were left stunned by what just occurred. Neither side was prepared for the sheer amount of destruction that could come from unleashing this magic. Shadows swirled around me as I stood in the middle of the field. Looking out at the power I had just unleashed.

I was the weapon. Me.

I jolted awake as Tyran sat up with me, noticing my shadows were dissipating and nearly sparkling with starlight. My heart was pounding as he held me to calm my fears of what I had dreamt.

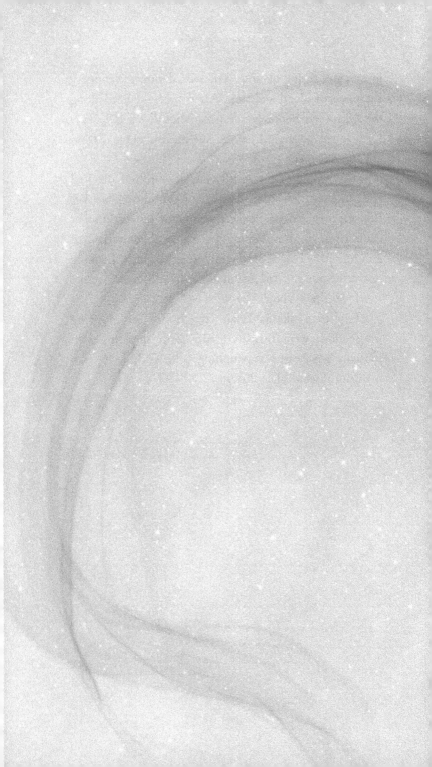

CHAPTER 26

Tyran grabbed my hand tighter as we crossed into the main building courtyard. It had taken some convincing from Bergen, but Viggo allowed Tyran to cross into the Sentinel grounds. It was unheard of to allow a soldier from outside of Gaelfall to witness the inner workings of our defense base, and many of the Sentinels were keeping a close eye on him because of it.

A branch of the Sentinels were gathered between the armory and the central building, readying weapons, repairing any armor that needed it, and gathering enough supplies for the group that we'd leave with. It didn't take long before I noticed that many weren't just sizing up Tyran, but also looking at me. I could overhear them talking about how I took down an Abomination. That I had ancient magic within me. I wasn't sure if it was fear or uncertainty of the power, and if I should worry they too would want to kill me for it.

We met with Viggo in the central building's war room where his closest Watch stood near him while they went over a map of the Hidden Forest. Small carvings of what would be a representation of our unit were gathered together at the edge while they talked about the best paths to get to the Ancient Battlefield. We moved around the table as Viggo only looked in our direction to acknowledge us being there before turning back to speak to his Watch. Viggo was dressed in battle gear. His armor was on, with the additions of pauldrons, a belt that held a sword and a horn crafted from a tusk of some beast, and a fur trimmed cape.

The way the Sentinels worked together methodically planning where to land our attack was mind blowing. I quickly saw that training and learning how to fight was only one small part in what Sentinels actually do. The ability to understand terrain, what locations to approach from, all while engaging in combat, and how to gain the best advantage left me without words. It all went through Viggo and his remarkable ability to spot any weaknesses or flaws in plans, and then quickly correct it with a new idea.

"Does your Guard go this in depth too?" I whispered to Tyran.

"Each town does. If not, they would be left with a wide weakness. It would be recognized by others, and used to their advantage."

"You'd think you'd want to help them and not take advantage of it." I replied.

"In conflict and war, you take whatever edge you can to protect what is yours," he said solemnly.

I twitched my mouth in disapproval, but understood what he meant. It reminded me too much of how the Red Kingdom felt.

Viggo and his watch seemed to come to an agreement on the plans to enter the Ancient Battlefield and made his way over to meet with Bergen who had just come into the room. We followed them as Viggo started talking about the plans that were laid out.

"We will enter the Forest at the southeastern edge, my watch has been tracking beasts' movements in the forest, and we will need to take a few out as we work our way toward the Battlefield. We've got a half dozen Archers who will take them out early enough, but any others that are too close we'll need to be on our toes and take them out quickly."

"I trust they will be dealt with quickly and quietly from your well-trained soldiers," Bergen responded.

Viggo nodded, "After that we will need to make our way through the marsh, there are some clear paths, but we need to send a few soldiers ahead to check for quicksand along those paths, and from there on out, we should be able to make it to the outskirts of the Battlefield by late afternoon. We will set up watch, and rest as much as we can, and hopefully catch this bastard before he attempts to do whatever it is within those grounds. Hopefully, before the stars begin to streak across the sky."

I felt the twinge of sadness radiate through me as I thought about my birthday, the Aurarius Lights, and how I wanted to watch them tonight. The eerie quiet of being in the middle of the Ancient grounds with magic amplified within it as the golden lights streaked through the sky would certainly be an experience. I wondered if Tyran and I could break away from the group once all was taken care of, enjoying a moment alone under them. I was used to having small celebrations for my birthday, but I really had looked forward to spending this year with Tyran.

Bergen agreed with everything Viggo laid out, and we walked out of the central building to meet with the soldiers who waited for their next orders. They stood at attention when Viggo moved to the center, directing them to meet at the western gates, and our small army moved into formation to head out of town. I kept in stride with Viggo as he grabbed a pack and took position, rounding up the back of the group of Sentinels that marched forward.

"What do we need to be most concerned about while going through the Hidden Forest?" I asked while we marched.

"The beasts roaming nearby are fairly easy to take down, minus one or two that might give us a fight. I don't want you spiking it with your shadows, your reputation with the soldiers makes them nervous enough," Viggo said with a half smile.

"Noted, and here I thought it was because a Necromancer Guard was among us." I said jokingly, trying to push out the thought of the Sentinels finding me dangerous.

"Aye. They didn't like that much, either. They respect my orders, and soon enough we can get back to minding our own business." he said.

I saw how he maintained his composure, talking about something that could rile him up. It was small steps that I hoped would be permanent in allowing him to see the good that I saw in Tyran, and what he was sacrificing for the better of our people. I knew he was also doing this for me. It was his way of showing that he cared for me, in that deep fatherly love.

The town was quiet in the early morning hours as we moved through. Few townspeople were up and out in the cold air, and those that were went quiet at seeing the group of soldiers march to the gates ahead. I breathed in the last smells of the town, of the wet dirt and dried dead leaves that gave that late autumn scent. We gathered at the gates and Viggo moved to the front, giving the signal to head out with a blow of the horn that had been attached to his hip.

I moved my hand to Tyran's, interlacing our fingers as we marched forward. I felt the small surprise, then approval from the shadow magic that we shared. My necklace felt cold against my skin that I kept tucked under my shirt. Tyran's grip tightened gently, and I didn't care if the Sentinels saw. I wanted them to. To see we were working together as one.

It took longer than the previous journey with Viggo to the edge of the Hidden Forest. Not only were there more people to march with, but also some supply carts being pulled. As per the plans, once we reached the trees we were called to stop, and a band of the Archers moved forward for a period before a call of all clear allowed movement forward again. I didn't see every beast they took down, but the familiar dark fur off in the distance of a stop let me know wild Ursendirs wandered a lot closer to my home than I wanted to know.

The sun broke out from the mostly cloudy sky for a small part in the early afternoon, and the light filtered through the misty floor of the forest. It made me think of it being nature's way of representing the shadows that dwelled within Tyran and me. I ran my fingers across the wisps of the light gray mist, feeling the cool dampness of it. Such familiarity, like the shadows within us, but the difference was that there was also an inner warmth within our shadows. The life of the magic that changed it from nothing more than a cool mist to another extension of what made us.

We approached the marsh and Viggo sent a few of the soldiers ahead with polearms to check on the solid ground portions we would be navigating. The risk of stepping in quicksand and becoming a victim to it was high, and from the hushed talk from the surrounding Sentinels, there were river beasts that lurked within the waters that we would be lucky not to meet. We broke into three groups and maneuvered around following the lead of those with the polearms, poking and prodding the ground before placing a foot, then the other, testing for solid grounds.

There was a slip of a step by a Sentinel, and he was swallowed whole into a soft patch of dirt that looked no different from what we had been testing. Viggo lept for him and his upper half was consumed by the sand. The Watch on either side of Viggo pulled at his legs as they tried to work him out of the liquified sand. I couldn't breathe in the moments Viggo and the soldier were submerged.

I looked for a way to get over there myself, to help pull him out with the other soldiers, but before I found a path to them, Tyran was already moving. He moved without hesitation in their direction and helped the soldiers by pulling Viggo out by the waist of his pants.

Slowly they emerged, first Viggo's torso, then head, as he sucked in a large breath, followed by his arms that were hooked under the soldier who was not breathing. They laid him out, and Viggo immediately started pumping his chest and breathing into his lungs. A muddy cough and retching from the soldier had them turning him on his side as he tried to clear his airways of the thick, murky sand.

Tyran helped Viggo to his feet, and I saw a look of gratitude, only for a brief second, come from Viggo. Tyran patted his back and turned back to my direction as the rest of the group composed themselves to continue. It was another small moment that I would keep in my mind of the kind acts that Viggo accepted from the Necromancer. My Necromancer.

The clouds kept the sun hidden for the remainder of the journey through the marsh, and the swamp land's thick canopy of trees that covered much of the paths we traveled, kept the temperatures to a chill. Tyran and I moved through the marsh, staying close to one another, ever ready to leave this place behind. It wasn't much further until the sweet feeling of firm dry ground greeted us and we felt the lingering layer of chill that clung to the marsh leave the surrounding air.

It was another hour of travel until we finally reached our destination. The clearing of the Ancient Battlefield spread out before us, as soldiers separated into the groups that Viggo assigned back in Gaelfall. We were stationed along the southern treeline of the ancient grounds, and the Sentinels were already unpacking the carts taken with us. Placing stations of weapons, medical tents out of canvas that were painted to match the colors of the surrounding trees, and setting up watch points to keep a view on the expanse of the battlefield that spread out ahead. It had a haunting silence to it.

No creatures wandered the empty field, no birdsong, no movement of any kind beyond the breeze that caught what was left of the dried and nearly dormant grasses. Giant boulders looked as though they erupted from the ground, pushing their way up to the sky, and I thought of the points of protection they could offer if needed. Places we could push forward to. Trees surrounded all sides of the baleful clearing, and I felt like we were in a bowl where giants could look down and view the battle that happened here, almost like they would be watching a game.

I found a boulder to rest on at the edge of the trees, eating a couple snack balls consisting of rolled oats, peanut butter, and chocolate pieces. I tried to imagine what this place would have looked like during the Originals battle. Even this very spot where I sat could have been an active site of their fighting. My shadows shifted within me as they felt the energy of our environment. It was as though my magic recognized something about this place, but wasn't entirely welcomed to it.

Tyran came to sit beside me, and a gentle calm came over my magic with his own so close.

"Well, there are no spirits, or wailing wraiths out here like we were told as kids. Might as well go home," I said.

Tyran took a bite of his jerky, smiling at me. "Hmm. No, but it doesn't make this place any more welcoming."

"True. And here I thought we'd be spending the evening in a lovely field under the stars."

"Happy Birthday, Wren," Tyran teasingly exclaimed.

"What better way to spend the day than some old fighting grounds," I quipped.

It was nice to have a moment of laughter, but I shuddered at the thought of us walking through the kind of magic left here. Maybe the stories weren't wrong, and maybe Tyran could sense something more about the dead and the life in between out here than I knew. I shifted back to the matters at hand.

"So what if it's just Rhonin who comes out here? How would you like to deal with him?" I asked.

"I know what he's been capable of, and he won't be alone. I'm willing to bet he'll bring an army of his own with him." Tyran took a moment. "Whether that's alive or dead is yet to be known. I'm concerned if there has been a shift in allegiance within our town, and no one has caught on."

I didn't know he was concerned about his people like that, and that this was of that magnitude to worry about for him. For hating being the Baron's son, he was good at thinking of his people.

"I'll do what I can so that everything is right in the eyes of Reapford. So that you can explain everything to your people when you return. I wish we had more time, so that you could assemble your Guard and talk to Gunnar. I know this is hard fighting without them."

Tyran smiled, and I could see a hint of pain at the thought of him doing this without his people. Gunnar was unable to pull away and get a group of soldiers out here to help, they had too many eyes on them at the moment, and Rhonin had yet to be seen. Tyran was out here alone, fighting against one of his kind, his father of all people, and along with that, he was fighting without them at the same time. I could feel how conflicting it would be for him even without it being his father.

I want to meet them one day. Reapford. Your people, I said, letting my shadows speak.

I want you to as well, He said softly back.

A cry rang out as a raven flew across the field from the north. My heart stopped at the sharp noise that broke the quiet.

CHAPTER 27

Tyran and I were standing within a moment, scanning the northern treeline for movement. Silence met us. The Sentinels had gone quiet as well, and we awaited a sign from the lookouts. Tyran was tense, and I realized he was more aware of something.

The raven? I asked.

He knows we're here, he said, and pulled his sword from his back.

The call from a lookout at the far western edge of our position made me look at the other end of the northern field. Small movement, as I barely noticed the brush and trees moving, then more movement happened. It spread along the treeline to the north, and my knees went weak at the sight.

Out walked the first line of reanimated dead. Old soldiers that wore tatters of red fabric and armor I didn't recognize. They marched out to the first quarter of the field as Viggo called orders behind us. I could faintly hear what he said as the details of the dead came into view.

Some were barely made of any flesh, others were partially reconstructed, and some looked whole. I wondered how it was even possible. Black tar-like substance, the same as what bled from the Abomination, dripped from the parts that were without flesh, and I had to steady myself against Tyran as he protectively stepped in front of me.

Another band of reanimated soldiers moved out of the northern treeline, followed by a third, and I quickly realized we were outnumbered. Panic soared into my throat as I tried to swallow it down to ready myself for what more could come. Tyran pulled my hand forward, moving me next to him, and it helped me sharpen my senses to what we were facing. I needed to push my fear down and ready myself to fight what was before us.

A single figure was the last to emerge from the northern treeline. It was Rhonin, who remained hidden behind a black cloak and a hood that shrouded his face. Viggo, Bergen, Tyran, and I moved to the front lines of the Sentinels, while Viggo called out commands as they had weapons drawn and ready. My ears were ringing as the adrenaline pumped through me. I realized the magic here was thrumming, causing that deep magic inside to pulse along with it.

"What have I told you about mingling with people outside of our pure lines, Tyran?" Rhonin shouted as he pulled back his hood, "Come now, help me finish what I've started."

Tyran remained standing by my side, his breath becoming uneven. "You are responsible for the deaths of our own Guard. For the deaths of the Witches and Mages. You set up our town to be attacked, to burn innocent people's homes and torture them, all to hide what you were doing! You will be charged for everything you've done."

Rhonin rolled his eyes and sneered at Tyran. "You've no idea the power I'm about to wield. You are too busy getting lost with those so far beneath you. You choose to be weak."

A flare of rage hit me at his words. My shadows flickered in response. Tyran's own shadows swirled angrily behind his narrowed eyes as well.

"Enough. We will defend these lands, and you will answer to the court of Reapford." Bergen spoke loudly.

An evil smile broke over Rhonin's face as he returned behind the waves of reanimated soldiers that silently waited for his command.

"I don't think that'll be the case, Wizard. You'll love seeing firsthand what we've gathered here for."

Rhonin pulled the small black obelisk from his pocket.

With a gentle flick out of his hand, the first wave of dead readied their weapons. Viggo launched into a call to ready his own army. I pulled my sword from my back as well and waited for our command.

Rhonin launched his attack simply by dropping his hand back to his side while continuing to hold the obelisk in the other. The guttural noise of the first wave rang out as the bones and flesh of whatever was left of these humans. I closed my eyes and took one last breath before hearing Viggo's command to attack, as both sides advanced.

I moved in a seamless dance of blade and fire. Meeting the first wave with a skill that felt fine tuned from the recent training and sparring. Tyran stuck by me as we took down our enemies. His shadows snaked down his forearm to his blade as he sliced through the reanimated, while I burned the ones I attacked. I moved back to set fire to any of those the Sentinels took out while the injured reanimated were left writhing and attempting to continue fighting.

Another wave was ordered by Rhonin as Tyran and I separated more. I moved in Bergen's direction to help him with the new wave that came crashing into us. Bergen fought with a skill better than I'd expected from someone his age. He moved with precision and speed as he jabbed and slammed his staff towards the corpses that came charging toward him. Shockwaves of air radiated from the crystal, blowing enemies who came too close into pieces, while others further back were blasted back from the wave that emanated.

I lit flames and shot bolts of fire, burning the bodies on the ground, ridding our path forward of anything that would stop our soldiers. Sentinels called out for help, as many tried to fight off two to three living corpses at a time. I had to help the ones closest, and pulled back any that were injured, as the medical unit moved in to retrieve those who needed immediate attention.

The first and second wave continued their attack and caused more separation from Tyran. I saw he and Viggo were closer as they fought near the front of the lines at the initial advance. I could feel the shadows swirling in me as we moved into the center of the battlefield. The deep, dark thrumming of the most dangerous part of what I held grew louder, and I had to push it back in my mind to keep it from overtaking my ability to focus on what I fought through. More reanimated, and more black blood spurted and pooled at my feet as I continued my dance through them with my blade and fire.

Rhonin stood at the back of the last and largest wave of his reanimated soldiers, holding his obelisk and chanting an incantation. I let my focus drop for a moment as I noticed the obelisk glowed a faint green in the dying light of the day while we battled on. I was slammed to the ground in a split second by a reanimated soldier and quickly tried to pull my dagger from my side to thrust into the side of its skull before kicking it off with the help of a fireball. I stood quickly and was met with another, and another, as they continued their attacks.

More Sentinels called out for aid, and others helped where they could. Viggo still moved up ahead, closer to the back line of the first and second waves that had been sent. I hoped we could survive the final line of dead soldiers that still stood waiting before it grew dark.

Viggo moved with the absolute skill of the warrior I saw before. His ability to sense attacks on him while only having use of one eye always impressed me, but today was an intense show of his abilities. He worked through the reanimated, severing heads and limbs as he moved inward back towards his soldiers, then pushed forward with them once again.

Tyran had advanced nearly as far up as Viggo now, while both of them were picking off the corpse soldiers on either side of the attack line. Tyran showed no slowing in his attacks as he continued to fight through, slicing with his blade encased in his shadows, while those that met with it went still. The closer he got to the front the more I noticed that Rhonin's attention went to the shadows his son held.

"Tyran, I always thought you had something different within you. I knew there had to be some way to coax that out, and how lucky for me it is happening here tonight," Rhonin shouted.

It was hard to hear him with the sound of clashing weapons and slamming bodies, but it was enough for me to turn my attention to see Rhonin walking out toward his son. It was the second time I let my guard drop, and I was tackled again by a fully formed reanimated corpse, he didn't have a weapon but held my arms down to my side as I fought to get my knees under him. His dead, milky eyes moved closer to me as he leaned in and bit my shoulder. Pain radiated through me as I screamed, while it tore a chunk of my flesh away.

I thought I heard Tyran call my name as another corpse dropped on me, blocking my vision of the sky above.

CHAPTER 28

Tᴀᴇ sᴛᴇɴᴄʜ ᴏꜰ death and the bodies of reanimated piled on me as I cried out. I could feel the tearing of my flesh and hear the inhuman growls around me. Faintly, a familiar voice rang out.

Viggo and… Rhonin?

I couldn't make out what was said, but the yell from Viggo sent a jolt of adrenaline through me as I freed my hand and positioned it under the belly of the corpse on top of me. Shadows shot through, solid like weaving vines, spiking through those around me that kept me down.

More familiar shouting, this time Tyran and Viggo. The panic that came from Tyran as he cried out at Viggo sent waves of panic through me. I had to get up. I had to help. I felt the coursing thrum of that deep magic within me growing as I made more vines of spiked thorns through every last corpse until they went still. Bergen shouted something in a shocked tone, and I couldn't help but feel the fear of what I wasn't able to see happening ahead of me. The sky was nearly dark as stars started to appear.

The heaviness of the bodies weighed on me as my shadows evaporated from where they impaled the reanimated. I pushed with all my strength to move them off and saw the familiar faces of two Sentinels as they pulled more off me. I screamed at them to help as I writhed under the weight. I had to help. Viggo and Tyran's voices were still raised, and I couldn't see what was causing the panic between them.

Rhonin let out such a vicious laugh at what was playing out in front of him. I kicked and twisted out of the remaining bodies as the Sentinels grabbed my arms and pulled me up. I looked out to my left and saw Bergen standing still, staring at what was occurring in front of him. My ears were ringing, my heart beating loudly, and I couldn't adjust to the echo of noise before I turned to see what it was.

It happened in a mere matter of seconds, as my soul broke apart.

Tyran was holding the hilt of his sword as the point pierced through Viggo's chest. I watched as the blade went through him. Tyran's echoing yell shattered through me. How? Why?

I watched as my father, my friend, and the one who cared for me from the moment he saw me, sank down to his knees, and life left him. The man that helped repair me when I didn't know how to overcome my self-doubt, the trauma that plagued me, and the weaknesses that I let in. The man that helped me find my worth in order to give that to others, laid with a blade through his heart. My father whom I loved. Gone.

And the man that I shared a connection with, that went deeper than our magic. The person to whom I gave myself, who I opened my darkness and light to, was the wielder of that blade. The man who I loved, who now climbed to Viggo's side, had held that blade. I couldn't see beyond those two, as Tyran knelt before Viggo.

I couldn't breathe. The echoing thrum of the ancient magic grew deafening within my ears. The heat of anger, sadness, pain and sorrow, all with the question of how and why, combined into that dark matter that erupted from me. I opened my mouth and let it all out.

Shadows burst from me as I saw the tendrils rise high into the air, and the swirling of mist and smoke enveloped me, placing me into the eye of what I was creating. An orb of destruction and pure pain. I let out a scream. A wail so loud and powerful that the ground shook under me. A shockwave erupted from my body, blowing all those around me down.

I willed it to kill every last reanimated thing as I fully exploded at the loss of my friend, my Dad. I couldn't stop the scream that radiated from me until I felt a familiar touch from Bergen reaching for me through the mist that surrounded me.

He crawled over to me, using his staff to withhold a shield of air and enter through my shadows, reaching for me to stop. I fell to my knees then, and he held me as the tears came. I was still entirely formed of my shadows as if they were trying to protect me as the pain of loss flowed through me. I couldn't stop the rising of anger, and the flood of hatred at what I just witnessed mixed with the sorrow like a deadly poison. I barely made out Tyran's shape through the dark shrouded mist as he stood from where Viggo lay.

My mentor, who opened his heart to me and told me how he lost the love of his life at the hands of a Necromancer, now lost his own in the same way. The one that accepted my choice to allow a Necromancer into my life, and I pushed to work together with, did so all because he cared for me and wanted to believe in my worth. In his last weeks of life, I made this man open himself to that which he protected his heart from for so long. I couldn't handle the anger that rose as I focused more on Tyran.

"You. Why? Why did you kill him?" I sputtered toward Tyran.

His eyes were wide with shock, "He wasn't stopping. He wouldn't have stopped."

I couldn't stop what I said as the heat of deep power radiated within me. The hatred fed it, sending it through me. I pushed away from Bergen's grasp, still kneeling on the ground.

"How could you do that to him? To me! My Dad!" I said through gnashed teeth.

"Wren. Let me explain." Tyran tried to plead with me.

"You are dead. Your blood is next."

Tyran opened his mouth in protest and tears started to well in his eyes as he kept walking in my direction.

"I will kill you!" I screamed, as my shadows swirled around once again.

"Leave!" I heard Bergen yell at Tyran.

There was such hurt, such pain in his gaze, before he placed a rune and disappeared.

I went back into an uncontrollable sob, and Bergen moved back to place a hand on me. It was a worse pain than I ever imagined. My heart was smashed. My chest hurt. Everything hurt. I had lost Viggo, and now Tyran, too.

Pushing off the ground, I couldn't feel my own body move as I ran towards Viggo's body. He had been left alone. I couldn't allow that. My hands and knees slammed down on the ground next to him. He was left on his side with the blade still in him. I noticed his hand was wrapped around the strong part of the blade and had bled from how hard he gripped it. The tears continued to flow as I laid down facing him and felt the last warmth of his blood soak into my clothes. He looked peaceful, such a juxtaposition to our surroundings, as I slowly put my hand on his cheek. A continual flow of tears fell, blurring my vision.

"I had a feeling that my son had something within him, but I didn't know there were two," Rhonin spoke as he stood from the destruction I had unleashed.

The protection rune cast before my attack rippled as he walked out from it.

"It appears you were just what I needed." He held up the obelisk, glowing radiantly with a green light from within. Power thrummed from it, and light and dark magic grew heavy around us. My shadows were still formed around me and responded to the power felt by churning and pulling toward it, "As you can see, the power it contains calls to you. You will be the perfect outlet for this concentrated magic."

I didn't have the strength left to fight. I wanted to stay next to Viggo and allow the life to be sucked from my body. Shouting from behind me echoed as I listened to the Sentinels and Bergen advance to protect me from Rhonin. He was the only one left, as I had killed his army in that explosion of power.

"Join me and let me show you just what we can do together, with the harnessed power I hold, and your ability to channel it, we could rule these lands," he said as he held out a hand to me.

I stayed still, staring back at Viggo's lifeless face.

Bergen and the Sentinels came closer.

"Maybe not tonight, but the battle has only just begun," Rhonin said while he placed a rune on the ground and disappeared.

The steps of the Sentinels rushed to our side while I kept my hand on Viggo. It went quiet again, and Bergen touched my shoulder as he knelt next to me. New tears formed in my eyes as I let them silently stream from me.

Golden light streaked through the sky as the Aurarius Lights began. They illuminated us as I spent the last moments of time next to Viggo before my shadows fully withdrew into me. The light moved across our bodies as they shot through the sky above us.

This should have been a different night for Viggo. He should have been here with me; with his Watch and Sentinels, but he was gone. I was numb as Bergen helped me up, and two of Viggo's Watch brought a stretcher to carry his body back with us.

It was a deep sorrowful quiet as the golden light continued to pour down from the sky. The torches carried by the Sentinels lit our path through the forest. It was almost as if the beasts and monsters of the forest knew of our pain and hid in our presence as we journeyed back through the Hidden Forest.

I kept a hand on Viggo. I couldn't try to get myself to even think beyond his body next to me. All I could feel was emptiness and a cold and alone darkness as my body moved with the motions of everyone around me. A small group of soldiers stayed back to attend to any who had died in the battle. Lighting pyres and sending them off with the Sentinel's chant.

By the time we made it back to town, the sky changed to a faint hue of pink on the horizon as the last of the star-fall flowed. I didn't want to leave Viggo's side as they took him into the central building, but with some gentle coaxing, Bergen got me back home where Endora woke quickly and took over.

She held me as choking sobs flowed from me again. I couldn't speak, and Bergen gave her the report of events that happened. We sat on the floor as we both cried for what felt like hours. Endora kept me close, rocking and humming softly to me. I could feel the drops of her own tears on my head at the pain we endured together.

The morning sun rose over the horizon as Endora tucked me into bed and closed the curtain on my window, hoping to get me to sleep any amount that I could. I hadn't spoken once, but gently squeezed her hand to thank her for the care she gave before she left my room. I laid there in the dim and quiet as birdsong had started.

Wren. Please.

Tyran's voice rocked through me.

I couldn't stand the pain, it was as if I was watching another death all over again.

Please talk to me. He pleaded.

You killed him, Tyran. I choked out.

I would never. Rhonin had control—

Go back to him. Finish out what you were planning to do all along with your father. I cut in.

Rhonin is going to pay for what he did. I can't return home. I won't until he's dead. Please, meet with me and talk to me.

I was going mad with that hurt. I felt as though I was drowning. I did the only thing I could think of that would stop it. My heart broke all over again as I pushed that connection with Tyran behind the mental door I had locked that magic behind before I knew what it was.

I blocked the ability to communicate with him, shielding myself from his access to me. I threw everything I had to barricade that door from opening. My shadows mourned as I pulled part of what they were away from them, of that link we had so intimately shared. As the final lock went into place, I was met with a deeper, chilling silence.

CHAPTER 29

IWASN'T SURE HOW many days went by, only noting that my wounds had closed, and the day we lit the pyre for Viggo's funeral ceremony. Bergen, Endora, and I stood in the forefront to say our goodbyes. Every Sentinel soldier was in attendance and chanted the ritual prayers to the afterlife that each soldier received when being honored.

"May the Valiant Prevail!" Their voices echoed around us as the fire was lit by his Watch.

I couldn't shed any more tears that day. I hadn't eaten, let alone barely left my bed, since coming home.

Endora faithfully worked around the clock to care for me, taking time away from her duties at the orphanage, as I became a husk of who I had worked so hard to be. Hollow and empty from the inside, the hatred for myself and for what happened sunk its ugly teeth into my mind causing such pain of knowing things will never be the same.

Oona came often when Endora had to go to the orphanage. She would sit with me in the quiet, telling me about her day and what was going on at the library. Not once did she ask about Tyran or what had happened between us. She brought books that soon piled at my table, and eventually she took it upon herself to read to me. She would crawl into my bed beside me, and read many of the stories she knew I would love to hear again. Anything to get me to come back to them.

It was a rainy morning when I woke up clearer than I had been in some time. A pale blue light of the early start of the day filtered in as I got up and dressed to go outside. I hadn't checked if Endora was still in bed, or had already gone to work, and stepped out into the cold.

I kept my jacket buttoned close to my body as the familiar roads awoke me. I felt like I was floating toward the training grounds. The pathway soon came into view and I walked down the muddy dirt road towards the rail fenced arena that Viggo and I first trained in.

The soldiers outside gave a nod of respect as I entered that small arena. The grass was now dead and flattened to the ground. There was a mixture of fresh rain and a faint smell of smoke from the fires that burned within the barracks that I barely registered as I plopped down in the center of the ring looking out to the other fenced in fields beyond.

I waited to feel him. Anything to bring me one shred of him to my senses.

Why had he attacked Tyran?

Why had Tyran killed him?

I struggled to pick out anything to remember, but the bodies of the reanimated piled on me kept me from seeing anything more than what I had. I struggled at remembering the voices. The tones and words that I could make out. I shook my head after realizing I was reaching. Trying to fill in blurs with information that just wasn't there.

The wave of sadness rolled through me again.

A familiar large blue-gray tuxedo cat, still wearing an empty harness, rubbed against my back before climbing on my lap. He purred and slowly closed his amber eyes before settling down on me. His gentle rumble moved up my stomach as I slowly put my hand on him, noticing the details of the harness.

It was Viggo's details. He was more than just a messenger. He was Viggo's cat while he spent so much time here.

I couldn't help but smile at Newt as he slowly curled his paws independently against my thigh, and pet his soft fur as he continued to purr sweetly. It was at that moment that I finally started to feel again. A piece of Viggo I was so desperately reaching for came to me.

Ambient noises became more noticeable and the cold ground I sat on was damp enough I needed to stand and head back home to change. Newt followed me as I left the arena. I paused, wondering if I needed to tell anyone at the Sentinel camp, but no one looked alarmed as we walked out together.

Coming out of a warm bath, and a happy cat that rested on my bed gave a shocked Oona all the information that things were turning. After dressing in some warm fleece lined leggings and a thick sweater, I asked if Oona would take me with her to the library, to which she eagerly agreed to. Endora had baked some poppyseed muffins the night before, and I ate the first solid thing in nearly a week as we left the house.

Oona was cautious about how much to talk as we strolled down the street. I saw her hopeful, but still concerned, look as I drifted in and out of thought while I ate. A small sliver of healing occurred. Something that made me feel a glimmer of what I once was, happened when sitting on those grounds and finding Newt, but there was still such a dark expanse that was left completely dark and unknown.

I wasn't sure if I'd ever be able to open that door I locked him behind in my mind. If I could even begin thinking of Tyran without questioning his motives. I quickly pushed it aside, knowing that it would only bring the rage and pain to the surface again.

A rush of warm air escaped through the opened doors of the library as we entered. It had seemed like it had been so long since I had come through those front doors. The familiar smell of books, glue, and wood, mixed with the sights of the great quartz pillars and marble-checkered floor. It reminded me of a much different time, as we walked to the back of the great room. It had been nearly fully restored and only a few minor items were left to replace. Oona hugged me and I let her know I'd be right back as I walked to Bergen's office.

He sat behind his desk with pen and paper, writing and keeping records of the many things that we had experienced. It was part of his duty as the Wizard of our town to keep history, and what happened that night needed to be recorded, too. His crimson robes were trimmed in a white thread that stood out against the mahogany wood. I set my bag on my small desk and looked at what work had been stacked there for who knows how long.

Bergen nearly jumped from his seat with a shout of surprise. "Wren! You're here!"

I could only smile when I looked his way while I finished assessing the work to accomplish for the few hours I could manage.

"I'm so glad to see you," he said, standing quickly and coming to my side.

"Hi Bergen. I thought I'd maybe get some work done today, if that's alright?" I managed, still sounding hollow, unsure of the proper tone.

"Yes, of course; but I want to talk for a moment if you're able to?" he stumbled over his words, something he didn't normally do, and I slowly nodded.

His breathing was a little heavier than normal, and tears formed as he looked at me, trying to smile. I couldn't help but feel the burning in my own eyes as we stared at one another before he spoke again.

"Wren. I'm so very sorry. I can't even begin to express the sadness we've all felt from what happened, but for how much it has hurt you."

I was definitely going to cry.

"We can't take back the actions that led to what happened, but we need to work through them, and it doesn't have to be today, or even this week, but if, and when, you are open to this we can talk, and more needs to be talked about." he said.

I closed my lips tightly and looked down at his feet. I knew he was right, but it still felt so fresh. I wondered what Viggo did after he lost Mikhail. How long had it taken him to recover? How does a warrior overcome sorrow like this? I knew he would want me to press on, but out of anyone who would push me in the ways he did, he also would understand the time taken to get to a point where things could be understood.

"Soon. I don't know if I can now, but... Soon," I said, looking back up to Bergen.

Bergen gave a nod of understanding as he clasped his hands together and turned back to his desk.

I shelved books, walked the halls, ate lunch with Oona, and helped her at the front desk that afternoon. We got into the groove of what it was like before I was diverted to attending combat and magic training. She told me about her new interest in a Sentinel that stood watch around the library, telling me about how they have become closer and were going out to dinner this evening.

It made me smile to know of the happiness she was experiencing amidst what had occurred, and what more could happen. It made me think of all the people in town who may not know of the things that had happened, and what loomed with Rhonin still on the loose. I thought of their blissful happiness at their day-to-day activities and the joy that their lives brought. It gave me another shred of Viggo back, thinking of what he put aside to protect his town and his people for those moments.

I knew we didn't have much time before Rhonin would strike again. He would want to unleash whatever powers he spoke of, and from what I gathered in my haze, it'll either be channeled through Tyran or me. I needed to save what I loved, and keep those that experienced such terror from the attacks safe. We had to figure out a way to take down Rhonin, and ultimately that would fall on the one Necromancer we knew who could tell us what was happening. I would need to work with Tyran again.

The moments of clarity and being present within our world would still come and go from time to time. I would be fine part of the day, then feel numb and empty for the other part. It was a process learning how to adjust back to what life would be like, doing the familiar things that normally included people in your life that no longer would be there, and yet, you were supposed to continue to do those things when they weren't there any longer.

It would be simple things, like cleaning up from cooking a meal, or walking through town, and you would realize they weren't with you. Then there was the fear of wondering if you were forgetting them if you hadn't been thinking of them. The hardest part, though, was knowing one was truly gone, and the other you had shut out.

CHAPTER 30

IFINALLY FELT READY to move on and see what we needed to do to prepare ourselves for when we face Rhonin. Bergen was wearing plain natural linen robes when I arrived in his office that morning, which told me he was planning on traveling out today.

"You and I are going to the Village of the Witches today," he said while stacking a couple of books on my desk to take with us. "Agatha has sent their Vulpini Bats for us, they should be here shortly," he said and a smile of excitement came over him, "I've always wanted to ride one."

"Do we know what we are meeting about?" I asked, very intrigued by our transportation.

"We have a few things to speak about pertaining to Rhonin, and well… You," He said, with a more serious smile.

A small chill rose along my spine as I thought back to Rhonin's offer when I nearly had given up while laying next to Viggo that day. He needed me, or someone like me, to channel the power the obelisk contained. I wanted to stay as far away from it as possible, and what was worse is that his own son could also be used as someone to channel it.

There were so many emotions that I felt about Tyran. I couldn't bring myself to open those shields and closed doors yet. There was still too much anger and pain associated with him.

Bergen grabbed his staff, and we walked out of the library to the main road. He let me know we would avoid the pageantry this time and the Vulpini Bats would land outside the northern gates. Our pace was quicker than normal in excitement for those fox bats.

The large billowy clouds moved across the sky and light left rays shining down onto the expanse of fields around us as we walked through the gates. A flicker of gold and red light soon came into view as three Vulpini Bats flew overhead. One Battalion Witch hitched two of the vulpini either side of the one they rode. With a swooping descent and fluttering of wind around us, they landed gracefully.

The vulpini greeted us with excited chatter and fox-like calls as I took in their lean, graceful bodies. Sliding into the leather saddle harnessed to one, I couldn't help but pet along their coarse guard hairs that parted to give way to the smooth undercoat. The one I was on gave a trill-like sound at my touch, and I could feel the energy within it that let me know it was eager to fly.

The Battalion Witch welcomed us with a smile as we gripped the handles of the saddle before calling out a whistle to lead us into the sky. The cold wind whipped at my face and hair as we spiraled up into the air. I gritted my teeth at the speed, and my knuckles went white at how tight I was grabbing my saddle handles. The whistling of the leather-tipped wings cut through the air was like a beautiful song as we soared. I looked to my side to see Bergen hanging on for dear life as well.

As we flew over the lands, I recognized the familiar small villages that laid between our two main towns. The Quarter Moon Village was beautiful from above, and I searched for the rooftop of the inn, only to feel a mix of sadness. It was only a moment after that we were nearing the forest that I was chased by the Ursendir. I couldn't help but check if there was any movement within the trees, but we flew by too quickly.

A rise of anger dug into me as we crossed each of these locations, not just because of what happened there, but these were two places where I couldn't escape the memory of Tyran. I still wanted to hurt him for what he did, and it hurt how he plagued my memories of these places.

The anger quickly simmered as Briaroak Village came into view. The library at the center of town rose above the buildings as a new and shining pillar of the center of their town. We landed in a staging area for the Vulpini Bats in a part of town I saw when I last visited. We were met by another two Battalion Witches as they gave us their welcomes and led us into the center of town.

The library was no longer bare wood frames and scaffolding along the outside. The red terracotta roof almost glowed in the sunlight. White wooden cladding that matched many of the homes and buildings around that rose through its tall center. Rich maple wood that framed the corners of the building were carved with intricate vines, flowers, and celestial elements of the stars, moons, and planets. The entrance doors were just as carefully carved as the maple frames, and two cloaked witches opened them for us as Agatha waited in the entry.

"Simply wonderful!" Bergen breathed out as he walked into the library.

"I'm so glad to have this space back in our village." Agatha beamed.

The interior of the library was completely different from our own. Rich maple panel molding decorated the walls with large tapestries depicting landscapes of their town hung inside of the large frames. Dark red velvet swaths of fabric hung from the tall coved ceiling as more support beams stretched across the width of the space. Bookshelves lined the walls that didn't have landscapes on display, and rows of bookcases in the center of the room stretched to the back wall.

I noticed that many of the townspeople were still working to place books back on the shelves, organizing them how they saw fit and making sure they could fill their ample space as best as possible after losing so much. I almost wanted to walk down one row to help them before I heard Bergen calling to me to keep up with where they were headed. I hurried my stride on the lovely red and gold rug runners that stretched down the walkway to a door at the center of the back wall.

Agatha led us into her office. It was simple, made of the same maple wood as the rest of the library. Her desk had delicate carved wood legs, and open hanging shelves on the back wall where she kept the ancient texts she preferred on hand, flanked by two floor to ceiling windows.

We took a seat at the chairs in front of her desk as she sat in a more substantial leather one behind her desk. Bergen and Agatha continued the small talk of pleasantries and compliments of the new building before beginning the real reasons for our meeting.

"It's wonderful to see you again, Wren. I want to extend our sincerest apologies for your loss," Agatha said kindly.

"Thank you. I'm processing through everything, and I'm glad I can be here today," I said.

"We have been working together to find out what Rhonin obtained within the obelisk that day on the battlefield. We have found some very concerning information along with a few things we need to speak to you about," Bergen said, while I listened closer. "It appears that Rhonin was stealing old texts and ancient books to research how to store both light and dark Aura. Our idea that he's looking at creating a weapon was right. He wants to use a weapon so powerful, and so great, that only those who use shadow magic can channel it."

"Well, he's going to be waiting for a while because I don't know how he thinks I'll be willing to channel that sort of magic," I said with a sharp tone.

"We aren't worried about you wanting to, but what we've found is that he can still use this incredibly dangerous weapon even if you aren't willing." Agatha said grimly, "All he'd need is to tether you to the obelisk through proximity and a spell, then he will be able to use it at his command."

"Why would it only work with shadow magic?" I asked.

"Shadow magic can use both light and dark magic, and not become consumed by its effects. You already have a balance within the magic that doesn't seem to tip one way or the other. Aura becomes just Aura, whether light or dark for you. The magnitude of light and dark Aura contained in the obelisk would tear any other kind's mind apart," Bergen said. "From what we've learned, Rhonin is preparing an army and he'll stop at nothing until he finds you… or Tyran."

Heat flashed through my cheeks at Bergen's pause before saying his name, "If he even thinks of going back to his father, I'll kill him."

"Have you spoken to him?" Bergen asked softly.

"No. I don't plan to ever," I said, seething with darkness.

A part of me knew I'd have to, eventually. I'd have to open that door and reunite that other part of my shadows once again. We needed Tyran away from Rhonin to defeat him. I just didn't feel ready to confront those emotions yet.

"I think it's time we talk about that day, Wren," Bergen said as he straightened in the chair next to me. "That battle was a blur, and I can't give you a definitive answer as to just what occurred in those final moments," Bergen cleared his throat, "but I firmly believe what transpired was not fully Tyran's doing."

I shot a glare at Bergen. I couldn't help it. I was so protective of those emotions that this could bring. I was just able to bury them away, and yet we were opening them up fully.

"How could you take his side?" I shook my head at Bergen.

"I'm not choosing a side, but merely telling you what I saw," he said, remaining cool and neutral. I wasn't sure I could hear more from him.

"If we want to have a true fighting chance at taking Rhonin down, we will need to keep tabs on you and that boy." Agatha said to me, trying to move forward beyond what was left open and raw.

I sat in silent rage as Bergen and Agatha started talking about logistics, what armies should be notified, and what we could do working together.

The Battalion would offer aid and fighters. It was an incredible thing to have, as they could provide the Sentinels with easy access to elixirs and potions that could make recovery in battle quicker. They talked about sending out scouts, some in the air and some on the ground to see what movements we could detect. As of right now, our Sentinel soldiers were being led by three Watch members that were closest to Viggo. We would need to clear everything with them ahead of time, but the ability to have a plan, and a new lead of the Battalion to work with would prove helpful to them in their newly appointed roles.

We spent a couple of hours going over details until the discussion came to a stopping point when we had a loose idea of what we could do to prepare. I thought we were near saying our goodbyes, but Agatha seemed to have something on her mind she finally wanted to address.

"Before you go, Bergen and I need to offer you something."

She went to a large wardrobe cabinet that resembled one to store coats and jackets, but when she opened it, a large rectangle box was inside. Bergen helped her bring the box out and placed it on her desk, turning it so the clasp that held it closed faced me.

"We've kept this hidden for centuries. So long in fact that the history of it became partly unclear, and through our research to fully understand its importance, especially with the showing of your magic, it's come at a time where the stars are aligned to who this needs to go to." She finished and held out a hand, prompting me to open the box.

One small click and the box hinged open slightly. A smell of old velvet, and cedar filled the room as I opened the top of the box. Against the deep blue velvet sat a leaf-bladed sword. Arcane runes were carved on the hilt, like small etchings of protection and something too old to make out. The blade had a mirror-like finish with a hint of iridescence to it. A gentle thrum of magic stirred, as that deep magic I unleashed so wildly on the battlefield responded to the blade that laid before me. I gasped at how it soothed me, and yet empowered that wild, deep magic I held.

"It calls to you." Bergen said, realizing the shift in magic around us.

"It has always belonged to you," Agatha whispered in amazement.

My fingers slowly moved to touch it, and white light appeared, as if it were an inner glow waiting for our connection. I pulled back, hesitating for a moment, before giving in, and grabbed the hilt. Stars burst from within the blade as it went fiery white. I squinted at the glow but quickly adjusted as I felt my magic channel through it. Bergen and Agatha sat with mouths open as they admired the blade in my hand.

It had a comfortable weight and the size of the blade was what I was familiar fighting with. I noticed the sheath it came with tucked into the top of the box and pulled it out to place the blade inside. It was a leather strap that I could wear on my back, much like I did with the swords I wore of the Sentinels. I thanked Agatha for the gift, not entirely sure yet what powers it will hold, but only that it definitely spoke to the shadow magic within me.

She offered another time to speak in the coming days about the blade and my magic. I wanted to train with the blade and understand how my magic worked with it. Agatha walked with us to the doors before a waiting Battalion Witch took us back to the Vulpini Bats to fly us home. The gentle weight of the sword against my back felt like it was a part of me I didn't know was missing. Something felt so right having it on me as we flew into the sky and back towards town.

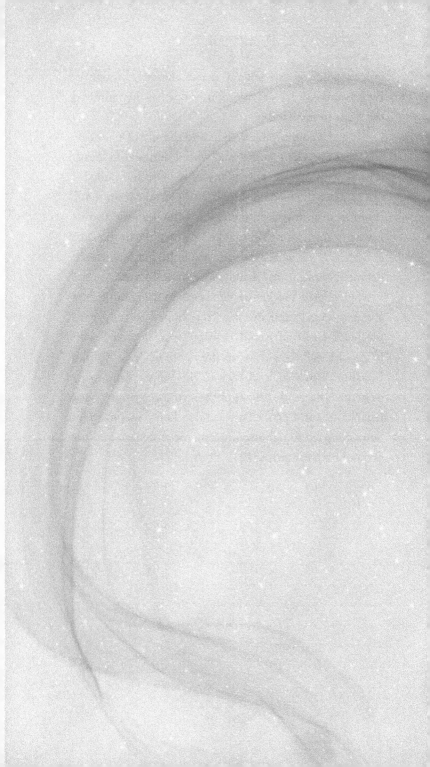

CHAPTER 31

I FELL INTO A rhythm for the next few days of working in the library, mixed with the time spent with Bergen preparing ourselves for the next battle. We kept in regular contact with Agatha as we worked together and continued to share information.

"Tell me more about my shadow magic? What else do we know beyond what I've learned from Bergen?" I finally asked one day after Agatha had stopped in to see Bergen.

Agatha took a seat in Bergen's office and began.

"Shadow magic is why the blade calls for you. It belonged to an Original. An ancestor of yours." Agatha said.

"I'm from an Original." I said, repeating what I already knew, and Bergen had already gone over with me, but it still felt more real hearing it from someone outside of who I regularly kept my secret with.

Bergen and Agatha silently nodded.

"And Tyran?" I said hesitantly.

Bergen spoke. "From what we've been able to surmise from our ancient texts, it appears the three Originals who carried shadow magic had specific roles. Marion, keeper of Life, Jareth, keeper of Death, and Ismael, keeper of Immortality." He went on as he pulled the corner of his beard, "Your magic calls to the Life ancestry; of Marion, and we can assume Tyran is a descendant of Jareth, of Death lineage."

Agatha moved back to the main point. "It's unclear as of now of Ismael's lineage, we surmise he didn't have any descendants before he was killed, removing the shadow magic to bind immortality, but we hope to continue learning more while we keep researching."

All this was so much to process. Much of which I couldn't wrap my head around without having time between learning of my father and what I'm now a part of. Tyran was as much a part of this as I was, and I wasn't sure I could handle it all.

"Thank you for all you've done to research this. I think I need some time. I'm going to get some fresh air if that's alright," I finally said, leaving the room as they nodded.

I hadn't been out to the Sentinel training grounds since that morning Viggo's cat found me. It was yet another step in my process of healing as I entered the ring with the training dummies. I stretched my legs and arms out before using my new blade. It took some time to get into rhythm, feeling that such a large part of me being here was missing. I missed our jokes, our conversations, and just having someone with me. I unsheathed my blade and started with practicing stances and basic attacks.

It was as if I felt lost again, almost as if I wasn't doing something right without Viggo watching me and training me, offering insights and corrections to my movements and attacks. I paused after a set of attacks to catch my breath and thought about what Bergen told me in Agatha's office when he witnessed Viggo's death.

I had to go back to my own memories and what I witnessed. The way Tyran was on his back, both hands on the hilt. Viggo's choice of grabbing the blade, and causing an injury to his hand was a reckless move. Why had he done that? The tones of voices that were blurs in the drowning tones of everything occurring around us.

My blade started glowing white hot and drips of what looked like starlight fell from it as I held it at my side. My breath was uneven as my anger rose again. I played back the reactions of what I saw, how Bergen may be right. It didn't make sense for Tyran to be the one advancing on Viggo, and Viggo wouldn't have truly tried to harm Tyran like that. There was something more.

Still, I couldn't get past the anger and hatred for it being Viggo's life that was lost to a Necromancer's blade. Starlight continued to fall from my weapon, and shadows weaved down my arm before I heard a gasp from a soldier as they ran past the training ring. I had to calm myself.

I knew what I'd have to do to overcome this pain, and to think clearly once again, but I knew that would mean I would have to confront what I kept shut away. The emotions I tried to keep suppressed kept rising on their own. I would have to open that door I locked Tyran behind if I wanted to help our lands. Fear crept in me as I left the training grounds, knowing what I was about to do.

I got home that night and went up to bed early. Endora noticed I was feeling off and tried offering some gentle advice that it was normal to feel some stress and very much recognized that it could be hard on me after being at the training grounds. She was partially right, but it was something much heavier that I knew I was going to confront tonight. I climbed into bed after getting ready for the evening and tried to clear my mind of any residual emotion that could keep me from opening that shielded and locked part of me.

That dark space within my mind opened to me, my shadows following me as they longed to be reunited with Tyran. The darkness cleared to the door I imagined I had locked, and I slowly placed a hand on it and waited. I could feel life on the other side, faint at first, but once it knew of my presence, the shadows licked at the door, begging for freedom. I turned the handle and opened myself once again to it.

The rush of both sides of our magic convened into me once again. I gently allowed those shadows to swirl around me in the happy reunion, knowing too well I was using it for something that wouldn't bring the same happiness. I sent out the wispy vines, searching for the familiar figure I so easily had found on the other end before.

I found him after a moment, laying curled on his side. My shadows touched him softly as his form became clearer in my mind. He sat straight up, almost instantly recognizing me, and shouted down the line of our connection.

Wren? Shadows moved quickly from him as he sought me out.

Don't. I said.

I didn't want him near me like that just yet. It was painful enough to feel him on my own.

Please, Wren. Let me see you. He nearly begged.

Tell me where you are.

He paused, hearing my cold tone.

Meet me at New Moon Inn tomorrow.

It didn't feel like he had been staying there this whole time; the surroundings felt more distant and unfamiliar. My heart raced for a moment, wondering if he had given into his father's control, and if he was back at Reapford. My anger grew then, as it sunk its fangs into me. If he was there, and giving in to his father's will. I would kill him. I quickly shut the connection once more before I couldn't control the deep magic.

It was hard falling asleep that night, and the sleep that did come was fitful. I kept dreaming of his voice. The deep seductive way he talked when we were closest, his laugh and the way we made each other smile, down to the pleading sadness as I shut our connection behind that door. It hurt to still be so attracted to it. The pain radiated in my bones; of want and sorrow, of anger and frustration.

I woke in a cold sweat to his gentle whispering; *I love you.*

I left early that morning knowing it would take the better part of the day to get to the New Moon Village. I sent Newt with a message for Bergen that I would be out for the day. I didn't tell him where, though.

My sword was strapped to my back, and I packed my satchel with extra food for the journey. I wore all black. My boots, thick leggings, long sleeve undershirt and sweater, followed by a slim fitting jacket were all dark as night, as I moved through the pathway that would loop me towards the similarly dark town. I pushed myself to not feel really much of anything, including the cold, as I tried to not think of what I was about to do. What I did know was that I didn't want to weaken myself by getting lost in thoughts along the way.

I stopped only to eat lunch before the stave church-style black buildings came into view. The sun was getting lower, as the shadows stretched towards the hills and treeline to the east. It was almost as if winter had set in, leaving the air cold over the path while I kept my pace. I hadn't let my shield down or opened that door to allow Tyran in yet. Once I crossed the gates to the village, I would open the door.

I could feel him nearby as my shadows swirled and pulled me. They longed to be reunited physically once again. My steps crunched along the pathway as I turned a corner to the inn. My emotions were rising to where my lungs burned. I knew I had to control myself, but I wasn't sure how easy it might be once I saw him. I immediately felt his presence in the tavern as I entered the inn. I could only nod quickly at the innkeeper as I searched for him.

Another shot of pain deep within my bones shook me as he came into view, sitting in the back corner of the room. He looked drained, and completely lost compared to his usual confidence. I opened that mental door, and his hazel eyes met with mine immediately. I saw the sparkle of red in their sea of hazel once again and had to steady myself as I walked through the empty tables to sit across from him. He reached out for my hand, but I pulled back.

I was shaking. It hurt so much seeing him, my heart ached. The rage built within me once again, trying to replace the pain. I wanted to push it aside, but I couldn't escape the image of him holding the blade, and Viggo's heart being pierced.

"We need to go somewhere else out of this town before I erupt and blow apart a building," I said, continuing to shake.

Tyran's expression turned to stone, not underestimating what I could do as we stood to leave. It was well into the evening by the time I arrived, and people were filling in the empty spaces of the tavern for dinner and evening plans. We went outside before he placed a rune on the ground, appearing only a short distance near the treeline of the hills to the east.

Tyran tried to touch me again, and I slapped his hand away.

"You don't get to do that." I snapped as the anger kept flowing. "You killed him!"

"Wren, please let me talk to you," he said firmly, before I slammed my hands into his chest, pushing him back.

"How could you!" I screamed, as he stumbled.

I went to swing a fist at him, and he blocked it, but didn't counter-attack.

"I won't fight you, Wren," he said as I moved on him again.

I swung at him and landed a hard fist to his side, making him cough out at the blow. I went to throw another punch, and he blocked it, backing up as I kept advancing. The anger boiled as I threw out another punch, making contact and turning to kick him before he grabbed my leg and let it go.

"Fight me! Show me what you did to him!" I yelled as my shadows radiated from me.

"I told you, I won't hurt you, Wren. I tried to stop—"

My shadows wrapped around him and threw him to the ground before he could finish.

"You killed him!" The sting of hatred in my words.

"Never once did I try to kill him!" Tyran yelled back, now matching my anger.

All the emotions I suppressed turned into something so violent that I pulled my sword from my back and pointed to his chest while he was still laying on the ground. He stayed still, looking up at me with those beautiful eyes. The point of my blade was close to breaking his skin, but he didn't move.

"He was under the control of Rhonin. My father tapped into dark magic and used a mind control method.

You have to believe me, Wren." Tyran said, trying to remain calm.

I scoffed, still fighting the urge to crumple right here and now, letting my shadows completely consume and tear me apart.

"You know he was a warrior. He would have been able to disarm me, or kill me first. My father's control affected his ability to fight."

I paused. He was right. Viggo was skilled and would have had Tyran disarmed. While I didn't put it past Tyran being a good fighter, Viggo was a true warrior. The Aura channeled through him like magic, but in pure physical prowess.

The sword glowed against his chest as I stared back at him. My breathing was ragged and grew heavy at the scene before me. Those emotions toiled together in a powerful mixture from the rage, and surfaced more of my sorrow and pain. It was at the loss of Viggo, but also the sorrow and pain of missing Tyran; of believing he wouldn't do that to him or me. The emotions shifted so quickly that I couldn't help as I let them spill from me, seeing what was before me. The man I loved laid there as I was about to pierce his heart. What was I doing?

I was about to lose him too, and it would be completely my fault. This was all my fault. The hurt stung deep, and I pulled the blade back. I buckled to the ground, landing hard on my hands and knees, and crumpled before Tyran. Tears ran down my face as a sob escaped my mouth.

My heart was still shattered. Utterly broken at the events, and the monster I had turned into; all the pain and sadness I held onto came out of me in a deep release, pouring from me as I mourned. Tyran was next to me in a second, holding me close as my emotions tormented me.

He softly stroked my hair, telling me he was alright, and that we were safe. I tried to climb out of the sudden depth of emotional despair that rocked me since I shut him out. I put my hand against his heart where I had held the point of my blade, promising to myself I would never do anything to hurt him again.

Tyran gently kissed my head before I pulled back to truly look at him. He was full of such empathy toward my hurt, and I could see the pain he held as well. His eyes were red, and I realized he had cried with me. I slowly raised my hand up to his cheek as he leaned into it.

"I'm so sorry, Wren." he nearly whispered, kissing my palm. "I am so sorry for that day."

"I know. I didn't want to, but I know now," I said, looking back down for a moment.

"Wren, I tried to keep him back, push him away, anything to fight him off, but Rhonin had a hold of his mind." Tyran repeated from sheer relief of being able to tell the truth, "Viggo confronted him, but Rhonin saw something within Viggo that he used to control him. When Viggo came after me, he wasn't himself any longer."

Tears began streaming down my face in quiet mourning, remembering that day again. I was finally accepting the reality of what happened.

CHAPTER 32

WE ONLY SPENT a short time in silence out at the treeline before a howl came too close for comfort, and Tyran placed a rune, taking us back to the New Moon Inn. He took my hand as we walked in and asked for a room to continue our conversation. The room was familiar with the ashen wood furniture and soft black bedding.

I pulled off my sword and sweater, grateful to be back in the warmth after realizing how cold it got sitting in the dark with Tyran. He wore his usual white shirt that opened into a V-shape, exposing the top center of his chest. A hint of those intriguing rune tattoos could be seen. I grabbed the comforter and wrapped it around me as I sat on the bed, taking in his beauty I missed so much.

"Where did you go? After everything?" I finally asked, hoping he didn't say anywhere near Rhonin.

"I needed to find out what Rhonin did with the obelisk on the battlefield. I went to the Warlock Camp and asked

Mennew for sanctuary while I did some research," he said, lying on the bed next to me.

"What did you find out?" I pressed, hoping for anything to help us.

"A lot of which we already know. It is an obsidian obelisk used to absorb different magic, Aura, in this case. He wanted to absorb the amplified light and dark magic that night with the Aurarius Lights so that he could use it as a concentrated weapon," Tyran replied, looking at me solemnly. "He chose the Ancient Battlefield because of the level of dark magic that still lingered there."

I thought for a moment how I might have affected the obelisk when I unleashed my powers. If that would have done more harm than good, then I would be responsible for whatever terror he planned to rein down on our lands. I didn't know what this deep ancient power within me was, but I had been allowing it to feed off the dark more than the light.

I knew I would have to tell Tyran about what I learned of our shadow magic from Agatha and Bergen. It worried me to think that Rhonin may even be a descendant of shadow magic himself, and if he truly knew of Tyran's power only because it came from his lines.

"Have you spoken to Gunnar or the Guard at all? To know what is going on in Reapford?" I asked hesitantly, trying to prolong the conversation.

Tyran sighed, "I got word to Gunnar about what happened. He's been relaying information to me about what's been happening. It's not good. Rhonin returned and commanded that people obey him, or he'd have them killed, and then forced to obey him in death. People are afraid, but those of pure blood lines are reveling at his insanity."

A chill rose through my spine and prickled down my arms.

"We still have a large unit of the Guard who don't want to follow Rhonin or his plans, but for their safety, they are forced to follow suit until we can figure out how to get control of him."

"So, can't they just attack him? Get him at a weak moment and grab the obelisk from him?" I asked.

"When Necromancers give in to dark magic it becomes incredibly powerful as it drives them mad. They become consumed with it, and it will take hold of everything that makes a person who they are, to a point where it becomes an extension of them. The things controlled, the dead raised, are always watching, and that all is linked to the wielder. Rhonin sees everything that they see, hears what they hear, and once one dies, or is attacked, he knows."

There was a yearning in his expression of wanting to be there, and to help in any way he could, but we both knew the danger that would lead to. Rhonin would find any way possible to use Tyran along with the obelisk to finish what he set out to do. The loss of choice for his people on how they chose to live and what to believe hurt him deeply. I laced my fingers in his.

I couldn't keep it in any longer.

"Agatha and Bergen have been doing a lot of research about our shadow magic. About where it may have come from."

Tyran turned to me as I continued.

"Apparently I'm a descendant of Marion, a keeper of Life."

"And that makes me… a descendant as well?" Tyran asked, trying to take everything in.

I nodded, "They think you are a descendant of Jareth, keeper of Death"

Tyran continued to stare at me, then joked "I mean, naturally, right?"

"I think the good thing is that we aren't from the same line." I joked in return, but was entirely relieved that we weren't of the same Original. His half-smile had me relax a bit.

"I… don't know what to say…" Tyran spoke slowly, feeling very much as I did over this.

"I know my father had to hold the shadow lineage, do you think your father has any shadow lines in his family?"

I was afraid to hear the answer. I knew Rhonin was maniacal over pure bloodlines, and I worried it was because of the power we had. What he could have.

"No. He's traced his family lines all being Necromancer," Tyran said quickly. "But my Mother…"

I watched him go far in thought, searching for anything he may have known about her.

"I wish I knew more about her. There were times I'd beg Rhonin to tell me more about her, and if she had any family alive I could meet with, but he told me she had closed them out."

That was a pain I knew all too well.

"I'm sorry. I feel like I pulled you into something that, had we never met, it might not have come to the level that it has," I said.

There was a sharp pain in my heart that I had brought up memories about his mother that had him feeling how I did about my parents. He has the added level of not knowing anything about her. I didn't want to be the reason he might feel anywhere near what I did. I could feel my cheeks growing warm.

"Do not for one second think this is your fault. Rhonin had to have known something about her. He's chosen to keep those parts of her ancestry hidden from me, and now I can see why. He knew something was different about me no matter what, and hoped that if he pushed me enough, I'd finally give in to his desires to embrace dark magic and allow the shadow magic to flow along with it. He wouldn't give me a chance to learn about her, and her ancestry, if it meant they would protect me, if they knew what she held."

I touched my forehead to his, smelling his familiar scent and allowing our connection to soothe the sadness. I would never tire of that ginger and bergamot smell he carried on him. He moved to kiss my brow and pulled me closer to him.

"I was so lost when I couldn't feel our connection. It nearly broke me. I tried for days speaking to you, and sending out my shadows only to be met by a wall I realized you put up."

My eyes stung, I wanted to say I was sorry, but he continued as he stroked my cheek.

"So many times I weighed the risk of going to you, to see if you were okay, but I knew you had shut me out for a reason. I didn't want to break that barrier you put there," he whispered. "I reached out for you, called for you every day through our magic, hoping you'd answer."

"I was going to hurt you. I couldn't do anything else that would protect both of us."

"I know, and I was going to wait for you, endlessly," he whispered.

"I don't deserve it," I said nearly inaudibly.

I didn't deserve it. He hadn't done anything to intentionally hurt me, but I had. I shut him out when he was hurting as well, when he needed someone too, and I wasn't there for him.

"Wren, if I could enter your mind and defeat every one of those thoughts that you aren't worth it, I'd make it my life's work." He tipped my chin up towards his face. "Do you even know how beautiful I find you? Inside and out? I'm so lucky to have the time I do with you."

"I'm so sorry I shut you out." Tears welled in my eyes.

"You had to."

He kissed me with such passion after he spoke that I nearly forgot everything that weighed me down in that moment. There was no sadness, guilt, or pain. It was just us in a sea of shadow and stars as I kissed him back. There was something about our connection, especially now that we understood it more, that made being together even more intense. I wanted to stay there, in that sea of stars, escaping this world and the hurt and danger it presented.

But we couldn't yet.

An idea sprang into my mind.

I slowly pulled back from his kiss. "You can get a message to Gunnar then, right? Can we trust that the Guard could help if we want to take out Rhonin?"

"I can get a message to him. What are you thinking?" he asked.

"We have been working with the Witches to prepare our armies for battle, if we could get intel from your Guard, we could cut Rhonin off whenever he plans to attack," I said.

Tyran thought for a moment, "They won't be able to leave, or desert the orders he gives them. They'll have to play along until the last second, and even then, the risk to them is great. If Rhonin finds out, they'll end up dead and have to obey his orders, no matter what."

"If we can work together and have the Guard turn against his armies at the right time, it can give us an opportunity to get that obelisk from him."

The pieces fell together as I spoke.

"It will have to be worth a shot. I'll send word to Gunnar in the morning. It might be risky to get him to slip away from his patrols, but he'll be willing to try," Tyran said, becoming more open to the newly formed plan.

"We won't leave each other's side this time."

"No. Not anymore. Never again." Tyran kissed me again.

"It'll be too risky for Rhonin to get control of one of us if we separate. Besides, you need to protect me with that new blade you have." Tyran tipped his head towards the sword I had tucked in the corner.

"It's from my however-many great-great relative. I call it my star blade," I said sarcastically. It was so regular looking when it didn't glow with my magic. "I'm sorry, I shouldn't have pointed it at you."

"I'm glad I didn't meet an end to it, and I know how hard that was for you. However, I'd be forever grateful if we didn't end up in that position again," he softly joked.

I couldn't help but shake my head at him, as I placed my hand on the side of his face and pulled him to my lips.

Stars burst forth in our misty dark as we dropped all conversation and gave into wanting to be fully consumed with each other. I missed this. I missed him and told myself I'd never cause that silence between us again. I couldn't get enough of his mouth on me, and of him as I ran my hands down his strong back and up to tangle into his hair as I pulled him toward me. The dark wisps of shadows shimmered as our magic danced around us.

CHAPTER 33

Tʜᴇʀᴇ ᴡᴀsɴ'ᴛ ᴀ better feeling of waking up to his warmth next to me and hearing his soft rhythmic breaths as he peacefully slept. His smell of spiced citrus clung to my hair and skin, as I laid there listening to the rain pelt against the window of our room in the New Moon Inn. It was a dark storm, and I couldn't be entirely sure it was actually morning. But judging by the hours we spent entangled in one another, and waking from a deeper sleep I hadn't had in a while, I knew it had to be.

Despite everything we talked about and the dangers that we were about to face, I let myself sink into this moment of tranquility. I moved closer to Tyran, as he sleepily pulled me to his chest while I listened to his heartbeat. I wanted this moment every day for the rest of my life. To disappear into our own world far away from anything that could tear us apart. He was mine, and I was his. My wicked Necromancer, and I, his Dark Star.

A flash of light and a crack of thunder startled Tyran more awake. I tried to stay in place when the thunder finished its rolling rumble, but he had other plans upon realizing I was awake and lightly tracing his runes.

By the time we made it down to get a message out for Gunnar, it was well into the afternoon. The sky was still pouring a cold rain as we dodged between building covers and open space to make it to a restaurant to eat and let Bergen and Agatha know about what we had planned.

"Think I can make that blade glow too, if I use it?" Tyran asked between bites of his roasted chicken.

"No way. It definitely claims me and only responds to my touch," I teased. "It'd probably zap you for even trying."

Tyran smirked. *I can think of other things that respond well to you.*

I could feel my eyes go wide at his words in my mind. *Wicked. Wicked Necromancer.*

We runewalked to the outskirts of the northern gates, deciding it would be best to be fully transparent bringing Tyran into town with me. I wasn't sure how the Sentinels would react after everything that happened. I didn't know where to begin, helping them understand the truth of what happened, and that I trusted Tyran. I hoped I could escape causing further sorrow and pain to them.

There was a brief shift in the Sentinels' stance as we walked up, but the soldiers remained in their spots, keeping eyes on us as we walked through. I gave them a nod of greeting but didn't want to look too hard at their expressions, not wanting to feel the emotion they could be masking. It didn't take long before one spat on the ground and muttered something about Necromancers as we had our backs to them that I realized I was holding my breath. Once we were a good distance past them, I let out a sigh louder than I expected.

"I'm here. We've got this." Tyran weaved his fingers in mine as we walked.

I smiled weakly, "It will take some time, they are hurting too, and they don't know what I do."

Tyran nodded, knowing that Viggo was lost by many in town.

The library came into view and we went through the side door to avoid the faces of the Sentinels that stood at the great doors. I wiped off the small droplets of rain that collected along the surface of my jacket as we walked down the warm hallway to Bergen's open door.

Bergen nearly fell out of his chair, much like the day I came back to work, when he saw Tyran walk in with me, still hand in hand. He quickly caught his glasses from slipping off his nose. His bushy gray eyebrows were raised higher than I had seen them in some time as a large smile came across that full bearded face.

"Oh my, my, my. I didn't see this happening any time soon," he said.

"Good afternoon, Bergen." I gave him a smile as I walked over to my desk and placed my blade atop it.

"We were wondering if we could talk about a few things?" Tyran asked.

Bergen was up in a moment, coming around his large desk, and clasped his hands around Tyran's shoulders. "Forgive my excitement. I understand this must be a hard time for your kind, but it truly is good to see you again, Tyran."

Tyran smiled in return as we both went to the empty chairs in front of Bergen's desk.

"We might have a way we can keep track of Rhonin's movements by the Necromancer Guard. Tyran has sent word to his closest trusted friend, and we're hoping he can let us know when he can slip out and meet with us," I said. "We've asked that he send a response if, or when, this might happen to our library if that's alright. I understand that could be a risk, but with Rhonin already knowing our involvement, I figured it was the lesser of those risks."

Bergen nodded as he took his seat behind the desk.

"I let Tyran know about the Battalion's help, and if we can get enough soldiers between us, the Witches, and a portion of the Guard, we could take Rhonin on before he makes moves to gain the power he wants," I said.

"What's the status of Reapford?" Bergen asked Tyran.

"Rhonin has put out a decree that all are to join him on his crusade. They either can do so willingly, or they will be killed, and forced to follow him in death." Tyran frowned, "Many have already tried to flee, and have been met with death, only to be reanimated and put on reserves for his army. Those that fought against him are now also living corpses."

Bergen's eyes showed a flash of sadness at the loss of innocent lives.

"We are hoping a turning of his own Guard will surprise him enough to where Tyran and I can grab the obelisk from him before he turns it into the weapon he's hoping for," I said.

"It would be an incredible risk to have you two confront Rhonin," Bergen said warily.

"We can't give him the opportunity to get to one of us alone. If he can channel anything like what Wren did that day on the battlefield with a concentrated amount of Aura, we don't know how much damage that could do," Tyran warned.

Bergen thought for a moment, "We'll need to speak with Agatha, her army will have the advantage of flying soldiers that could help play into the role of distracting Rhonin long enough."

Tyran talked to Bergen about what he learned when he stayed at the camp of the Warlocks. What he found out about the obelisk and that the Warlocks would not be willing to help us fight Rhonin. I was confused as to why, but Bergen seemed to have an understanding of them, explaining that they were an advantageous kind, and would rather sit back and see where things played to get the upper hand with whatever victor emerged. They knew that they could work with Rhonin, offering more power together, or if we defeated them, they could remain silent and continue in a peaceful land. It sickened me to see them so complacent.

It wasn't until after dinner when we saw a stray skinny tabby cat come slinking through town; he rubbed against the doorframe of the library as we were leaving for the night with a message.

"Gunnar can meet with us near the Forest of Weeping Willows tomorrow afternoon," Tyran said, folding the paper and lighting it on fire at a nearby flame of a light post.

"And you trust this isn't a trap?" I asked, knowing he trusted Gunnar, but couldn't shake the idea of either of us being tricked and captured.

It was as cold as early winter near the high walls of the Great Northern Sierras. A skimming of frost still hung in the shadows, and frozen yellow leaves still clung to the willow trees. Tyran and I runewalked here and kept within the shadows to remain unseen from anyone that could have followed Gunnar. My body gave involuntary shivers at the breeze caught in our space, as Tyran kept watch and listened for any noise.

It wasn't much longer until a soft whoosh was heard and we both stopped breathing.

"I can literally hear her bones rattling together," Gunnar said, stepping out from behind a tree. "You should at least offer her your jacket, Tyr!"

"I offered! She's stubborn!" Tyran said playfully.

They met each other and hugged, both so happy to see each other again. Gunnar looked strong, but much slimmer built. He was nearly a head shorter than Tyran, much closer to my height, and his black hair was kept short.

His golden brown skin and brown eyes complimented the softer features of his face.

"I've heard a bit about you, Wren! It's nice to meet the lady who's been tearing this guy away from barking commands at us," he joked. Tyran punched his shoulder playfully.

I smiled as Gunnar reached for my hand and kissed it dramatically. I couldn't help but laugh. Even in the face of what Gunnar and his Guard have had to endure while being subjected to Rhonin's demands, he still had humor and positivity radiating from him.

"It's nice to meet you too, Gunnar. Tyran has told me a little about you as well, and I'll agree you're definitely the stealthiest person I've met." I said.

Tyran found it the perfect time to gush about his friend, "For what he lacks in minimal Necromancy magic," Gunnar shot him a glance, but Tyran raised his eyebrows to let him continue, "Gunnar is an incredibly skilled fighter with daggers. He's light on his feet, smooth, and calculated with his attacks; I've even seen him take down monsters twice his size without a scratch."

Gunnar gave him a nod of appreciation. "That's true, I've had to save your ass a few times."

Tyran rolled his eyes, but laughed at his friend. A best friend for sure, but then got more serious as he spoke.

"Anything new from town? Has Rhonin been still demanding his ultimatum to the people?"

"It's not good, Tyr. Your Dad… He's gone wild with the dark magic. It's at a point if anyone even shows a sliver of fear, he'll siphon their life from them. It'll be in front of their partners, or kids, it doesn't matter." Gunnar looked away.

"I can't think of him as a father right now." Tyran growled.

"Our unit is still intact. We're fully committed to taking him down, but he's growing stronger the deeper he's going into the dark magic, and that object he's keeping with him; it's glowing and I swear it's siphoning magic or something. It's dangerous," Gunnar said of the obelisk, fully perceptive to the evil surrounding his home.

"The Sentinels and the Battalion are working together to build up their army to defend Caldumn. Do you think we have others outside your unit we can trust to take part in a plan to turn on Rhonin and any of the living that support him?" I asked.

Gunnar rubbed the back of his head in worried contemplation, "I don't know, it's dangerous to even talk about attempting a coup like that. I'm going to have to single out some soldiers to see how far we can trust them, but I know we can get a few more together."

"It can help divert his attention so that we can grab the obelisk from him and hopefully prevent him from unleashing anything that could decimate our lands," Tyran said.

"You know you have my support in what will keep Caldumn safe. We are on the side that needs to win." Gunnar looked at his best friend. "We're brothers in this."

Tyran hugged him again, "We'll be prepared this time now that we know who and what we're facing. Thank you, Gunn."

"We'll need to work quickly, Rhonin's army is growing, and he's ready to move out by next week toward the villages, then the main towns."

I could feel Tyran and I both tense. Gunnar finally told us the most important piece of info to this whole meeting.

"I should slap you for holding that till now," Tyran said wryly.

Tyran spoke to Gunnar only a moment longer about the Guard and what training they were being told to do by Rhonin, trying to get the idea of where they would be placed, and what location would be best for them to be in to turn on Rhonin's army when the time was right. We agreed to send another messenger cat if either of us had heard anything more, and we parted ways.

Gunnar left with a goofy goodbye, as he kissed me on the cheek and welcomed me into their Necromancer clan, leaving me laughing, but also warmed at the depth of the welcome. Gunnar disappeared back into the shadows of the forest, and I could feel Tyran's heart nearly break after he hugged his friend. I moved my hand into his and held his arm as we stood watching the space where Gunnar had been.

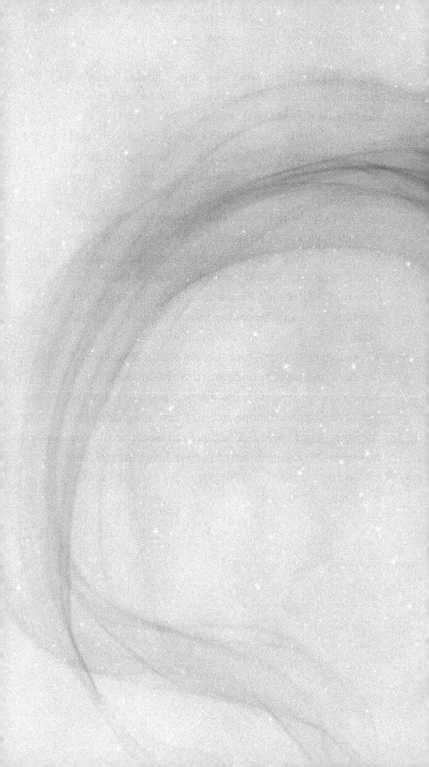

CHAPTER 34

OUR NEXT FEW days were a whirlwind of working with the Sentinels, meeting with Agatha and the Battalion, and waiting on word from Gunnar. Tyran kept busy, but I could see the lack of response from his friend was wearing on him. I trained more with my blade, understanding the magic that I could channel through it, while Tyran helped step into Viggo's shoes of being a teacher and sparring partner for me.

We spent time in the war room with the Watch as we looked at the maps of Caldumn and where the best strategic spots would be to intercept Rhonin's army. Where our weaknesses would be, and what we could do to prevent them from taking certain paths. Reinforcements were given to our town's borders, as well as bolstering our defenses at the harbor, and Oona was called to help with shields and wards around Gaelfall's gates.

The nights couldn't come soon enough where we would be too exhausted to allow any anxieties over what all this work was leading up to. Eating together in front of the fire, spending time with Endora, and sleeping next to one another for these final nights before our very way of living could be changed forever.

"Tell me more about these." I said to Tyran, as I traced my fingers across the runes on his chest.

We decided to stay the night in my room, too tired to go to the inn.

"My form of rebellion against my father's wishes of remaining pure in blood, body, and magic," he said lightly, smiling at my touch.

"Did they hurt?"

"Mm. Branded and then tattooed. It didn't feel great, but they were imbued with ancient protection spells that went back to a time where Warlocks and Necromancers shared rituals."

"Is that why you went to them after the fight?" I asked.

Tyran let out a breath. "I was more worried they would have my head for what my father has been doing, but I had nowhere else to go that would answer my questions. Mennew has kept an open relationship to our kind, as our ancient magics tend to work symbiotically, and he was the one I sought my runes from in the past. I knew he would offer me sanctuary by giving him information on what my father did."

"Let's hope these work," I said, gently kissing one point of the rune.

Tyran's low groan had me moving over to kiss the other one as well, but I could feel a part of him still disconnected from the moment. I stopped to look into his strong face. The chiseled lines of his jaw, the stubble that lightly appeared, his soft lips. His eyes were on me, anticipating my moves, but I could see the small part of them showing concern.

"Tell me your thoughts," I said sweetly. "I see there's something there you haven't said."

"I haven't heard from Gunnar yet. It's unusual for him to take this long getting word back, even if progress hasn't been going well," he said as he stroked my auburn hair that tumbled down onto his chest.

It was hard to believe that he would be in danger. I knew from what Tyran told me and seeing the way he moved, even playfully when we met, that he could easily handle the task at hand, but I could see that Gunnar was Tyran's one connection to his town and his people, and to not hear from him like he was used to would be worrisome.

"He's earned your friendship and trust for a reason. Maybe he's noticed it's too dangerous to get a message to you just yet." I tried to help ease him, "With Rhonin's preparations, I'm sure more of his armies have moved to the front lines, and perhaps even within the Guard."

Tyran nodded. "Perceptive, and a very real possibility, but I know he'd try what he could to get word out."

"We can't let ourselves spiral to those negative thoughts," I whispered, as I placed my fingers against the side of his jaw and moved up to kiss him.

He gave another low rumble, "Keep me occupied then."

I laughed as he rolled me on my back and started kissing my neck. A familiar purring sound erupted. Newt leapt on the bed and heavily stepped over us, curling his paws a few times on the comforter, and found the most inconvenient spot to lay. Tyran gently picked him up and sent him on his way out of the room before closing the door.

The air was unseasonably warm, giving a small reprieve from the layering of undershirts, sweaters, and jackets. I wore a deep red tunic top that went to my knees, and belted at the waist, with leggings and boots, and smiled at the warmth of the sun as we walked down the sun-warmed cobblestone paths to meet with Bergen. My sword lightly patted at my back as I pulled my braid to the front of my shoulder.

Bergen was waiting at the bottom of the steps of the library, and let us know Agatha was meeting with us one more time before we called on the Sentinels to move north to meet with the Battalion. It wasn't more than a few minutes later until Agatha and her Battalion escorts came swooping in on the familiar flying fox creatures and gave us a happy greeting.

We didn't meet in the library, instead bringing Agatha with us to the central building of the Sentinel base. The Watch gave a respectful salute to her as she nodded in return. Agatha's Battalion General took to one side of the table with the large map of Caldumn pinned to it and got to work talking to the Watch about the Battalion's locations and where to meet at. The Watch listened closely and gave information and suggestions as to the final arrangements and preparations needed for a seamless joining of our units.

Weapon types were checked on, how many flying fighters we could expect, and medical units with various magic and potion supplies were counted between the two armies. Soon they turned to Tyran to hear about news from the Necromancer front and if we could expect their Guards support. He straightened himself and cleared his throat, shaking off the nerves before going over the last news, or lack thereof.

"We are currently still waiting on news of how many more units of the Guard we could expect to turn on the armies when the call is made," Tyran began. "The Guard will be placed midway through their units. We expect reanimated and more disposable units to advance on the front lines."

Tyran paused before I could see that hint of concern. "I ask you to please hold your attacks on those that are living. If we don't get word on their status, we can't know for sure if they will be on the side of Rhonin's or with us."

The Watch and Battalion General had mixed expressions to Tyran's request.

"We can't just hold our attacks if we have an advantage in taking out the armies that support him," one of the Watch said.

"You have not heard from your contact within the Guard since your request. We can't trust that he's been compromised," said another.

"Please, Innocent lives are at risk. They are prisoners to Rhonin's demands, and I ask that you use restraint before attacking them willingly. We have to give them the opportunity to act on the plans we gave them," Tyran nearly pleaded.

The Battalion general took a step toward Tyran. "We will hold our vulpini aerial assaults from those living that aren't attacking, but we cannot be responsible if innocent lives end up lost due to unfortunate positioning."

"Just give my contact time, I trust there will be a shift within the Guard that will allow us the advantage," Tyran said once more.

The Watch and Battalion looked at one another before nodding in agreement.

"We will assess our positions before making the choice to attack those within the Guard that you are waiting to hear from," the third Watch member spoke.

Tyran breathed a sigh of relief as Bergen and Agatha thanked the Generals for the meeting. We walked out and back into the warmth of the sun as we finalized everything we would take with the armies in the morning. I couldn't help looking off in the distance, hoping to see a sleek messenger cat arrive with word from Gunnar, but it never came.

CHAPTER 35

I STAYED CURLED IN Tyran's arms for as long as I could before we both had to leave the warm embrace of the bed's comforter and get changed into a base layer we'd wear under the armor. I packed a few changes of clothes in my satchel and pulled my sword over my back, and went downstairs to see Endora busy with full breakfast preparations.

"I know something is happening, and even if I don't have the full details of it, I want you to be careful, and I'm not just talking about between you two," she whispered, tipping her head at Tyran who was finishing getting ready in the upstairs washroom.

"Tyran and I have something different for sure," I smiled at her, not wanting to go deeper until I knew exactly how we should refer to one another. *Boyfriend? Partner? My Wicked Necromancer?*

There wasn't any doubt that we both felt the magic strengthened the more we spent time with one another, but there was an intense connection beyond the magic. It was physical and emotional, and our ability to joke and laugh with one another were moments I'd never find with another. He was my friend, and my love.

"There's a lot that I have been learning about myself and about what I'm capable of these past couple months." I whispered back to her, "I know it's hard to not know everything, but I will be protected, and will protect those I'm with, too."

She gave me a long look, I could see the emotions running through her. Of understanding, of love, of uncertainty. She looked back at her breakfast.

"I can't ever thank you enough for all that you've done for me, Endora. You gave me a place in the orphanage, and continued to foster my growth with Viggo. You are someone I can always come to when I'm broken." I said softly, "But the most important thing is you gave me a place to heal."

Endora pushed her lips together, and I saw her fighting back tears. She grabbed my hand in hers. The dark umber tone of her skin against my pale skin was always something I loved seeing, even as a little girl.

Tyran came down, greeting Endora and grazed his fingers along my braid as he came to sit at the table. Endora was up and piling a plate with an assortment of breakfast food for him, before grabbing her things and getting ready to leave for the orphanage.

She turned as she opened the door, "I only ask of you one thing, Tyran. Take care of her."

I didn't have a chance to look at her leave, and I felt my heart ping at her words. She knew we would be involved in something dangerous soon, and it was hard for her to not be able to do anything about it. She and Viggo had been watching over me for seventeen years out of the now-twenty that I've been alive, and now with Viggo gone, she saw that this was somewhere that she couldn't protect me.

Tyran had a look of full acknowledgement at what she asked of him. His eyes moved from the door back to me with genuine care in them that made my stomach flip.

The town was quiet, but more busy than normal at this hour. Many townsfolk offered to assist preparing our Sentinel soldiers for the journey ahead, and I couldn't help but look around with pride at the community that had become my home. Many were carting food, extra blankets, supplies of various needs as we walked to the Sentinel grounds. The Sentinels were already organized, setting up checkpoints for those that offered their various donations as last-minute things to pack and take with us, while others stretched in the training grounds and readied their weapons.

I grabbed my armor and suited up near a few of the later waking soldiers, and gave them a nod of support. They nodded back, and nervously looked to Tyran as he dressed in his Guard armor, which plated him in all black. I knew it was hard for some soldiers to see him here after what happened. Many of them wouldn't even look in our direction, while others glared with hate in their eyes. I would honor their feelings, as long as they didn't come for Tyran.

We entered the central building as the Watch finished rolling up their maps to store into scroll cases, ready to be moved with us to the battlefield. Bergen entered shortly after and gave news from the Witches that they were prepared and on schedule to meet us at the time originally given. Even with all the organized movement going on, it felt chaotic. A hint of tension and excitement was palpable in the air.

"We need to be clear about what to expect from the Guard." Bergen said to Tyran as we walked back outside with him.

"We will know when I get a visual of Gunnar," Tyran said sternly.

"I'm sorry if this doesn't go as planned, but we are going to try our best," Bergen said.

"We'll wait until I can actually see him. I'll know then," Tyran said, ending the conversation.

After doing one last round of arming myself with weapons; a dagger at my side, and a small knife to hide in my boot, along with my blade at my back, I felt more ready to leave town. There was a small ceremonial goodbye from the townspeople that showed up as we marched out of the northern gates. Many were crying, many cheering, and others stared with both pride and concern as we marched out of town and into the fields beyond.

We marched for a good part of the morning, making it to the Quarter Moon Village to stop for a break. It would be a few hours' march to the northwest before we met up with the Battalion who were going to head west out of Briaroak Village. It had been the first time Tyran and I had come here since hearing it was attacked by the bandits during their onslaught, and we immediately headed to see Jurna after we were given a set time and place to assemble again.

The building was in working order, but part of the tavern was boarded up and unusable from the destruction that was brought here. I knew it was going to take them months to get things repaired and rebuilt. Jurna nearly cried when she saw us and embraced us both as she ushered us over to a table for some food. I knew it would be devastating if Rhonin's forces made their way back here. This wonderful town and its people were just now getting back on their feet.

We are coming back here to help them when this is over. I said to Tyran.

Exactly my thoughts, he said, taking a bite of the food Jurna brought.

This town had a special part of us, and I couldn't bear to think of leaving it to the small group of people who lived here. It was something that I tucked away to look forward to after the war.

Time passed too quickly as we finished our meals and walked through town bidding our farewells, and fell back in line to our continued marching. The sun broke from the cloud cover for a period before we saw shadows flying overhead. Sentinels ducked at the shock of the large size, but it was a familiar shape to me.

Vulpini Bats and their riders swooped overhead as they flew in the direction we marched. The heads of a sizable army came over the hill to the east as the Battalion met with us. The three Watch Commanders walked up and shook hands with the Battalion General and checked on the size of each of our joining armies. The General let us know the sky watch had a run-in with Rhonin's army when they tried to get a visual on them. Sadly, they lost two of their riders to arrows. They were moving within a forest to the north, and the attack came as a surprise. It's no more than a few hours' walk north and we could cut them off at a large clearing.

My heart raced as I thought about how soon we might be fighting. It was going to be early evening by then, and wouldn't leave much daylight if we were going to attack today.

I hooked my arm into Tyran's as I spoke. "How much do we have to worry about Rhonin attacking tonight?"

"The Guard will need rest. It won't be practical for him to push."

"But what about the reanimated? Do they need rest?"

Tyran hesitated. "No, however, if I know the generals within the Guard, even if they are siding with Rhonin's cause, they will ask for a night of rest."

I swallowed hard and hoped he was right.

It was careful planning and surveying from the riders in the sky, but the Watch and Battalion General had planned correctly, and we were in a favorable position in the treeline before the clearing where we had planned to attack. The elevation of the Central Plains gave us a good view, and we had Sentinels and Battalion flyers regularly watching for any movement along the horizon line.

The soldiers were calculated with how they set up camp. It was a considerable task compared to the small setup that I saw when we first confronted Rhonin, before we even knew who and what we were dealing with. Tents of various sizes, battle staging areas, kitchen areas, medical units, and blacksmithing anvils with portable forges were set up to repair weapons. I never witnessed what a war would be like at this magnitude. Some of the older soldiers definitely saw what the earlier battles over territory were like, and it chilled me to think that we were doing something once again that had been so long ago.

Fires were lit as the sun set behind the mountains of the Great Northern Sierras as they loomed in the background. I had been so busy getting our sleeping quarters situated, and checking over my weapons and practicing my fighting positions with Tyran that I didn't have time to think about whether we had received word on Rhonin's advancing Guard. It came at dinner, when the stars were glowing brighter and the purple of the twilight into night was nearly full black.

A birdsong shot out, and the Vulpini Bats that sat hitched to the temporary posts cried out in a warning chatter as I shot to my feet and ran to the front lines outside of our camps. Small fires were lit at the horizon, and I could barely make out movement in the dark. I grabbed Tyran to brace myself as I saw the long line of small lights that were lit intermittently along their camp. It looked massive.

"A tactic to worry us, it's why they didn't advance until night. So we didn't have an aerial view," One of the Sentinel Watches said to me, noticing my unsteadiness.

"We're going to tear them apart," said a Battalion Witch. I hoped he was right.

CHAPTER 36

THE WIND SWEPT through the open flap of the tent as I pulled my hair up and tied it back. The rustling of soldiers moving about outside woke me up from a very uncomfortable night's sleep on the thinly padded mats on the ground. I knew it was the adrenaline keeping me from feeling my exhaustion, and I thought about seeing what the Witches may provide to keep me further stimulated. Endora's coffee with an elixir mixed in to give the focus I needed would do.

Tyran had woken when I did, and I could sense he felt the same about the comfort of the previous night. He stretched as he woke, then changed into the battle gear, before coming over to help me with adjusting my blade's leather strap to avoid it bouncing against my back like it had been. I took a moment staring at his face as he focused on tightening the belt around me.

I had already memorized the strong lines of his jaw, where his stubble grew along his face, the way his lips curved in such a dreamy way, and how beautiful those multifaceted eyes were. The mixture of green, brown and blue with the flecks of red that reminded me of shards of rubies when they caught in the light.

When my belt was secure and he looked up at me, "We stick together today."

"You won't leave my sight," I said, promising to him, and myself.

He kissed me with a sweet softness that reminded me of our first kiss. A gentle love as he moved from my bottom lip to my top and back. I met him with the same slow movements, relishing in one of the last moments of privacy we might have.

I love you, my Dark Star.

I love you, my Wicked Necromancer. Always.

We held each other for as long as we could before we heard the faint call of order from the Sentinel Watch.

The smell of fires and food being cooked wafted through the cold air as we walked to meet with Bergen and the Generals. Agatha had stayed back to protect their library and town, and I thought about the charge Oona had been put in protecting ours. I couldn't think of anyone else who loved our building and history more than her outside of Bergen. So many faces of fighters, fully armed, many with black cloaks and many who wore the familiar brown leather armor sat together while eating the last of their breakfast.

Bergen was at the edge of the treeline with the generals. The light of the day shone through the thin cloud cover that kept the morning dim. Bergen and the Watch had their backs turned, looking toward the battlefield, blocking the view, before I finally got close enough, and my stomach dropped.

Small, thin lines of smoke trailed up from the fires that had been lit the night before across the field. I was hoping to believe what was said about it being a tactic to make their army seem larger than what it was, but sadly it wasn't. Small black figures of Rhonin's army filled the horizon line, assembling into units and groupings, preparing for our meeting of blades and magic.

Another call rang out from the Watch, and our Sentinels and Battalion organized, moving beyond the safety of the treeline and coming into view of Rhonin's armies. The Vulpini Bats began circling above the assembling troops as the riders took the time to get them to get their wings stretched and moving. The Watch spoke to Bergen, letting him know our armies were maybe just over half the size of what Rhonin brought, and set to work figuring out the body count and ease of killing reanimated and the first line of defense.

Our high attack soldiers took the first line of defense, followed by two flanking units of secondary Berzerkers, who were highly efficient dual-wielding short swords. The third line of defense included our Archers, and the last couple rows were of the defensive units who would be in charge of picking off any of the attacking lines that made their way through. Tyran and I took a position between the Archers, hoping for the opening needed to push towards Rhonin.

There was an eerie quiet that went across the field as our armies marched into position on the battlefield. Rhonin's armies approached, and I realized the sheer size of the reanimated that he controlled, making my stomach churn even more. All those lives who had to fall subject to his command even after death, left to meet another death—another form of suffering and pain. I hoped that whatever part of a soul these had, didn't have the wherewithal to comprehend this sort of torture.

Beyond the line of reanimated came vile beast Abominations. Three massive creatures constructed of raw flesh, fur, tails, teeth, and eyes lumbered forward. They walked on four legs, and had another four arms, some holding weapons, while other arms looked like they were the weapon. I remembered how the last Abomination fought, using its appendage as the weapon against the Sentinels that braved the attacks, and how quickly they met their end.

"We need to focus on the Aboms first," I said to Tyran, knowing it would save a large part of our troops.

Tyran agreed as he stood next to me with an energy I hadn't felt before. He was a trained fighter, being part of the Guard. He knew what he was up against with his own people on the other side. I saw him looking beyond the Abominations scanning the line of the living members of the Guard.

They wore black armor, like his, with pauldrons and small silver rivets adorned them, keeping the plating flexible. So many of them stood out, some wide eyed with fear at their own units, others glazed over and lost to what was to come. Tyran's body stiffened, and I saw who he found.

Gunnar stood near the front side of the Guard. Many of them with expressionless faces, standing and waiting, looking beyond our very own armies that were meeting with them. He was completely still, no movement or signal of noticing us as we searched for any hint of knowing in his face or eyes, even some small glance to let us know he was aware.

"He's alright," I heard Tyran breathe out in a whisper.

"He's not under any sort of control, is he?" I asked, still searching for any recognition of what he showed me before.

"We need to get to him." Tyran said.

I nodded, making a mental image of the path we would take, trying to save as many of our units from the Abominations, followed by a push for an opening to get near the Guard, helping Gunnar, or at least getting him away from danger, and then we'd have to confront Rhonin. Three things that may seem so small on paper. But facing it head on? I didn't know how we would accomplish it all in the chaos that was about to be unleashed.

As for Rhonin, we hadn't been able to get sight of him yet as we marched forward towards his armies. The lines of soldiers kept advancing from their starting point and I thought maybe he would be near the very back, biding time until he could make his advance with the obelisk. It would be a long day of fighting just to make it beyond the troops that we could see clearly, and knowing that there were even more beyond was hard to accept without feeling the worry of defeat.

Tyran stayed focused on Gunnar, as if he were trying to speak to him in the unspoken way that we could to one another. I looked at the Guard that Gunnar led, knowing that they were the people Tyran were closest with as well. All sharing the same stone-cold expression. Not one of them with fear, or panic, or even anger in their eyes, just a forward look beyond anything.

"I'm seeing something between all of them," I said hesitantly, not wanting to give up hope. "Gunnar and the Guard he's with, they aren't acting in the same way as the others."

Tyran gave me a sidelong look as we kept moving.

"Look at the others, fear, aggression, or that glazed look you said Viggo had, but Gunnar and his unit…" I trailed off.

"He is alright." Tyran said again, a hint of excitement in his eyes.

I nodded. "I think we can expect him to stick to our plans."

Tyran turned back to Bergen who still stood in the treeline. Barely visible, but a whistle and a wave from Tyran gave him the signal that was needed to let our Generals know that the Guard, or at least some of them, would be with us.

One final call, and both sides stopped advancing. Our Watch and Battalion General made their way to the front lines, calling out orders and raising morale. They felt too close to us, seeing all those that were reanimated. They soon parted to a cloaked figure that walked through. His hood covered his face, leaving an ominous feeling in the air as even our own armies and leader grew quiet. Slowly, Rhonin removed his hood and stood before us.

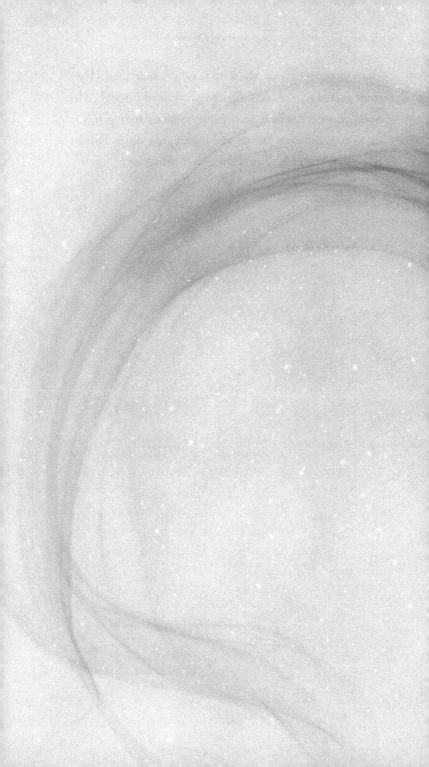

CHAPTER 37

"My, I expected more from two major towns joining forces," Rhonin yelled with utter arrogance. "And not to be surprised, but my very own son is still fraternizing with the enemy."

Rhonin let out a tsk of disapproval as he looked at us.

"I will give either of you one last chance to willingly submit to me and join what will be our new future."

Tyran spat at the ground in defiance as I held my place next to him, allowing the gesture to be our answer to the offer.

"Manners, my dear boy." Rhonin sneered, "Very well, we can do this the long and interesting way. You'll have to watch as I slowly dismantle all those around you. The suffering you'll witness and the blood spilled will be on your hands."

"You know that's of your own doing!" Bergen's voice boomed, as a Vulpini Bat landed in the middle of the second grouping of soldiers allowing him to dismount.

"Ah, Bergen. So lovely to see you again," Rhonin said with feigned welcome. "Those fox wings would make a lovely addition to my creatures, just imagine their power if they could fly as well."

My body shook with rage at the thought of him harming such a magnificent creature.

"Rhonin, we are standing united to stop you from your attempts at tyranny. You must turn over the obelisk and allow your people to live without dark magic control. You are to be tried for your crimes against Necromancers and Caldumn," Bergen commanded.

An evil smile spread across Rhonin's face as he began laughing. "You think I'll listen to an old Wizard? Kept locked up in their glass towers with their books and knowledge to be shielded from the world? Oh no, dear friend. It's been far too long that the Necromancer people have had to hide our true power and ability. We are the chosen who can wield both light and dark magic. Too many have succumbed to the ideas that society has placed on us being weak, and that changes now."

Bergen opened his mouth to speak, but Rhonin cut him off.

"I will rule these lands and take over the North. My power will know no bounds. I will harness Aura, contain it, and create the most powerful spells. I will rule you all."

"Those spells can tear our lands apart as well as your mind. You will have nothing to rule if you use it in the way you plan to!" Bergen shouted.

"Well, let's find out just how powerful this can be then, shall we?"

Rhonin pulled out the obelisk and moved to the back lines of his army, controlling the reanimated with a whisper of commands. They readied their weapons as he retreated to the back of his armies, leaving Bergen alone in the front. Unnatural growls and moans of the dead soon reverberated through the field and they charged forward.

The shouts of attack rang forward from our units as our front lines launched into battle. Bodies slammed against that of the dead and partially decayed. We ran forward to reinforce the lines that speared through the dead. The strategic positioning of our units in the v-shape allowed not only for us to make the opening to Rhonin, but to split the enemy and weaken them.

Sentinels battled with blade and sword, while the Battalion fought with magic, shooting bolts of light, and teleporting around the enemy slicing them with enchanted daggers and other weapons. The Vulpini riders swooped down, throwing glass orbs of blue flame that erupted in the front lines. Our Archers took aim, raining arrows down on the Abominations that made their way into the first line of our attacks.

Tyran and I fought side by side, slicing through enemies in a dance of death. Fire flew from my fingers, burning the bodies that were killed by our soldiers, as the back line brought torches forward to keep the reanimated dead. A loud bellow erupted from one of the monstrous creatures as it slammed two of its arms up, trapping a Vulpini Bat and rider in its palms. It ripped them in two with ease and kept moving forward as I gasped before having to battle forward with our armies.

What started as only bodies of the reanimated dead that we stepped over in our advance soon became tangled with bodies of our own. Soldiers' faces, some whom I had recognized fell at the hands of Rhonin. I wrapped the initial reaction of horror behind the drive to continue fighting for them as we made it to the first Abomination that was tearing through our troops.

Tyran and I sent our shadows out, making it drop one of the Battalion Witches from its grasp. Swirling skulls scraped at its outer layers as it tried to bat them away, while I drove a spike of black onyx into its skull.

The shriek that arose from it before being drowned out in the thick black blood that poured from the fatal wounds alerted the second as it kicked its back legs and charged at us. Tyran ran forward to meet it, twisting sideways and slicing an appendage off with his blade wreathed in his shadows. I encased its lower limbs in blocks of solid shadow, hearing the bones snap at the sudden halt of movement of its legs while the rest of its large body followed through with the forward movement. Another cry before Tyran gave it a death blow with his blade, beheading it.

Between us and the final Abomination were enough reanimated dead to slow our forward movement. I heard Tyran shout for Gunnar as we neared them. Gunnar and all the living Guard remained still, not being called to attack yet from Rhonin. For a moment, I saw the glint of something in Gunnar's eyes before having to block an attack that came from behind. I couldn't make out what that look was. One of sorrow? One of yearning? I had to quickly push that out of my mind and focus on the task ahead.

The final abomination was decimating our right flank of Berzerkers. It moved with more agile skill than the other two, looking to be made of part predatory cat, with two heads and long narrow jaws filled with sharp teeth. Its claws were like talons from a large eagle as it sliced soldiers in half, and slammed its other appendage that ended in a stump down, crushing them into the ground. A long whiplike tail of a giant lizard sent others flying back, their bones breaking upon contact.

Tendrils of shadow climbed out of either side of my shoulder blades and flowed out. Tyran ran forward, sending his magic to circle around the beast and lock it in place. My sight darkened as the shadows formed closer around me. Guards who stood watch became uneasy and watched on as I became consumed in my shadows. The giant beast roared as it realized it was trapped within the shadow rune that Tyran set, as he had to fight off some of the reanimated that tried to protect the beast. My tendrils hardened at the tips, forming large spikes. I shot them forward, continuing to solidify them in long, narrow needles. The soft sound of piercing tissue, then the crunch of bone, followed by a mash of flesh as I ripped them out and pulled the beast into pieces.

Tyran was back to my side after finishing the rest of the reanimated that were nearby, while I reeled my shadows back, and shouted for Gunnar. A horn blared out from Rhonin's side.

"It's the call for the Guard to advance," Tyran said.

Only the far left side of the Guard charged forward as they wrapped around our tactical formation to our defensive units. I braced myself for the incoming units that Gunnar stood before, but they didn't move.

"Necromancer Guard!" Gunnar's voice rang out clear, "We are the protectors of those who walk in life and death! We are the valiant, the courageous, and the strong! We are the keepers of death itself! We oppose those that sink into darkness and evil! We are Necromancers and we protect the living and dead!"

Tyran and I stood in absolute awe.

"Attack!"

Gunnar's whole right flank of the Guard turned toward the rest of the reanimated and began their assault. It was an incredible sight to see the plan play out. A flank of soldiers moved to the left, intercepting those that charged forward, others turned around to fight the rest of the reanimated, and another group came to aid our soldiers still fighting. Tyran's eyes were nearly glowing with excitement as he watched his people fighting for what was right in this world.

We joined Gunnar in his advance.

CHAPTER 38

Rhonin stood on a rise of a hill that overlooked where the Guard flanked and attacked their own. His mask of confidence wavered, seeing the damage it caused from behind. I kept my eyes toward him, trying to see the path we could clear to him while moving in his direction.

Tyran remained steadfast at my side. Our blades sang a song of demise to all those who met it. I used my short sword and dagger until now, not wanting to draw attention at the glow of my blade on my back. We reached a point where we found our moment to make a break for Rhonin. It was then that I pulled out my star blade.

Tyran saw the path as quickly as I did, as we broke free from the bodies of the reanimated and ran around the outcropping where Rhonin stood, finding the slope that allowed access to the top. We were met with an ambush from his bandits, the Butchers of Drog.

I fell to my knees as my shadows shielded me. The cracking sound of the mace slammed down on my shield and my magic flared in anger at the blow it protected me from. An unnatural low growl escaped from the bandit as I opened my eyes and saw Tyran engage two of them.

Shadow and rage poured through me as I swiftly spun with my blade and sliced toward the assassin. It twisted to barely avoid my strike and swung at me again with his mace. My shadows grabbed at its weapon, wrapping themselves tightly around it, and pushed the weapon off its path of contact.

A clashing of my blade against his mace clanged as we met each other's strike. A death-rattled roar erupted from the assassin while I cloaked myself in my shadows, disappearing from its sight. I willed my mist to move and appear behind it, swinging my blade once again before it could react and block the slicing blow I landed from his shoulder to the other side of his ribs. My ears rang as the bandit writhed from the open wound I created, but no blood escaped. Only the thick black viscous substance, much like the Abomination, began flowing from it.

I searched for the other bandit, and saw the largest bandit standing back, almost enjoying our fight. I had no time to react before the bandit I sliced turned and charged. The powerful reanimated crashed into me and I blasted his body away with a fireball, falling back from its tackle. I immediately began scrambling to my feet before it came back with its mace raised for another strike.

I blocked it once more, just in time, as the slam vibrated through my blade and down my forearm. I gritted my teeth at the powerful pain felt down my bones with the hit. I threw my tendrils forward around the assassin's feet and solidified them, as I pulled them back, knocking him on his back. I slammed my blade down and severed the head of my opponent.

Turning to help Tyran with the other two, I formed large spikes of ice and shot them towards the back of the assassin that was ready to slam Tyran with his shield. With a loud fleshy thud, the ice slammed deep into its back, giving Tyran the chance to land an attack of his bone spikes into its chest.

The clashing sound of metal and bodies, blades with weapons, and fists with flesh covered the battlefield. We fought with a heightened skill as I thought of Viggo as I fought. How he moved on his opponents, and what skill he had in these moments.

My shadows grew around me as I ran to assist Tyran before the fourth bandit joined in, pulling the dagger from my side and slicing at the sensitive flesh under the assassin's raised arm causing the bandit to drop his blade. Tyran rushed at the attacker, locking its head into his arms as he twisted, severing the spine and muscles that kept it upright. Within a second of it hitting the ground, I had a ball of flame erupting on it as more wails rang out.

Tyran turned only to have the leader of the pack ready with an attack he narrowly missed. Much larger than the others, the assassin's black eyes flamed in sheer rage at the deaths of his brothers. Shadows swirled around Tyran as he fought. Bone spikes shredded into the large undead figure as he slammed his blade against Tyran's.

It felt as though time slowed while I walked to Tyran and our shadows intertwined, sharing power with one another. The darkness grew around us as we fought. Two shadow forms of what shouldn't be here, now alive once again.

A swirling of smoke and shadow moved at the feet of the bandit as I saw Tyran's attack take shape. The mist rose as our weaving shadows formed at our backs and stretched out toward our enemy. The assassin hadn't realized it was trapped within the rune of darkness until Tyran formed his shards into skulls that swirled around it, scraping at its outer layers. Spikes formed at the ends of the tendrils that moved above me, and I plunged them into the head and chest of the leader. It twitched before becoming still, all while continuing to be consumed by the onyx skulls that ate its flesh.

We barely had time to catch our breaths before running up the slope to stop Rhonin. My legs felt heavy as we moved up the back of the hill and saw his cloaked back come into view. Rhonin was focused on chanting a spell as I realized the bodies of our dead were being raised to fight against us. I couldn't hide the noise that escaped me as I froze, seeing Sentinels and Battalion Witches reanimate and turn to attack our people. The fear and confusion sent many into a frenzy, fighting off anyone near them. Some fell victim by not recognizing that the dead of their own side were attacking them.

"Father! Stop this immediately!" Tyran shouted as we neared Rhonin.

"My son. Crawling back now that the tides have turned?" Rhonin spoke while turning to see us nearing the top of the slope.

"Give us the obelisk and I'll take you back to town to be tried for the criminal you are. For what you've done to our people, and those of Caldumn." Tyran gritted his teeth.

"Dear boy, have you not seen the power that I hold? That you could have surpassed had you even listened to me?"

"Did you know what magic my mother held when she gave birth to me? Was I just part of your plan for power?" Tyran growled.

"Your mother lied to me about her history. I knew what she and you held even before I saw those shadows swirling around you while you slept one night as a child."

"You gave yourself to the dark."

"You could have ruled this all. Could have taken over everything that I would leave you." Rhonin curled his fists at his words.

"Your world isn't one I want anything to do with," Tyran shouted.

"Enough!" Rhonin snapped, pushing his hand forward, sending an invisible force that knocked Tyran backwards.

I whirled around as Tyran was thrown down the hill, slamming into the trunk of a tree. A green, iridescent rune grew around Tyran as he remained stunned from the knock to the back of his head. Faint green chains encircled him, keeping him against the tree. I screamed out for him as he tried to get up, but the chains held him tightly.

"You are weak, Tyran! You've wasted your talent, and now you don't have the power nor ability to show anything for your efforts. You ruin my reputation the longer you spend with those lower than what we hold. I should kill you now, but I want you to watch the only good thing you did for me. You brought me this little gem, someone who isn't afraid to show the power I saw in you so long ago." Rhonin turned to me.

I couldn't stand hearing him call Tyran weak. The barrage of abuse from words that I had once thought of myself, and to hear them being directed to someone I cared so much for gave me a fire within that I hadn't felt before.

I steadied myself and readied my sword as he walked towards me, my shadow shield was still intact and I had hoped it would hold against a blow like the one he gave Tyran. He smiled at me as I growled, feeling the power rise that I had unleashed at the death of Viggo. The blade burned brightly as drops of stars fell from it, dripping in my magic.

"You will enjoy this so much more if you come willingly, girl," Rhonin warned.

"I'll never side with you." I spat. "You will die to a blade through your heart, as Viggo had done to him."

"Oh, did that warrior mean that much to you?" He questioned with evil delight, "You see, when you allow rage to fully consume your mind, it makes quick work for dark magic to infiltrate and turn you into a pawn to whatever the wielder wants of them."

I shook hearing his words. This monster, no more a human than the creatures he created. He was responsible for Viggo's death; commanding him to attack Tyran. Making it appear like Tyran was responsible for his death.

My eyes stung with something deeper than the sweat of battle.

Rhonin finished. "You can make them do what you want, even help to pull a blade into their very heart."

A hidden power suddenly slammed against my shield. Something violent and invisible. His own attempts at controlling my mind, knowing the pain and anger he had risen in me at the truth of Viggo's death. His mouth curled up at the realization of my shield.

"New trick of yours? Shadow magic, no doubt. Show me, girl. Show me those shadows deep within you."

I ran at him in a wild rage, raising my blade and going straight for his head. I couldn't think clearly, as his words blinded my ability to consider anything more. He dodged the strike and spun around, slamming me into the ground with an invisible shove of power. My shield weakened as I felt the continued pressure of the invisible weight on top of me, the ground sunk a few inches below me as my shield struggled to hold.

I turned to the side and shot out spikes of ice toward Rhonin, surprising him enough to let go of the force that was holding me down. I quickly got to my feet and sent a wall of fire toward him. I let it burn in his direction, as the flames rose high and completely covered his figure. Another laugh broke out from him as he walked through the fire, completely untouched by my spell. The flames died out and I saw the remnant of a protection rune he had placed.

I lunged at him again with a blast of cold air, and slicing with my blade. Rhonin anticipated both moves and sent me flying into the ground again, dragging my body along the dirt and mud with his magic hold. The star blade flew from my hand and went sliding down the hill while I continued to get thrown around on the ground. My shield finally gave in from the constant attacks, allowing the ground to cut at my skin.

I erupted with shadow, trying to envelop me and make me invisible. Hoping to escape his hold and get to Tyran to unbind him from the tree.

"There you are," he said, lifting me from the ground before I could escape his grasp.

The unnatural strength of the magic coursing through him was startling. Rhonin lifted me like I was a doll, turning me towards the battlefield that we overlooked.

"Let me show you exactly what I can do."

Rhonin wrapped an arm across my chest and held me against him as the obelisk floated in the palm of his other hand in front of us. A violent connection pulled at my shadows, as I tried to keep them within me. The pull was too great, and my control slipped as it gave in to the power that the obelisk held.

A dim green light glowed from the center of the obelisk as I felt the magic connect. A mixture of sheer bliss and joy, mixed with a deeply destructive and hateful power. Both so magnetic to the shadows as they consumed the power it held.

My body became paralyzed from the connection as Rhonin held me before the armies fighting. Sound and sight became clouded and fogged as a deep thrum of the magic rose from within.

It was like floating in the same dark rooms that I dreamed of when using my shadows. There was a small point of light that grew larger as I watched. The battlefield appeared in view with a glassy filter over it of green and black swirling shadows, almost as if I were trapped in the obelisk itself. He whispered something in my ear that I couldn't understand past the echoing of the magic within the obelisk as I unleashed something completely out of my control.

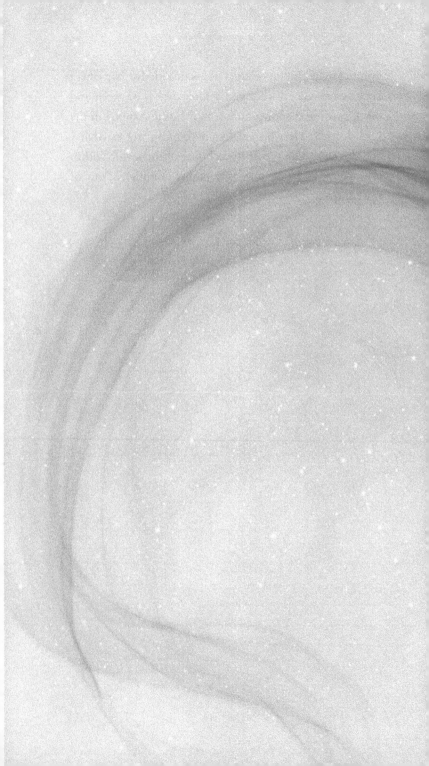

CHAPTER 39

I WAS CAUGHT FROZEN in terror as a magic so devastating emitted from what my mind was contained in. I had absolutely no control over the shadow, smoke, and dark lightning that flowed outward from me and onto the field below. I was screaming as I watched the powerful beam of lightning strike and turn anyone in its path into dust. Rhonin gave no care who it targeted, as he used me as a tool to kill both our soldiers and his own. My body ached at the pressure that was released.

The images of my dreams came to me, as I realized I was playing out a real version of it. I was the weapon. I was leaving a path of death to those of Caldumn. Tears gathered in my eyes as I watched, unable to stop the power that continued to flow through me.

It felt like an eternity as the magic radiated from me, feeling as though part of my own life was leaving with it as the tears fell down my cheeks. The obelisk grew dim and I was suddenly released from his hold, falling to my knees completely exhausted. My shadows stayed fully formed around me, but I couldn't begin to will them to attack, to protect, to do anything other than keep my form shrouded in its opaque mist.

A silence had fallen across the battlefield. The destruction that was unleashed shattered me, knowing that so many were killed through my magic. Rhonin stood in a shocked scoff at the magic he controlled. The obelisk was pulsing with a dim green energy, and I knew it was going to consume the Aura and magic unleashed from me once again. I had to do something before it was too late.

"Feel that power of light and dark. Let it flow and consume you," Rhonin whispered, kneeling down next to me.

"You are mad," I gasped.

"I am what will be feared. No longer will we be hiding along the borders, protecting that which shuns us, who look down on the power we hold as a weakness more than the strength that it is. The pure line of Necromancy will reign and those who stand in our way will perish, and be used as the great army that will serve us forever. The Red Kingdom will realize their weakness and fall to my hands, and I will rule you all."

I shook at the conviction he had, knowing that he wouldn't stop, and I wouldn't be able to take him down in my weakened state. I wanted to escape the despair, the insanity that came from him. I couldn't allow myself to be a part of this.

"Now, you see what you'll be, my precious pet. Weakened and so easy for taking," Rhonin said.

I felt the claws of control work their way toward me, attempting to consume my mind completely. I used every bit of magic I had to shield my being from them; the last attempts to not become his puppet. They sliced at me in a mental attack that felt as though my flesh was being ripped from my body.

I couldn't help but think of Tyran, how I needed to fight for him, fight to save him. I thought of the people on the battlefield who gave their lives for our cause, who continued to fight for our lands and our people. I couldn't give in. I used every ounce of magic I had within me, but the claws still tore through me, removing every layer of protection I built.

I looked at Rhonin and opened my mouth to scream.

The cold steel hilt of my blade slid to my side, and I faintly heard Tyran's voice as I reflexively reached out and grabbed it.

Rhonin's hungry gaze went wide before I slammed my glowing blade into the side of his neck, slicing clean through, and down the other side of his torso. My scream fell silent as I watched the top half of Rhonin's body slide diagonally to the ground from the blow. Tyran's face appeared standing directly behind where Rhonin's body once was, consumed wholly in his own shadows.

I choked out a cry at the sight of him, dropping my blade as he knelt down and pulled me up to him. Hot tears stung at the scrapes on my cheeks as I grabbed at him, never wanting to let go.

A faint cheer erupted from below. Tyran and I looked out to see the reanimated who had once been attacking, now falling over and becoming still at the death of

Rhonin. The Battalion, Sentinels and Guard that were left standing, cheered in pure relief of the battle ending.

I scanned the faces, hoping to see Bergen. His gray robes blotched in dirt and black blood came into view. He used his staff to keep himself straight, but I could see he was safe. I sighed, knowing he was alive.

Tyran shouted Gunnar's name as he caught sight of his friend, who was helping one of his Guard limp through the piles of bodies that littered the floor. So many of those in familiar cloaks and leather armor lie on the ground. It hurt to see the loss we sustained, but the relief of it being over tried to numb the sting.

"You saved us," I said as we still held each other.

"I ripped the trunk apart." He breathed out. "When I saw what he did to you, I couldn't control the rage, and my shadows erupted. I broke through the chains and found your blade."

"You saved me, again." I said, still processing, looking back at the tree nearly torn in half, and the divot of power left in the ground from Tyran's escape. "You did that?"

"He was hurting you." He chuffed as he kissed my forehead.

A thrumming of power loomed in our surrounding area, and I realized the glowing obelisk laid near the body of Rhonin. I slowly pulled away from Tyran's arms and watched in wonder at the pulsing power it held. A pool of Rhonin's blood around it reflected the green glow of light and dark Aura. I couldn't help but feel the pull to hold it in my hand.

My fingers reached for it as my shadows swirled. It was as if it contained its own source of gravity. I could feel the vibrations of all that was holy and unholy within it, the draw of ultimate power, to protect us from anything else that could stand between Tyran and I. My fingers nearly grazed its cool surface before Tyran placed his hand gently over mine.

"Wren. We can't." He whispered.

"I… But we can use it to protect us." I said, not fully in control of my thinking with the allure of the obelisk so near and calling to me, "Think of what we can do to leave the grasp of the Red Kingdom."

"Nothing good comes from the use of dark magic, even when mixed with the light."

I couldn't look away from it as the truth of Tyran's words sunk in.

He was born into the ability to use both light and dark, and had to watch as his people succumbed to its darkness driven mad with the power it swallowed them in. He could do so much with his knowledge and skills he already wielded within his magic, and yet, he chose the light. He chose the good and was a pillar of what is right in the world to me.

I pulled my hand back with his as he looked deep into my eyes.

"We need to destroy it," he said.

I nodded, knowing the truth of it, no matter how hard it was to turn away from something that could eternally protect us from any more evil in this world. I knew we had to choose the light.

Tyran picked up the star blade from where I left it and handed it to me. My heart raced as I grabbed the hilt. The runes illuminated to life, something I hadn't noticed before. The shining steel of the blade reflected the ground below before it went white with my magic. Tyran joined my side as we stood over the small obelisk that held so much power.

I raised my blade above my head with both hands and slammed it to the black obsidian carved stone.

A shattering crack of my blade to the obelisk released a blast of green and white starlight from the hill that we stood, sending Tyran and I to the ground as he moved over me to shield me from the release of magic. It sounded like thousands of souls screaming in one final breath before it faded away into silence. The thrumming of magic continued for its final moments, slowly disappearing into the surrounding environment, before we got back up on our feet.

It was done. The battle over, and the enemy as we knew it, defeated. Something stirred in me that this wouldn't be the end of things, that peace wouldn't reign for the rest of our long lives. Rhonin mentioned taking the North, and if they knew of his plans, along with our escape due to him stealing the obelisk, we would soon find out.

But we had peace for now, and we would need to do as much as we could to restore it with the people. Tyran slid his hand into mine as we walked down the hill to help our soldiers and allies in any way we could.

CHAPTER 40

THE WEEKS THAT followed were that of mourning the loss of those great soldiers who gave their lives to fight against Rhonin. Towns had become even more divided on whether they supported or pushed the Necromancer kind away. Tyran returned to Reapford, only to be thrown into whether he should be put in the position of Baron.

He worked hard to track down where his father had stashed the ancient texts stolen from the surrounding towns and returned them in good faith that Reapford wanted to keep things peaceful. Agatha and Bergen were quick to understand, but it did little to soothe the divide within the townspeople.

Tyran was mostly concerned about the writings his father had left. Much of it related to the Red Kingdom, and how he came to know about where to search for the ancient texts. It seemed as though someone may have planted the information in an effort to cause Caldumn to fall to Rhonin, only to step in and relinquish it from him.

Tyran needed to know more and sought the only ones he knew who might know.

"How do you think they'll react knowing we smashed one of their obelisks?" I asked Tyran as we made our way toward the Warlock Camp.

"I imagine they'll accept the reason we did what was needed. On top of the information we can give them about my father." He smiled.

"Why don't they have a name for their town?" I asked, "Warlock Camp is all we know it by?"

"It has a name, but it's kept between Warlock kind only." Tyran shrugged.

"Think I should get branded and tattooed while we're here?" I joked as we walked through the tall pine trees that surrounded their camp.

"Mmm... As much as I'd like seeing protection runes on you, I think the recovery time for it to heal would be torturous for me." He gave a sly grin. "It's already hard enough not having my hands all over you."

I rolled my eyes and laughed at the truth of it.

We certainly had spent more time being wholly consumed with one another than before the battle. In the space of time between coming home, helping the Quarter Moon Village rebuild where we could, we spent nearly three days not leaving our room at the inn. Jurna was a saint, leaving breakfast for us at the door in the morning, and would act as though nothing was obvious to our giddy behavior as we would come down for dinner, only to head straight back up to our room. When the duties of getting things back to normal couldn't be procrastinated any longer, it only left us yearning to plan another retreat as soon as we could.

Tyran opened his shirt to reveal the tattoos he also had, and they only took a moment before nodding and allowing us through. The town had a feeling of ancient magic as soon as we crossed into its inner streets. The smell of pine twisted with a hint of brimstone within the streets.

We strode to the tall building that loomed over the rest in the center of the square. Tyran led the way as I stuck close to him, unsure of how to react to the Aura that hung with an unfamiliar allure within the city's walls. The soldiers opened the double doors without hesitation as we walked up and we entered their library.

The walls were the same slate stone as they were on the exterior with torches placed throughout. Large black iron looped chandeliers hung from the ceilings with candles lighting the inner portion of the room. Instead of seeing the initial rows of bookcases and shelving, there were pillars of stone with small relics of power that floated a few inches from their top surface.

Various stones, some carved and some appearing in raw form, sigils of precious metals in shapes and forms I didn't recognize, and finally a couple pedestals stood near the back with librams, old books I had only ever read about, that had a glowing purple shield around them. I couldn't help but feel like I was in a museum in another world looking at all their valuable pieces of their identity.

There was another thrum of energy I could feel, though. One that felt like my sword. I looked around trying to find where the magic led me to but before I could put much thought into it, Mennew appeared.

"I see you brought a friend this time," the Wizard said, greeting us.

He was adorned in robes, much like Wizard fashion when serving within the libraries. The deep green he wore had gold thread that was intricately embroidered with flames and what looked like burning souls reaching from the tips of the fire. I couldn't quite place if they were dancing or suffering.

"We have come with news about my father," Tyran said respectfully, "and need to ask you for information."

"Ah, a trade. Tell me, which of us will benefit most?" Mennew questioned. I could have sworn I saw a hint of his skeleton glowing from within.

Tyran didn't answer his question, and went into giving him what news we had, "We met Rhonin on the battlefield and defeated him and his reanimated forces. He is dead, and I am to assume the responsibilities of Baron. The obelisk artifact was destroyed during the battle, as it was tainted with dark energy."

Mennew didn't show a reaction to the news, keeping a neutral expression about his face and body language.

"We need to know more about my father's role with the Red Kingdom." Tyran finally said as part of our request for information came into play.

"Your father had fallen victim to becoming a pawn for those to the north," Mennew started, "but he had motives of his own, and fell victim to his own greed."

"What do they want?" Tyran asked.

"The North is shrouded with mystery, and much like Rhonin, they are driven by greed. They are, however, more calculated at getting what they want. "

I couldn't help the nagging thought of wanting to know why the Warlock's didn't help, why they wanted us to fight alone.

"Why wouldn't you fight with us? When you knew Rhonin was weak in his greed?" I blurted out.

A smile broke out on Mennew's face, his hollow eyes looked into my soul and I felt uneasy at the two conflicting emotions that rang through me. One to run, and one to stay and listen.

"We are the keepers of that which is ancient, and that which is beyond any current conflict from childish mortal leaders. We are a constant within the world, and we protect that which our magic comes from."

"Our magic was being harnessed by one of your relics to be used as a weapon, that would warrant help in my opinion," I said, getting angry at his cryptic way of speaking.

Mennew only looked at me with those hollow eyes until he finally saw it.

"You have something within you, you both do." his voice turned to one of interest,

"You will learn one day about why we act in the way we do, it is part of you, and those that are run by greed will tear this world apart looking for you. The Red Kingdom knew of Rhonin's plans, and allowed for the obelisk to be taken. They will continue on their path. Be wary of who you involve in your matters."

Chills ran down my spine as I grabbed Tyran's arm without thinking about the fear it showed at Mennew's words.

"We thank you for your time," Tyran said as we turned to leave.

"Seek me out when you know what questions to ask. I enjoy this game we play, Tyran. And now it involves you, too, Wren. Your magic begs to know." Mennew nearly whispered.

I wanted to pause and press to know more, but I couldn't push past the fright of him that had gripped me.

"They knew." Mennew called out as we began to leave. "They let your father take the obelisk. They aren't done with us, either."

Tyran paused, and nodded, taking note of the second mention of this.

I heard a small escape of a laugh from the Wizard as we quickly stepped out to the outside. I wanted to get out of this eerie place as soon as I could.

We didn't speak as we walked quickly out of the town, and as soon as we cleared their protection wards, Tyran placed a rune and had us back at the Quarter Moon Inn entrance in no time.

"Such doom seekers." Tyran finally said as we walked through the lobby of the familiar inn. It took a good while, even after being in our room alone with each other, before I felt safe again.

"Do you think he has any real idea of what is happening?" I asked, still nervous.

"Chaos allows for the increase of Aura energy expended in our world. To them, it's the lifeblood that runs their magic and ways of life. I think they look for any opportunity to push our world into chaos," Tyran said.

"Something is there in their village that is a part of our magic." I remembered the magic calling before Mennew entered the room.

"I felt it while staying there, too." Tyran said. "But I couldn't find what it was, there's a lot of old magic that they hang onto in that library."

I nodded, trying to release any of the residual fears and nerves that had shaken me.

Tyran pulled me close to him as we took a moment breathing each other in. We had yet to hear a thing from the Red Kingdom. Rhonin had made the poor choice to get involved in something far greater than he could handle himself, and it cost him his life. If the Red Kingdom thought to use him as a pawn, this would show them the strength of our people when they find out he's died at our hands.

My mind eased as I tried to think as rationally as possible about the position we were in. We were safe. We had fought and won. We had a treaty in place to keep the peace between the two lands.

I was safe with Tyran.

I looked up into his eyes as he felt my body melt towards him. For now, it was just he and I, and as long as there weren't any more threats of dark magic, we would keep our shadow magic between us. Something that could soon become part of legends and stories from those who witnessed it, or so I hoped. Many had seen what we had done, but if we could keep peace? Perhaps many could soon forget.

I want to see your home. I said as I kissed him.
Stay with me. Tyran deepened his kiss.
Always.
My Dark Star.

ACKNOWLEDGMENTS

I NEED TO FIRST thank my husband, Jackson, for his tireless positive attitude. The amount of patience it took to listen to me shoot down all of your help, only to go back later and reconsider, is trophy-worthy. To my little one, Archer. Thank you for your unshakable love, your creativity and imagination. Mom, you read multiple versions and cheered me on during the times where I needed it most. Dad, it means the world to see how proud you are of my work, and that you shared my journey with so many. To my brother, Dave. Thanks for inspiring me to listen to Brandon Sanderson's lectures, spurring my confidence. Thank you to Mark and Amy for the constant love, interest, and conversations of my writing. You helped so much while this world was born. To Chloe, for sparking my interest in reading once again. You lit a fire in me that was dimmed for quite some time. Erin Young, for helping me shape this into something wonderful with your editing skills. Rena Violet, you created the perfect cover art and images that spoke perfectly to this world. To Meg Price. You brought Wren's voice to life. Thank you. To my CP, Carrie Ann. You helped me understand the direction I needed to take with this story, and helped bring Wren and Tyran to life. To the many partial and full reads from beta readers. Thank you so much. Finally, I have to thank you, the reader. Those who are coming from our community. Thank you for taking a chance on my leap into writing. Thank you for the continual encouragement you gave me on the live streams. You are part of what will make this world come to life.

ABOUT THE AUTHOR

Jennifer lives in Southern California with her husband, a tiny human, and five cats.

Coming from a background in Content Creation, she and her husband livestream gaming content on Twitch and gaming content on YouTube, where you can find her playing World of Warcraft, and Diablo IV. She loves being out in her garden and tries her best to grow various fruits and veggies throughout the year among any flowers, bulbs, or roots she can get her hands on.

Keep up with Jen at:
www.jenniferbliton.com

Follow Jen on her social media:
@warcraftjen
on Instagram, TikTok and Twitter

Milton Keynes UK
Ingram Content Group UK Ltd.
UKHW021052020923
427894UK00016B/454